A WITCH IN TIME

ALSO BY ALICIA MONTGOMERY

THE TRUE MATES SERIES

Fated Mates

Blood Moon

Romancing the Alpha

Witch's Mate

Taming the Beast

Tempted by the Wolf

THE LONE WOLF DEFENDERS SERIES

Killian's Secret

Loving Quinn

All for Connor

THE TRUE MATES STANDALONE NOVELS

Holly Jolly Lycan Christmas

A Mate for Jackson: Bad Alpha Dads

TRUE MATES GENERATIONS

A Twist of Fate

Claiming the Alpha

Alpha Ascending

A Witch in Time

Highland Wolf

Daughter of the Dragon

Shadow Wolf

A Touch of Magic

Heart of the Wolf

THE BLACKSTONE MOUNTAIN SERIES

The Blackstone Dragon Heir

The Blackstone Bad Dragon

The Blackstone Bear

The Blackstone Wolf

The Blackstone Lion

The Blackstone She-Wolf

The Blackstone She-Bear

The Blackstone She-Dragon

This is a work of fiction. Names, characters, businesses, places, events, locales, and incidents are either the products of the author's imagination or used in a fictitious manner. Any resemblance to actual persons, living or dead, or actual events is purely coincidental.

Copyright © 2019 Alicia Montgomery
Edited by LaVerne Clark
Cover by Jacqueline Sweet

All rights reserved.

A WITCH IN TIME

TRUE MATES GENERATIONS BOOK 4

ALICIA MONTGOMERY

PROLOGUE

1810
London, England

REED WILLIAM ATHERTON TOWNSEND, MARQUESS OF Wakefield, glanced around at the other dinner guests, trying to stifle the yawn that desperately wanted to escape his mouth. It certainly wouldn't be proper for anyone to show boredom at such an affair, more so for him, being the future duke of Huntington and Alpha of London.

His inner wolf, too, was bored, and longed to be released from this stuffy dinner party. *We'll be leaving soon*, he assured his animal. *I'm as eager as you are to be back home.*

The wolf snorted at him, as if in disagreement. *Hmm*. He would think it would be even more anxious to get back home considering—

"I do hope Lady Wakefield feels better soon, my lord," Lady Louisa Abernathy interrupted his thoughts, peering up with her beady little eyes as she sat next to him.

"Your lovely wife is always a welcome sight at these

affairs," her husband, Lord Horace Abernathy, Earl of Chilton added. "She is very much missed."

"I agree," Reed concurred. He especially missed his wife tonight. Not only was she the most beautiful woman he'd ever laid his eyes on, but she had a vivacious nature that made these droll dinners much livelier. He knew the moment he saw Lady Joanna Aspen that he would marry her. He had been awestruck when he gazed at her from across the room. Golden blonde hair, the greenest eyes he'd ever seen, pretty plump lips made for kissing.

It was a boon, of course, that she was also a Lycan and had just come out for her first season. She and her mother were visiting his mother, the duchess of Huntington, hoping to have her favor to help in her debut to society. Her father was the viscount of Clearwater, but he also happened to be one of the Lycans under the duke of Huntington's protection.

As it turned out, Joanna didn't need any help with her debut. Reed spent weeks courting her, and their engagement was announced even before the season ended.

"Yes, her absence tonight is a disappointment. To everyone." His mother caught his eye as she took a sip of her wine. He didn't miss the slight smile that made the corner of her lips curl up.

He smiled at his mother knowingly. Before the dinner party began, he had told his parents the reason why Joanna was absent tonight: She was resting in bed because she was currently carrying his future heir. To say they had been thrilled was an understatement, and for what seemed like the first time since Reed announced his engagement two years ago, the duke and duchess seemed genuinely happy about their son's marriage.

When Joanna begged off for the evening citing fatigue, he didn't protest. Seeing as such topics were not discussed in public, they refrained from telling their guests the real reason the marchioness of Wakefield was absent tonight.

"I hope you all enjoyed dinner," the duke of Huntington said once the footmen cleared the dessert plates. "Shall we retire to the library for coffee and tea, and perhaps something stronger for the gentlemen?"

Everyone heartily agreed and followed suit as the duke and duchess stood up. However, before they could all leave the dining room, Reed stopped his father and mother with a hand on each of their arms.

"Father, Mother," he began. "I hate to leave so early, but I should check on my wife." He looked at the other dinner guests. "My sincerest apologies, everyone." Normally, these after-dinner refreshments went on and on until the late evening, and Reed couldn't stand being away from Joanna, especially with her carrying his pup and heir.

Lowell Townsend gave his son a curt nod and turned to the half dozen guests. "Please, do go on ahead to the library. The duchess and I will join you shortly."

Soon, the dining room was empty, as even the footmen had discreetly left, probably at the orders of their observant and efficient butler, Neville.

Now that they had some privacy, it was his mother who spoke first. "What's bothering you, my wee one?"

Though two decades living in England had all but eradicated his mother's Scottish brogue, Annabelle Townsend used it when they were alone. The soft burr reminded him of his childhood, when she would sing to him or soothe him in her native tongue.

His father laughed. "Our son hasn't been 'wee' for a while." He winked at his son. "Nothing about him is 'wee.'"

Reed had sprouted like a weed when he was fifteen, even towering over his own father by half a foot. Though he got his dark hair and ebony eyes from Lowell, his physical stature obviously came from his mother's side of his family. He'd met his Scottish uncles and cousins a few times, and compared to them, he was, indeed, 'wee.' His grandmother had bemoaned his size saying it was unfashionable for a gentleman to be of such height and width.

"He will always be my baby, not matter how old he is," Annabelle declared. "Now, tell your mother what's wrong."

"Nothing's wrong. I'm fine." He let out a deep sigh and ran his fingers through his hair.

"Ah, you're concerned about Joanna and your pup." Lowell patted his shoulder. "Absolutely understandable, my boy. When your mother was carrying you, I wouldn't let her out of my sight."

"He kept hovering around me. All the time." Annabelle rolled her eyes at her husband. "Despite the fact that I was practically indestructible, as I kept telling him."

Females who were pregnant by their True Mates could not be harmed, that was a known fact. Reed's mood sank, and it must have been written all over his face.

"I didn't mean—"

"It's no bother." He pursed his lips together. Although Joanna was a Lycan and carrying his pup, they were not True Mates. There was always that feeling that his parents were disappointed he didn't marry the one who was supposedly the other half of his soul. But to Reed, that never really mattered. He'd fallen in love with Joanna from the moment he laid eyes on her.

Annabelle looked despondent. "Reed, I've always treated Joanna like my own daughter, you know that," she insisted. And Reed knew his mother tried hard, she really did.

"And so what if you're not True Mates?" his father added. He put an arm around his wife. "What happened to your mother and me is rare. I mean, who ever heard about a Lycan who could immediately tell who her True Mate was?"

She smirked at him. "Ah, after all these years, you still don't believe me, *mo ghràdh*?"

Reed had heard the story a million times: that the Lycans of the Caelkirk clan knew their True Mates upon meeting them. It had caused quite a stir when Annabelle MacDonald, Alpha of Caelkirk, had met Lowell Townsend at a gathering of the Alphas of Europe and declared him her True Mate. They fell in love instantly and married only days after knowing each other. Growing up, he asked his mother what it was like to know one's True Mate. She would only smile at him and say, "Oh, you'll know, my wee boy, you'll know."

Perhaps if she had bloody told him how, he wouldn't have fallen in love with Joanna so quickly. But, blinded by her beauty, his feelings had run away. When his mother had asked him if he felt 'it' upon first laying eyes on Joanna, and he had only stared at her blankly and asked what 'it' was, the disappointment on her face had been obvious.

Though his father wasn't ecstatic about the news, being English, he was at least glad he was marrying a member of the ton and another Lycan, which should at least guarantee him a suitable heir to both the dukedom and the Alpha title.

As his father and mother continued to stare at each other with love and admiration, he cleared his throat. "In any case, I'm loath to disturb her sleep if I were to come home at dawn."

"I'm sure she'll appreciate your thoughtfulness, my boy." Lowell patted him on the back. "And just so you know, son, I'm happy for you. Being a father is one the best privileges I've had in my life."

Reed smiled at his normally stuffy father whose eyes were shining with tears. His mother, on the other hand, placed a hand over his, her expression warm.

"I know we said we thought you were too young to marry at twenty-one," Annabelle squeezed his hand. "But I'm glad you don't have to wait much longer to hold your pup in your arms."

"I should warn you, it will be difficult for you and your wolf," his father warned. "It won't want to be away from her. Mine would growl at me if I stayed away from your mother too long."

Huh. Reed thought that was strange. His wolf, at the most, was lukewarm toward Joanna, which he thought was normal, as that's what it felt for most people and Lycans around him, save for his parents and sister.

"You'll do well," Annabelle assured him. "I know it."

"Thank you, Mother." He leaned over and kissed her on the cheek. "If she's up for it, I'll have Joanna invite you over for tea."

Her smile was genuine. "That would be lovely."

"Grandmama will be invited as well."

His mother winced, though to her credit, not as severely as she used to. According to his father, the relationship between the current and dowager duchess of Huntington had mellowed over the years. If that was the case, Reed wasn't sure he wanted to have seen what it was like in the beginning, especially after his father had broken off his engagement to the Belgian Alpha's daughter when he met Annabelle. Miranda Townsend was probably not happy, but she didn't have a choice. In Lycan society, True Mate pairings trumped any other type of arrangement, sometimes even marriage. And knowing that True Mates conceived upon their first coupling, he wouldn't be shocked if that was the reason his father had procured a special license to marry his mother right away.

"Try to be surprised when Joanna announces her condition, Mother," Reed said. "You know Grandmama will be cross at me if she found out you knew first. Don't vex her, please? Or I'll never hear the end of it."

"I'll try." But the expression on his mother's face said, *not very hard*.

"Shall I bid Ellie goodbye?" His younger sister, Eleanor, was only fourteen years old and was probably upstairs in her bedroom. Growing up, he'd always doted on her, but since his marriage, he hadn't spent as much time with her.

"She should already be fast asleep," Annabelle said. "But I'll let her know you asked after her."

He nodded goodbye to them and pivoted on his heel, then walked down the long hallway of Hunter House, his parents' London mansion. Neville was already by the door, and no doubt, the trusty butler had informed his driver that he wanted to go home early.

"Good night, Neville," he said as he passed the other man.

Dressed impeccably, salt-and-pepper hair combed back

neatly, and his upper body stiff as a board, the older man gave him a short nod before opening the door. "Good night, my lord."

He headed directly to his coach and soon was on his way home. As a wedding present, his father had presented them with the lovely little townhouse on Cowley Street. Joanna was disappointed at the size and location, thinking that it was unfair of his parents to give them such a small place, especially compared to their sprawling mansion. He had to explain to her that Hunter House was the home of the Duke of Huntington, a title which Reed would not—and hoped not to—inherit for a long while, seeing as his father was still young and healthy.

It was really the only time he'd argued with her, as he thought she was being ungrateful. She apologized quickly, and that was that. Indeed, he counted himself lucky, as a love match was rare for someone of their standing. And now, he would secure his legacy with an heir, and maybe a spare if he was lucky.

His inner wolf let out a dissatisfied sound.

What the devil was wrong with it?

The coach stopping interrupted his thoughts. His driver opened the door and he quickly alighted, eager to be inside and slip into bed with his wife. His pacing was rather fast, so he did wait a few seconds for the door to open but found himself frowning when it stayed shut despite having reached it. Usually, the butler would have opened it by now.

That damned Foxworth. Joanna had insisted on taking on her family's underbutler to run their own house, but Reed had never liked him. Not only was he too young and inexperienced, but he had an air of impertinence Reed didn't care for.

Faced with the choice of standing outside the whole night or the indignity of having to knock at his own door, he chose the latter.

His keen ears picked up footsteps, followed by the sound of the key slipping into the lock. "What the bloody hell—my lord!" Wide brown eyes stared up at him, and Foxworth's face was as pale as a sheet. "W-w-what are you ... I mean ..." He cleared his throat and ran his fingers through his unkempt hair. "Good evening, my lord. Apologies, we—I was not expecting you home so early."

His eyes narrowed on Foxworth, and his sensitive nose picked up the scent of alcohol from his breath. Hopefully, the butler had his own bottle stashed away and hadn't been dipping into the decanter of fine Scottish whiskey in the office "I was feeling rather weary after a long day."

"Of course, my lord."

"Foxworth?"

"Yes, my lord?"

"Do you think I could come into my own home?" He raised a brow at the butler who was standing in the doorway blocking his way.

If it was possible, Foxworth got even paler. "Uh, of course, my lord."

As the butler stepped aside, he resolved to talk to Joanna tomorrow about finding a new butler. It really wasn't proper—

His wolf's hackles rose, and Reed instantly went on alert. His body stiffened, and his animal's ears perked up. There was unusual movement coming from the second floor—the bedroom. *Joanna*.

He raced up the stairs, using his supernatural speed to get to the bedroom in seconds. Still, it seemed like forever, and his mind raced with possibilities. A burglar who thought the house would be empty. Or maybe someone who saw him leave alone for the evening, out to target his vulnerable wife.

The door made a thunderous thud as it hit the wall when he threw it open. The bedroom was dark, but his Lycan eyes could see everything clearly. And the sight before him was not what he expected.

A shriek pierced the air, followed by a loud crash as a very male—very naked—body hit the floor. "I specifically said I did not want to be disturbed—" Joanna's eyes went wide as she yanked the sheet over her bare breasts. "Reed?"

Anger vibrated through him, and he turned his sights on the figure getting up from the floor. He stalked toward the man, his hands reaching out for his throat. His wolf roared, urging him on, and he let out a growl.

"No!" Joanna leapt from the bed, the sheet around her body and stepped between the two men. "Reed, be reasonable."

"Reasonable?" he choked out. The muscles under his skin began to contract and ripple as his wolf begged to be let out.

Joanna's eyes bulged. "He's ... he's not ..."

A quick sniff in the air told him what she was trying to say. *Human*. Using every ounce of his control, he tamped his wolf's instincts down. Thank goodness he didn't shift into his wolf form or their secret would be revealed.

Focusing his eyes, he recognized the other man. "Sherrington?"

Lord Jeremy Sherrington nodded as he swallowed audibly. "Wakefield," he mumbled. "I ... I must say this is awkward."

That word didn't even begin to describe the situation.

Sherrington scratched his head. "I suppose you'd like to call me out."

"Call you out?"

"Pistols? At dawn?"

He glanced at his wife. His cheating, harlot of a wife. Duel for her? Sherrington had to be kidding. "No, I don't suppose I will." He pivoted on his heel, his rage freezing over the white-hot sting of betrayal, and he walked out of the door.

"Reed? Reed!"

He was halfway down the hallway when he heard the footsteps behind him.

"Reed, please!" Joanna cried, her claw-like fingers digging into his arm. "It's not what you think—"

"It's not what I think?" He stopped, then turned to face her. "Then explain to me what I saw in there."

"It's just ... this is ..." Her face went scarlet, and she blew out a breath. "He was just a distraction, to pass the time."

"A distraction? From what?"

"Until I became duchess and Lupa!" she spat. "But with my luck, I'll be old and fat before I get to be called 'Your Grace.'"

Dear God, did she even know what she was saying? What it would mean for her to gain either title? She wanted his parents ... He let out a disgusted snort. "Get out."

Joanna blinked. "Reed?"

"I'm going to take a ride. One hour. By that time, I want you out of this house."

She sucked in a breath as her eyes filled with tears. "You're joking."

"I'm serious. One hour. If I see you, I won't be held accountable for my actions."

Stamping her foot like a child, she let out a cry. "B-but you can't! Think of the scandal—"

"*You* should have thought of the scandal before you jumped into bed with Sherrington." Did she really think he would just stay quiet to avoid gossip? She was a fool, then.

No, *he* was the fool. For being so blindly in love and not seeing what was obvious. And what his wolf was trying to tell him. His gaze dropped to her belly. "Is it even mine?"

She bit her lip, her hand going to her stomach. "I ... I don't know."

"Yes, you do." *He* knew. Rather, his *wolf* knew. That's why it didn't feel protective toward Joanna. And why, since she announced her pregnancy, it seemed even more wary of her. "For God's sake Joanna, Sherrington is human! What were you going to do when the child's wolf didn't manifest?"

"I ... I didn't think ..."

"You're right. You didn't think." Ice froze the blood in his veins as he pried her fingers off. "One hour. Not a second more." Without another thought or backward glance, he walked away from her.

The tentative knock on the door didn't break Reed's concentration as he stared at the column of figures on the ledger he was working on. For the last two weeks, he'd been busy with estate affairs. He didn't really care much about it while he was growing up, but he figured now was a good time to learn. His father hadn't objected when he asked for more responsibilities.

Continuing to ignore the next knocks, he stared at the neat numbers on the page, trying to make sense of them.

"*Ahem.*"

He peered up at the sound of the feminine cough. "Hello, Mother."

The duchess of Huntington stood at the doorway of his office, a tight smile on her face. "How are you, Reed?"

"I'm fine." He turned back to the ledgers, but they made as much sense now as they had an hour ago when he began. Feeling his mother's eyes on him, he looked at her again. "Is there anything else?"

She walked over to his side and placed a hand on his shoulder. It took all his strength not to flinch. "You know you can always talk to me or your father about anything. We are here for you."

Of course, they knew what happened. He didn't exactly have a choice. As he told Joanna, he went out for a ride and came back an hour later. She was gone, and he slept on the sofa in his office. In the morning, he told Foxworth to pack his things, as he did the rest of the staff because obviously, they all knew what had been going on and had some part in covering up their mistress's affair. It was sometime late evening when his mother and father arrived, perhaps wondering why the invitation to tea never came, and discovered Reed alone in the house, finishing the last bottle of spirits in his liquor cabinet.

He told them everything. They were shocked of course, and much to their credit, didn't tell him to go after Joanna to avoid scandal. In fact, they were quite supportive of him, tiptoeing around the subject for the last two weeks. And as for Joanna, he didn't really care where she was. She could go to the devil.

He didn't answer his mother, but instead, stood up and walked over to the window where he had a clear view of the street. "Did you come here to say 'I told you so'? To gloat that you were right about her?" he said with a contemptuous sneer.

"Reed William Atherton Townsend, I am your mother, and you will not speak to me that way!"

This time he did wince and turned to her, feeling like he was seven years old again and had just broken her favorite teapot. "Forgive me, Mother."

Her eyes softened. "Always, *a bhobain*."

My darling. He couldn't remember the last time she had used that term of endearment. He was probably a young boy, scared of the dark, unable to sleep until she told him stories about knights and kings who vanquished monsters and dragons.

"I know you don't want to talk about it," she continued. "But you must decide what to do. The ton will start to talk. In fact, there have been a few unsavory tales spinning the rumor mill."

"And do you care?"

She smirked. "Of course not." And why should she? Annabelle Townsend didn't give one whit to what the ton thought of her, a Scottish countess who had ensnared one of the most eligible bachelors in England. "But, your father and grandmother …"

Well, there lay the problem. His *very English* father and grandmother. The scandal would ruin the family, plus there was Eleanor to think of. Sure, she was a duke's daughter, and it would be a few more years until she came out, but the stories would come back to haunt them by the time her first season came about. It would definitely affect her chances of making a good match.

But what could he do? He could not be in the same room, much less look at that traitorous viper, not after what she did and said. It was obvious now. All she was after was the duchess's coronet and the honor of being called his Lupa. Did she ever truly love him?

"Have you heard from Lord and Lady Clearwater?"

"No." He could only guess that their daughter's actions had shamed them into staying away from him. At least Joanna had the decency to tell her parents the truth, not some convoluted version where he was the villain.

"You can't hide forever." She looked distastefully at the pillow and blanket on the sofa. "Or live in your office for the rest of your life."

He could not bring himself to sleep in their bed again. Indeed, he hadn't even entered the bedroom since that night. "If I had a choice, I would divorce her." His mother didn't react. "But I can't, not without bringing scandal to the family name."

"But you can't raise a child that's not your own. Especially not a human child who could never be Alpha."

And that was the conundrum. Damned Joanna. What was she thinking? If they were human, he could pass off any child as his own. But his family had held the Alpha position longer than they had the dukedom. He would either have to sire another Lycan child with Joanna or pass the Alpha title to another family. The thought of even touching that vile bitch again made him want to retch.

"So, we are at an impasse," he said glumly. Maybe he'd be lucky, and Eleanor would find a Lycan husband and have a son who could inherit the Alpha title, if not the dukedom.

"Excuse me, my lord," said the footman, Mercer, who had come to the door. After he had dismissed Joanna's servants, his parents had sent over some of their own staff for the time being. "You have a visitor. A Mr. Archibald Barrow."

Reed frowned. "I don't know anyone by that name."

"He says it's an urgent matter, and he must talk to you immediately. I can tell him you're indisposed and perhaps to call on you another time?"

He shrugged. It wasn't like he was getting any work done today. "Let him in."

A few moments later, Mercer escorted an older man with pure white hair carrying a leather letter case into the study. "I'm sorry to disturb you, my lord." His voice was scratchy and hoarse. "My lady," he said with a nod to Annabelle.

"My footman said it was an urgent matter. What is it?"

"Er, yes." He took out a sheaf of papers from his letter case. "My name is Archibald Barrow, and I work as a solicitor for the West Moreland Shipping Company. They've tasked me ... I mean, they ... my job is ..."

"Just spit it out, man," he barked. This man was trying his patience.

Barrow's spine went stiff as a board. "Your Lordship. I regret to inform you that your wife, Lady Joanna

Townsend, Marchioness of Wakefield was aboard the Voyager bound for the Caribbean when it sank a few days ago."

Annabelle's gasp was audible. "S-s-sank?"

"Yes, my lady."

"It's 'Your Grace,'" Reed snapped.

"Excuse me?"

"She's a duchess." His voice was flat, emotionless. "You are to address her as 'Your Grace.'"

Barrow's eyebrows shot up and he looked like he wanted to say something, but restrained himself. "Er, Your Grace. I mean, yes. The ship encountered terrible weather two days after they set sail from England."

"And you're certain she was on it?" Annabelle asked, her voice frantic.

"Her name was on the manifest, as was, er, her companion in the first-class cabin where she was staying."

"Companion?" his mother echoed.

"A Lord Sherrington," he said. "Before I came here, I spoke with his father, the marquess of Arden, and he confirmed that his son had indeed set sail for the islands."

"Dear God." Annabelle cleared her throat. "Mr. Barrow, I trust that all this information is kept confidential?"

"Of course, Your Grace," he said.

"Even so, my husband, the duke of Huntington, will have his solicitor call on you tomorrow morning."

"As you wish, Your Grace."

"You may go now."

"Thank you, Your Grace." Barrow bowed low, then turned to leave the room.

She turned to Reed. "*A bhobain.*" Her voice was barely a

whisper. "Say something," she said, her voice catching in her throat. "Anything."

Reed stared ahead at the rich, dark paneling that covered the walls of his office. He should have felt grief at the news that his wife was dead. Or, if he were *that* type of man, expressed relief that there would be no scandal to mar their name. But right now, he felt ... nothing.

Turning on his heel, he walked back to his large oak desk and sat down on the leather chair. Then proceeded to tally the figures he had left behind earlier.

CHAPTER ONE

"What do you think, darling?"

Elise Henney watched as her mother twirled around in the private dressing room at Bloomingdale's, the green skirt of her dress swirling around her slim legs. "You look great, Mom," she replied. "Just perfect."

"Oh, you should try it on then," Lara exclaimed. "If it looks good on me, then it'll look good on you too." They were, after all, identical in stature—same petite, curvy frame and flaming red hair, though Elise's electric blue eyes were inherited from her father.

Elise chuckled. "When you told me you wanted to go shopping, did you really mean for me or for you?"

"Why, for me of course, but you can pick up one or two things for yourself, you know. I mean, what are you going to wear tonight?"

Her mother was talking about Lucas Anderson's ascension ceremony, the reason they were in New York in the first place. Her own father was Alpha of the San Francisco clan and had close ties with the Andersons, but he couldn't make it due to a scheduling conflict.

So that meant her mother had to go, and she'd insisted on Elise coming to join her for the long weekend. She initially protested because that wasn't much time, but Lara was insistent. "We'll take the jet, fly in on Thursday night and leave Sunday morning," her mother had said. "Besides, we'll be staying with Daric and Meredith. She was complaining she didn't get to spend time with you the last time you were there." It wasn't like she could protest; it was an official function, and as the eldest daughter of the Alpha, she *had* to go.

"I brought something to wear," she sighed. "It's perfectly fine. Besides, I can't afford that dress."

Lara sat down next to her. "Then I'll buy it for you."

"No, Mom." She'd been on her own for nearly a decade now, and besides accepting rides on the jet to go to official Lycan functions and the occasional vacation with her family, she paid for everything she needed and wanted with her own hard-earned money. "It's fine. No one's going to be looking at me there anyway."

"Are you sure?" Lara said in a playful voice. "I mean, there will be lots of single—"

Elise stood up. "Maybe I will try it on." God, she would rather do that than have this discussion with her mother. Again. "Where's that personal shopper they assigned us?"

Lara's eyes lit up. "Wonderful, darling. But," she stood up and placed a hand over her daughter's hands. Or rather, over the gloves she was wearing. "Why don't you take those off? They don't exactly match the dress."

She yanked her hands away as if burned by fire. "No, I don't think so," she said in a flat tone. "I've changed my mind about trying on the dress. I'll wait for you outside. Take your time." Taking a deep breath, she walked out of the dressing room, closing the door behind her. She swallowed the lump in her throat and walked out to the main floor, pretending to browse through a rack of clothes.

Her inner wolf whined in a soothing manner. It was funny how she always felt at peace with her Lycan side. Her animal had always been a caring, sensitive creature, so in tune with her moods that some days it felt like it knew her better that she did herself.

I'm fine, she told it. *We're fine.*

She loved her mother, she really did. But sometimes Lara just didn't understand. Or maybe she was disappointed in her. Of course, she would never say it out loud, but Elise didn't miss the disappointed looks on her mother's face whenever the subject of her eldest daughter and magic was brought up.

But that's what she was. A disappointment. She was the first hybrid—half Lycan, half witch—child born of a True Mate pairing, and yet, she was squandering away all her potential.

"Elise!"

Painting a smile on her face, she turned her head and saw her mother rushing out of the dressing room. "Yes, Mom?"

"I just ..." Lara swallowed a big gulp of air. "Darling, I'm sorry. For being so stubborn about the whole ... I mean, I won't take you shopping again."

She knew that Lara didn't want to say the words. And frankly she was glad not to hear them. "It's fine, Mom. I do like spending time with you. And it's been a while since we had a girls' weekend. Just you and me."

She really was happy to spend time with her mother, and since they weren't in San Francisco, it didn't remind her of the past. After she came back to California when she graduated, she moved to Napa Valley where she worked for a nonprofit animal shelter. It was perfect for her—the location and the job. For one thing, she loved being out in nature, and her home in the middle of the vineyards meant plenty of privacy where she would often shift into her wolf form and roam the hills. And for another, she adored her job. For some reason, animals loved her; her brother often joked she must be some kind of Disney princess. Growing up, she had always rescued stray dogs and injured birds.

She couldn't help it, not when she was a child, and not now. It was like her inner wolf came with the nurturing nature witches naturally had. At least that was *one* thing she got from her magical heritage.

"I'm famished." Lara looped her arm through her daughter's. "Why don't we head back to the loft? Your Aunt Meredith said she's got lunch ready, and Aunt Jade's joining us too."

"Sounds great."

Elise grabbed a few of the bags from Lara, and they headed outside to catch a cab downtown. As soon as they stepped out of the air-conditioned building, she stopped.

Lara cocked her head. "Elise?"

Her wolf went into alert, and a prickling sensation crawled over the back of her neck. *Like someone stepping over your grave.* Or they were being watched.

Looking up, she saw someone across the street looking their way. A figure in a dark hoodie. A large truck barreled by and obscured her view, and by the time it moved along, he or she was gone.

She shrugged. "It's ... nothing. I just remembered something." Her inner wolf, however, was not calming down. Its ears perked up, and it sniffed the air as if trying to find a scent of *something*.

Her mother had raised her hand to signal a passing cab. "All right, let's head back."

Traffic during this hour of the day was surprisingly light, and soon they were walking into the loft in Tribeca where Lara's two best friends, Jade Creed and Meredith Jonasson, lived with their husbands. The large former industrial space was actually split into two separate apartments that housed the two families.

As she and Lara walked into the Jonasson apartment, Elise felt a wave of nostalgia. Growing up, she would visit New York often with the rest of her siblings, and she had lots of fond memories in this place. Playing dolls with Deedee and Astrid on the living room carpet. Going to the rooftop garden with Cross and Gunnar. Sleeping over at the Creed apartment and eating junk food and playing video games all night with Bastian and Wyatt. Or the big, family-style dinners they would have—and they *were* big since Lycans ate a lot.

And today was no different. It was Chinese takeout day, based on the white boxes heaped on the kitchen table. Two women hovered over the mountain of food as the kitchen TV blasted in the background.

"*And now, for news abroad,*" boomed the nasal voice of the famous gossip TV news anchor. "*It's been a few weeks since the death of his father, King Nassir Assam Salamuddin, but Prince Karim Idris Salamuddin still hasn't taken the throne. Is the playboy prince going to be crowned soon? Palace insiders say he doesn't want to give up his freedom, though official statements say that the coronation will happen after an appropriate mourning period."*

"And when is that?" the flamboyant co-host interjected. *"I'm dying to see His Highness wearing that crown."*

"Who knows?" the host replied. *"Zhobghadi is a such a mysterious country, and it's only recently they've even been on anyone's radar. As you know, the late king set the tongues wagging when he married an English—"*

Jade Creed grabbed the remote control and pointed it at the TV, silencing it. "Ugh, I don't know why you listen to this trash."

"Hey!" Meredith Jonasson protested. "I can't watch the real news anymore, it's too depressing. I'd rather learn about which celebrity is screwing who." When she saw Lara and Elise walking into the kitchen, she turned to them. "Did you guys get any good stuff?"

"A couple of things." Lara raised the shopping bags in her hand in the air.

Jade's light green eyes sparkled with mirth. "That's more than a couple of things." She walked over from where she was sitting on one of the stools and hugged her friend before turning to Elise. "Hey, Elise, did you survive shopping with your mom?"

"Mostly," she joked.

"Did you have Daric head to Shanghai for all of this?" Lara gestured to the food on the table. While most people would think that sounded crazy, it was a normal occurrence in the Jonasson household since Daric was a warlock who could travel great distances in the blink of an eye.

"Nah, he's too busy," Meredith said. "I got takeout from Emerald Dragon." She pointed to the empty stools. "C'mon, eat up."

Elise took the seat next to Aunt Jade, who handed her a plate of rice and a pair of chopsticks. She thanked her and began to dig into the vast amount of dishes piled on the table.

"How's Astrid doing?" Lara asked Meredith. "And the baby?"

"She's doing amazing, of course," Meredith answered through a mouthful of General Tso's chicken. "The job's stressing her out a bit, but I know she'll do well there too."

"I can't believe Lucas chose her to be Beta." Jade reached for an egg roll and plopped it on her plate. "I mean, I know she'll be great, and hello—a female Beta? It's about time. But it was still a surprise."

"To me too," Meredith admitted. "But I'm so fucking proud of her."

"And you let her know by arguing with her, right?" Lara snickered. "You guys are so much alike."

"Hey, she's the one who thinks she knows everything, while I've only been working as second-in-command for the Lycan Security Team for almost three decades." Meredith swallowed and turned to Jade. "Speaking of daughters, how's Dee? Is she enjoying the field work?"

Perhaps it was because of her sensitive, nurturing nature that Elise noticed the fleeting, pained expression in Jade's eyes. But the other woman quickly composed herself and took a sip of water. "She's doing great. Calls every few days, though I wish it was more often. But it's not like they have cell reception in the middle of nowhere." Deedee Creed was a professor of Archeology at New York University. Elise had heard from her mother that she had left New York a couple of weeks ago after receiving a grant to do some field work.

"What is she doing again?" Lara asked. "And where is she?"

Jade pursed her lips. "Her focus is on the ancient cultures of Mesopotamia, so she's going all over the Middle East. When she last called me, she was in Lahore. She'll be there for a couple of months before she makes her way to Afghanistan."

"Sounds exciting," Meredith said.

"And dangerous," Lara added. "I'm surprised Sebastian let her go."

"Well, she's a grown woman, and she loves her job." Jade looked around as if worried someone was listening in, then lowered her voice. "Don't tell anyone, but of course Sebastian has people looking out for her. He found out who was doing the security for Deedee's team and underbid them and got the contract instead. He's got eyes on her at all times."

"And Deedee doesn't know?" Lara asked.

Jade shook her head. "She'll be furious if she found out. You know how daughters are. They can be so hardheaded."

"Yeah, we only want what's best for them," Meredith said. "Why can't they just listen to us? And do what we tell them?" She shook her head. "Oh Lara, you're so lucky Elise is a good girl. She listens to you, right? And she's got a good, stable job that doesn't require her to go into dangerous situations?"

Elise nearly choked on the piece of broccoli that she was

chewing, but stifled the urge to spit it out until her eyes watered.

Lara laughed. "Elise has always been a dream." She smiled warmly at her. "You were never a fussy baby. Always slept through the night, rarely cried, ate anything we put in front of you. Plus, you were a straight A student and never got into trouble."

Yes, that's who she was all right. The good girl.

"And you work with animals," Meredith said.

"She loves her work, and she'll probably be made director of the shelter soon."

"Mom." Elise slapped a hand over her forehead. "It's not sure yet. My boss just talked to me about retiring the other day." Shelly, the current director of the animal shelter, had called her into her office and told her she was thinking of taking early retirement so she could move to Arizona to be with her daughter and grandkids. She wanted to see if Elise would be interested in the position. While she was flattered, Elise wasn't so sure she wanted to become director. It would mean spending more time behind a desk and less with the animals.

Meredith waggled her brows. "So, are you seeing anyone?"

"Meredith!" Jade sent her a warning look. "Elise doesn't have to answer that! She's got her career. A woman is more than the man she's with."

Meredith held her hands up. "I'm just curious. I mean, Elise is a gorgeous girl."

"And smart," Jade said.

"Yeah. But I heard how dating is so hard these days." Meredith's whiskey brown eyes lit up. "Hey, there are, like, tons of single Lycan guys here in New York. Maybe you'll find someone here."

"No thanks," Elise suddenly said. "No offense, but most of the single guys from the New York clan are like family to me. It would be like dating my brother. Gross."

"Hmmm, yeah, I guess that would be weird," Meredith said. "I mean, my brother's kids are all single, but you used to hang out with them a lot too." She paused. "Hey, aren't Alynna Westbrook's sons single? What's the name of the older one? The one who looks like his dad?"

"Nathan," Lara said.

"Yeah, he's only, what, a year younger than you, Elise?"

Elise wanted the earth to swallow her up. "Uh—"

"You know, Alynna and Liam went out on a couple of dates," Lara offered. "Wouldn't it be funny if—"

"Eww! Mom, that's even grosser," Elise cried. "And Donovan says he hangs out with Bastian a lot—no offense, Aunt Jade." Bastian Creed was a notorious womanizer, after all.

Jade rubbed her temple with her fingers. "No worries, I know my son well."

"Really?" Lara said. "I always thought he was such a quiet boy."

Meredith waved a finger at no one in particular. "Wooo, it's those quiet ones you have to watch out for."

Taking pity on her daughter, Lara changed the subject. "So, what time do we have to be at The Enclave for the ceremony?"

Elise sighed in relief, glad that her dating life was not under scrutiny anymore. *Not that I have one.* And really, she was fine being by herself. Because being alone meant she couldn't hurt *anyone*.

Pushing herself off the stool, she got to her feet. "I think I'll go lie down," she announced.

"Are you feeling okay, darling?" Lara asked.

"Yeah. Jet lag," she lied. "I'm going to go take a nap. I'll set my alarm and make sure I'm ready by the time we have to leave."

"All right, darling, have a good nap."

She left the three women, who seemed happy enough to chat and catch up by themselves, and headed to the guest bedroom where she was staying. As soon as she got inside, she strode toward the bed. *Maybe I will lie down for a bit.* Curling herself around a pillow, she closed her eyes and let sleep take over.

Elise immediately woke up from her dreamless nap. "Oh crap!" Sitting up, she glanced around her, her eyes focusing on the clock by the bedside. Her body relaxed and she sank back into the covers. Thank goodness, it was only three o'clock, but still, she had slept longer than she wanted to.

Uncurling her legs, she swung them over the side of the bed and got up, stretching her arms over her head. She walked over to her open suitcase to grab her toiletry case when she realized she had given her shampoo to her mom last night. *Better go grab it.*

Her mom was in the room just across from hers, so it wasn't a big deal. However, as she stepped out of the room, the sound of voices drifted down the hallway, and she stiffened when she heard her name. Was someone talking about her? Curious, she turned and tiptoed toward the living room.

The volume of Jade's voice strengthened as she got closer. "... and nothing's improved?"

"You've seen it for yourself. She's still wearing gloves. When I tried to take them off, from the way she reacted, it was like I was trying to peel her skin off."

Elise swallowed, hard. They were definitely talking about her.

"There has to be something we can do," Meredith added. "Maybe she just needs help? What does your mother say?"

"We've spoken about it at length," Lara replied, her voice despondent. "And we've run out of ideas. I just ... I wish I could have done more."

"No!" Jade exclaimed. "This isn't your fault."

"Isn't it?"

It was like an invisible hand clamped around her chest, making it hard to breathe. The walls were closing in on her, making her feel like she was being crushed. She didn't want to stay there, but she couldn't move either.

Of course, Lara wasn't disappointed in her, she was disappointed in *herself*. That somehow, *she* was the one lacking in trying to raise Elise as a blessed witch with magical powers. And that made her feel worse about the whole thing. But Elise knew the truth: Lara didn't lack anything. I'm *the problem, Mom.*

Biting her hand to keep from making a sound, she found the strength to move, slowly backing away to make her way toward her room. However, before she could reach it, she bumped into something.

"*Oomph,*" She spun around. "I—Uncle Daric!"

Even though she was all grown up, the sight of the Viking-like warlock never ceased to intimidate her. Of course, she knew Daric was as gentle as a lamb, but the power emanating from him sometimes hit her like a sack of bricks. Blue-green eyes the color of the ocean stared down at her. "Elise? Are you all right?"

"I—" Tears were threatening to spill, and she turned away from him. "I'm fine!" she cried as she raced back to her room. She rushed inside and closed the door quietly behind her.

Goddammit! She stared down at her gloved hands. Some days, she really did want to take them off. But she couldn't.

A knock on the door made her startle. "Y-y-yes?" she stammered.

"Elise," came Lara's voice through the door. "Are you awake?"

"Yes, Mom."

"Hurry up and get dressed then. Aunt Meredith's been called to The Enclave to help with security, and Aunt Jade and I thought it would be nice to get there early and see Frankie."

"I ... I ..." She didn't want to go. She didn't even want to be here right now. *I wish I was back in California.* Back in her home in Napa Valley where she could shift into her wolf and be at peace. "Mom, I can't be ready in that time."

"I'm so sorry, darling. I know it's last minute, but maybe you can move a little quicker?"

"Yeah, I'm not really ready." For any of this. But if her mother knew anything was wrong, she would be like a rabid dog. "You know, I've been to The Enclave dozens of times. I can get there by myself. I'll grab a cab."

"Are you sure?"

"Yeah."

There was a resigned sigh. "All right, we're leaving in an hour if you can manage to get ready by then, then you can just drive over with us."

"Sure."

Elise flopped down on her bed. The hour passed in an excruciatingly slow manner, and when Lara knocked again to check if she was ready, she told her that she wasn't and to go ahead without her. She listened carefully to the sounds outside—the three women rushing about and gathering their things, and the door closing behind them. Finally, she was alone. *Maybe I can—*

A knock on her door made her bolt up in bed. Who could that be?

"Lara, it's me."

Uncle Daric? Confused, she got up and walked to the door. "I thought you'd left with them."

Daric smiled at her weakly. "You heard them talking."

Her shoulders sagged. "Yes."

His expression became doleful. "She did what she could."

"She did," she shrugged. They all did. Him. Grandma. Even the powerful warlock, Lucien Merlin, couldn't do anything. "It's me. I'm the one who can't control my powers." Her gaze dropped down to her gloved hands. They had been a crutch, they said. It was all in her mind. She had the strength to control her powers, but she wasn't trying hard enough. Well, there was no way she was going to risk anyone's life again, which is why she resigned herself to wearing the gloves forever.

"I'm sorry there wasn't more I could do for you."

"I—" She stopped short, an idea forming in her head. Why didn't she think of that before? "Uncle Daric, when we were young, you bound our powers, right? All the hybrids?"

"It was a necessary precaution." The warlock's golden brows drew together. "Cross caused an accident when he was an infant, so we decided that all hybrids would have their magic bound until they were older."

"So ... could you do it again? This time ... permanently?" She reached out for that small bit of hope dangling in front of her. Without her powers, she could live a normal life. Maybe even touch another human without the damned gloves.

Daric shook his head. "I cannot, Elise."

"But why?" came her bitter reply. "The mages that you sent to the Lycan Siberian prison ... you bound their powers, right?"

"Yes, but that's different. They were pure magical beings. You, on the other hand, are a hybrid. Your powers are intricately bound to your wolf. I do not know what a permanent binding would do to your wolf in the long term or your ability to shift."

She could lose her wolf? So, her choice was to lose a part of her or to live like this forever. Living half a life, her powers within her reach but being unable to use them. "There *has* to be a way. Maybe if ..." The lump in her throat made it difficult to breathe.

"Elise, this is not the answer." He lifted up her gloved hands. "I know you can control your power. It's you who won't believe it. What happened was tragic—"

She yanked her hands away. "Please! I-I don't want to talk about that now."

The warlock nodded. "As you wish." A heavy silence hung between them. "I shall head to The Enclave. If you would like—"

"I'll find my own way, thanks." She yanked on the doorknob and shut it. It was rude to do that to her host, but she was too angry and disappointed to care.

She waited a few more minutes, using her razor-sharp hearing to observe the sounds in the apartment. When she could no longer sense Daric's presence, she sighed in relief.

What do I do? She didn't really know how she could stand being around people right now, or face her mother after what she'd overheard. But it wasn't like she could just not show up to the ceremony. It was tempting but disrespectful to the Andersons, one of their closest allies. There was going to be a lot of people there. Perhaps she could just blend in and find a couple of acquaintances. She knew Lucas's sisters casually, plus Aunt Cady and her family would be there too. *You're the daughter of an Alpha*, she told herself. And she had a duty to her clan to represent them.

She took her time getting ready, showering and putting on her makeup, then the plain, long black dress she had chosen. As she reached for the matching gloves, she paused. *Did she dare ...*

"No." She couldn't risk it, and put the gloves on. Grabbing her purse, she exited the loft and took the elevator to the street level to find a taxi.

Fifteen minutes passed and there was still no taxi. Elise grumbled. *At this point, I'll be really late.* Turning on her heel, she decided to walk a block up to try and catch a taxi before other people hailed them first.

"Excuse me."

She pivoted and found herself nearly nose-to-nose with a stranger. *Where did he come from?* "Yes?" she said, taking a step back.

The stranger was a man, about her age, dressed casually in jeans and a shirt. "Miss, do you have a light?" He raked a hand through his raven-dark hair and smiled at her.

"Uh, sorry, I don't smoke." Without waiting for him to say anything else, she turned around. She had only taken three steps when she felt her wolf's hackles rise for the second time that day. But unlike the first time when they were outside Bloomingdale's, this sensation screamed *danger* at her.

She attempted to spin around, but a hand going over her mouth and around her waist prevented her from any kind of movement. When she tried to scream, a coldness washed over her and her surroundings shimmered away. *Magic.* Magic was being used on her, but it was a strange kind. It felt different ... it felt unnatural and wrong.

There was a loud pop in her ears, and when she blinked, her surroundings changed. She was inside some kind of cavernous, abandoned warehouse. Summoning her Lycan strength, she broke free of whoever was holding her down.

"Get her!"

She whirled around but was met with a cloud of green smoke. It must have been some sort of confounding potion because she suddenly felt weak and lost control of her motions. Arms wrapped around her again, and her vision began to fade in and out. *Fight it,* she screamed in her mind. Her Lycan metabolism would be able to burn through it, but they might dose her with more of the potion if they thought she was regaining her senses. So, she remained limp.

"Excellent work, Malachi," said a voice on her left. "I can't believe they left her unguarded."

"The mother would have been better, but she will have to do," said the man who held her. "We don't know if the confounding potion will be enough to subdue her since she's one of those half-breeds. So make sure you have enough ready."

Malachi, Elise thought, filing the name away in her mind.

"Come on then, we can't waste any more time," Malachi said. "Hand me that knife."

Elise braced herself, anticipating the cut. Something sharp poked at her palm, and it was a good thing her mind was still cloudy as it didn't feel as painful as it should. Warm, sticky blood flowed out of the wound, but she didn't make a sound.

"Will her blood be strong enough?" Another voice, this time, female.

"It should," Malachi said. "All we need is the blood from the spellcaster. A drop of this one's blood and the spells used to protect The Enclave will be broken."

Despite the fogginess of her mind, fear rushed through her, paralyzing her as she realized what they were going to do. Long ago, her grandmother, Vivianne, and her mother had added spells of protection to The Enclave, to strengthen them and make sure no humans and magical beings would be able to enter their walls without permission. Since she was related to them, they must mean to use her blood in a spell to break the protections. And since they used blood magic, that only meant one thing.

Mages.

"That's it ... and now, break the spell and send us into

The Enclave. The ceremony should be starting which means the artifact will be out in the open."

Artifact? What were they talking about?

The arm around her waist tightened and propped her up. "Awake yet, little half-breed?" came the raspy voice in her ear. "Oh, this is even better than I planned. They won't have any choice now."

She let out a soft whimper but remained a dead weight in his arms. Her mind was almost free and the feeling in her limbs was starting to come back. *Can't let them know. Can't let them dose me again.*

Her heels scraped on the concrete floor as Malachi dragged her around like a rag doll. She opened her eyes to the tiniest slit she could manage and saw three figures in red robes surround them. They then began to chant. The coldness gripped her again, though their trip wasn't as quick this time. Her body felt like it was ripping apart and a loud sound rang in her ears like the shattering of glass. When her feet landed on solid ground, she opened her eyes.

"No one move or she dies." Fingers wrapped around her neck as Malachi held her tight against him.

"Elise!"

Her mother's voice broke through her confusion. *Oh no.*

They were standing in the middle of The Enclave. She recognized the main courtyard, all decorated for Lucas's ascension ceremony. The future Alpha himself was standing a few feet away from her on the dais where they had appeared.

The magic moving around her mother was unmistakable. Lara Henney was a blessed witch after all with the power to control air currents. Wind swirled around her, as did the power she was summoning.

"I said don't move!" The fingers tightened around her throat and she let out a choked sputter. She saw her mother's anguished face as she put her hands down and the magic surrounding her drained away. However, with Malachi's attention on her mother, he didn't notice two figures jump up on the dais and put themselves between him and Lucas Anderson. Elise recognized Julianna Anderson, one of Lucas's sisters, and Cross Jonasson, Uncle Daric and Aunt Meredith's eldest son.

"Don't hurt her," Lucas said in a calm voice. "What do you want, mage?"

Malachi laughed, the sound making Elise's flesh crawl. "I want *that*."

She couldn't move her head to see what the mage was talking about. What did he want?

"You can have it. Just let her go."

"You! Bring it here."

Julianna grabbed the something from her brother and held it up toward Malachi. It was a dagger with a green jewel at the hilt, the blade covered in blood.

"You stupid dogs!" Malachi sneered. "Using the dagger in your idiotic rituals. You have no idea what you've had all this time."

"Elise."

She froze, and her eyes met Cross's gaze. His eyes were so like his father's, though now they were a dark, stormy blue-green. And deadly serious. "Elise, do it."

"No, please, Cross," she begged. "Don't make me." She

couldn't possibly do it. He didn't know what he was asking her.

"Do it!" Cross shouted. "Elise, NOW."

The fabric covering her hands disappeared, and she realized he was 100 percent serious if he used his powers to remove her gloves. Malachi's eyes went crazy, and she felt his fingers digging into her throat, crushing her windpipe. And she knew, it was death or use her power.

And so, she chose to live.

She called up every ounce of magic in her veins and gathered it in her hands. White hot currents of electricity shot through her and to the mage. Malachi screamed as ten thousand volts of pure energy shot through him, and he let go of Elise. Threads of current kept them connected, and when she saw Julianna and Cross leap toward her, she screamed too, trying to warn them away. She tried to pull back her power, to stop the energy building and flowing out of her, but she couldn't.

It was too late. A hand held her on either arm, and her feet began to lift off the ground. Her body felt like it was being pulled back like a rubber band, then released, and she hurtled forward into a deep, dark tunnel, dragging Cross and Julianna with her.

CHAPTER TWO

Time seemed to slow down as Elise felt her body careen forward in an endless spinning vortex. Cross and Julianna kept their hold, and she gritted her teeth as her arms were nearly pulled out of their sockets.

"Ouch!" came a feminine shout.

They all landed in a tangle of limbs and bodies, rolling on the damp ground. Elise ended up on her back, and she blinked a few times wondering if she was hallucinating. Above her, the skies had turned gray and foggy, while the scent of earth and grass wafted into her nostrils. Her wolf immediately went on alert.

"What the hell—" Julianna gasped as she sat up and looked around her. "Where are we?" She turned to Cross. "Where did you bring us?"

Cross's golden brows knitted together. "I didn't bring us anywhere."

Only a handful of people knew that Cross had inherited most of his father's powers. Aside from changing the form of matter, which he must have used to remove her gloves, the other power was the ability to transport himself and others long distances. But why was he denying that he brought them away from The Enclave?

"Elise?" Julianna's bi-colored eyes—one green and one blue—zeroed in on her. "What happened back there?"

"Don't look at me," she answered.

"But your hands ... What did you do?"

Elise clenched her fists. "I used my powers."

"You can control electricity?" Julianna asked.

"I can *create* electricity," she clarified. Controlling electricity was another matter. "You shouldn't have done that," she told Cross.

"It was the only way, Elise," Cross said. "He would have hurt you."

"Well, I hope we got rid of that mage, whatever it is you guys did." Juliann got to her feet and brushed off the blades of grass sticking to her pants. "Let me see if I can call Papa or Lucas." She slipped her phone out of her pocket and tapped on the screen. An audible tone made her frown. "No reception. How about you guys? What carrier do you use?"

"Sorry, I must have dropped my purse." When the mages kidnapped me, she added silently. A shiver ran through her.

"I don't usually carry one," Cross shrugged.

"Damn. Hopefully we're not too far from New York." Her eyes darted around. "This place doesn't look too familiar. And, uh, why does it smell like shit?"

Elise's nose wrinkled. It did smell awful out here, worse still because of her enhanced senses. "Maybe we're near a sewage plant?"

"There should be several just outside the city," Julianna said. "Oh, I hear something ..." Her gaze moved into the distance, to a road just beyond the field. "What the ... is that a horse? And a carriage? Oh my God, are we in Amish country?"

Cross followed her gaze, then his entire body went rigid. "I think you two should stay here." His voice was oddly calm.

"Stay here?" Elise asked.

"We don't know where we are exactly," he said. "I think it would be better if I went and asked."

Julianna shrugged. "Fine, go ahead. Let me see if I can try to find one or two bars." She raised her phone up, waving it around.

"Yeah, we'll stay here," Elise said.

"I'll be back in a moment." Cross turned and suddenly disappeared.

"Jeez, I can't get over how creepy that is," Julianna said. "But you're probably used to it, being a hybrid and all?"

Despite the fact that they were both the daughters of an Alpha, Elise didn't really know Julianna Anderson too well, being a few years older than her. "Um, kind of. Why don't we try going up that hill? Maybe you can find reception there."

The hill was farther than it looked, but they managed to trudge up—a feat considering the ground was muddy, and they were both wearing heeled shoes. It took them a good thirty minutes, and when they reached the top, Julianna examined the screen on her phone. "Ugh, this darned thing. Hey, maybe you can use your electric powers to boost my signal or something."

"It doesn't really work that way," she said glumly.

"How does it work then?" She continued to move her phone around. "I mean, I've seen Astrid use hers while in training. It's pretty handy. How do you use yours? Can you, like, jumpstart a car or something?"

"Er ... I wonder where Cross is? He's been gone awhile. Maybe we should head back to where he left us."

Thankfully, Julianna agreed with her and didn't ask any more questions about her powers. They walked back down the hill, and as they approached the area where they landed, a soft pop startled both of them, and Cross reappeared in the same spot. "I have some ... news." He shook his hair, sending droplets of water everywhere.

"What happened to you?" Elise asked.

Julianna seemingly ignored the fact that Cross's shirt and pants were dripping wet. "Well? Where are we?"

Cross actually looked hesitant which made Elise worry. In all the years she'd known him, Cross was always so confident and sure of himself. "I'd tell you both to sit down, but there's no place to sit."

"For fuck's sake, Cross, just tell us where we are," Julianna said in an impatient tone.

"We're in England, just outside of London—"

"That's not so bad," Elise interrupted.

"In 1820."

"Where's that exactly?" Julianna asked. "Is that a zip code?"

Elise's head snapped toward Cross. "Excuse me?"

"We're in England. In the *year* 1820."

The silence between the three of them was deafening, and Elise thought she wasn't understanding him correctly. "We've ... we traveled through time?"

"That can't be right!" Julianna said. "You can't travel back in time."

"I'm afraid we did." Cross rubbed a hand down his face. "It took me a while to get back because I had to make sure. I traveled to London to this place I knew well and, uh, landed in the Thames."

"The river?" Elise asked.

"Yes. Uncle Sebastian has an apartment there, he lets me and Dad use it when we need a safe place to transport to." He shook his head in disbelief. "The building isn't there and I dropped straight into the Thames. After I got out, I walked around. I was definitely in London, but ..." He took something out of his pocket, unfolded it, and held it up. "See?"

It was the front page of a newspaper, and when Elise examined it closer, she let out a gasp. "Oh my God." The date definitely said 1820.

"What the fuck?" Julianna snatched the paper from Cross's hand. "What the fuck, what the fuck, what the fuck!" Her mismatched eyes trained back on Cross. "Is this really happening?"

"It is."

"Why? What did you do?" she railed. "Oh my God."

"Julianna, calm down," Elise said.

"Calm down! Calm down?" the younger woman exclaimed. "How can I be calm, Elise? We're over two hundred years in the past!" She turned back to Cross. "There must be something we can do?"

"I have a few ideas." Cross's jaw hardened. "And I'll tell you both everything. But first, we need to find some shelter. While I was going around London, I found an abandoned house at the edge of town. We could stay the night there."

Elise looked at Julianna. "I don't really think we have much of a choice."

Julianna opened her mouth, but only a small squeak came out. She clamped her lips together then spoke. "Okay."

Cross took their hands. "All right. Brace yourselves."

Elise closed her eyes feeling the coldness grip her. It was similar to the way the mages had transported her, but not quite the same. Cross's magic definitely felt more natural and familiar to her. When she opened her eyes, they were indoors in a dark room. The musty, damp smell reminded her of the attic in Gracie Manor, her parents' home in San Francisco. She let out a shiver.

"Wait." Cross waved his hand, and a fire began to blaze in the fireplace in the corner.

Julianna sucked in a breath. "I can't believe this." Surprisingly, her voice sounded much calmer. "We're really here. This is happening." Though she began to pace, she was no longer hysterical.

"I'm afraid so," Cross said. "There's no furniture around, but this place should be secure." With another wave of his hand, three sleeping bags appeared on the floor around the fire. "It's not much, but we can get some rest. I can make you guys some clothes, if you want."

"Whoa." Julianna froze. "What the—"

"Cross can change the form of matter," Elise explained. "Transmogrification." It was a powerful form of blessed magic, and as far as she knew, only Cross and Daric could perform it.

"Can you make anything?" Julianna asked.

"Not quite," Cross said. "For me to change one thing to another, I need know how it works and what it's composed of. For example, I had to study the composition of fire to create it"—he pointed to the fireplace—"and learn about fibers and sewing to make the sleeping bags. The more I make something, the easier it gets though." He waved his hand, and in an instant, Elise's black dress and Julianna's pantsuit turned into pajamas.

"Wow!" Julianna ran her hands down her new outfit. "Lined with flannel too!"

"Thank you," Elise nodded at Cross gratefully.

"Are you hungry?" With a wave of his hand, bread and cheese appeared on the floor as well as glasses with water. "It's not much. Cooked food is really complicated to make, because aside from knowing the composition of ingredients, I would have to know the recipe. Meat is especially difficult."

"I guess I won't be able to order a cheeseburger then?" Julianna asked.

"Afraid not."

"This is fine, Cross," Elise said. "Though I'm not really very hungry."

Julianna, on the other hand, was already stuffing half a loaf into her mouth. "Oh my God, I didn't realize how starved I was," she said through a mouthful of bread. She had already claimed one of the sleeping bags and was sitting cross-legged on top of it.

Elise, not knowing what to do, followed suit and sat on the sleeping bag on the farthest left. "Cross, why don't you tell us what you know?"

Cross nodded, then took the last open sleeping bag, curling his gigantic body down. "I guess I should start from the beginning." In the firelight, his ocean-colored eyes seemed to liquefy. "A year ago, my father felt a dark shimmer of power rising up. Then he began to have dreams of the future."

Elise shivered, despite the warm fire. "I didn't know he could do that."

"Neither did he," he said. "His premonitions only come when he touches someone. It's usually my grandmother, Signe, who has active premonitions. And she was having the same ones."

"What did they see?" Elise asked.

"That the mages would rise in power and finally defeat us." Cross's face turned grim. "So we went to the Alpha. Grant Anderson didn't want to cause any panic, so he sent me on a mission to find out more."

"The mages started attacking us a few weeks ago," Julianna said. "First, at Blood Moon, then at the first ascension ceremony. They also tried to get other Lycans to turn against us." She scratched her head. "Growing up, we didn't really learn about mages, but since those attacks, I've been trying to learn more."

"Mages are basically witches and warlocks who have gone against nature by using blood magic," Cross explained to Julianna.

"Blood is forbidden to use," Elise added. "Because you often have to hurt or kill someone to get their blood."

"However," Cross continued, "a long time ago, a powerful mage named Magus Aurelius was able to concentrate his power into three artifacts."

"Artifacts?" Julianna echoed.

"He infused three objects with the blood of six hundred humans and Lycans."

The words made Elise shiver. "Why?"

"So that his power would be preserved," Cross explained. "This was about a thousand years ago. Magus Aurelius controlled a large part of what's now Central and Eastern Europe, but he was losing his power because the people were rising up against him, with the help of the Lycans. So, he placed as much of his magic into these three artifacts, hoping that one day, the mages would rise up and rule the world. He sacrificed three hundred humans and three hundred Lycans."

Julianna's face went pale. "That's sick."

"They came back, but we defeated them," Elise said. "Rather, our parents did. In the battle of Norway, most of the mages were killed, then your dad gathered whoever was left and bound their powers before sending them to the Lycan Siberian Prison."

"A small faction survived." Cross's eyes hardened. "And they found out about the artifacts. It took them nearly three decades but they were able to get their hands on one of them. A necklace that could control people, even without the use of blood rituals."

Julianna's eyes widened. "Where is it?"

"It's still with the mages," Cross said. "It was used by the mages to try and frame Lucas for murder. They wanted to put him in jail so they could kill him and take his blood, but didn't succeed. They did manage to keep the necklace."

"What about the other artifacts?" Elise asked. "Where are they?"

"I've been trying to track them down, and I had my suspicions." His expression turned serious. "Now I'm definitely sure."

"Sure of what?" Elise's heart pounded in her chest as she waited for the answer.

"We had it all along. That is, the Lycan High Council had it."

"The dagger," she guessed. "It was the dagger."

"Yes," Cross said in a somber voice. "I was so close ... but I wasn't sure." He bowed his head. "I'm so sorry. This shouldn't have happened if I was certain of what the dagger was."

"But how could it have transported us here?" Elise said.

"I think ..." Cross cleared his throat. "Here's what my theory is: the mages have been desperate to get at Lucas and Adrianna—not to kill them or stop them from ascending—rather, they want their blood."

"But why?"

"I think it's because as children of two Alphas, their blood must have some special property. It didn't click into place until now, but I believe that when infused with double Alpha blood, the power of the artifacts is magnified. The necklace, as far as we knew, could control humans, but with Alpha blood, it could control Lycans. I believe the dagger would have allowed them to transport people across long distances."

Elise pictured the scene in her mind. Julianna holding the bloody dagger. The mage reaching for it. "But why did we end up here?"

Cross looked sheepish. "I didn't anticipate it, but it was you, Elise."

"M-m-me?"

"Your powers. I didn't know ... I'm really sorry. I think your powers must have amplified the artifact. Along with Lucas's blood ... it's the only explanation."

"Wait! Where's the dagger?" Julianna exclaimed. "That's our way home, right? All we have to do is charge it up with

Elise's powers." She slapped her palms together. "Badabing, badaboom, we're home!"

"It's not that simple," Cross said. "I did try looking for the dagger when I realized where we were. It's not here."

"No." Elise felt a dark despair take over her body. "We're stuck here?"

"There has to be a way," Julianna's eyes narrowed at Cross. "You have an idea, right?"

Cross nodded. "When I first suspected that the dagger could be one of the artifacts, I learned as much as I could about it."

"Why didn't you ask to see it? Or tell the Lycan High Council?" Julianna asked. "Why all this secrecy? You and your father should have said something the moment you suspected the mages were coming back."

When Cross didn't say anything, it was Elise who spoke. "Because he's a hybrid," she said in a quiet voice. "They wouldn't have believed him or his dad." Despite the fact that there were many hybrid Lycans now that the witches and Lycans were no longer on opposite sides, there were still a few who didn't trust either side. As a hybrid, Elise knew this and how it contributed to her feeling that she would never be part of either world.

Cross cleared his throat. "As I said, I learned as much as I could about the dagger."

"And what did you find out?" Julianna asked.

"Lycans didn't always use that particular dagger for ascension ceremonies. Any dagger or sword was used to cut the hand and make the vow." During the ascension ceremony, the future Alpha had to seal their vow to protect their clan by slicing their palms with the dagger. "The dagger the

Lycan High Council uses in our time belonged to the London clan. It was an heirloom from the Townsend family."

"Why do we use it now?"

A line appeared between Cross's brows. "The historical records are murky, but this is what I pieced together: During the ascension ceremony of one of the London Alphas, they were attacked by 'evil forces.' The London clan fought them off, but unfortunately, they killed the would-be Alpha."

Elise gasped. "Who killed him?"

"Like I said, the details are murky. But from what I could interpret, Reed Townsend never became Alpha. Since he didn't have any children, the title passed on to his nephew. But, the Lycan High Council wanted to honor Townsend, so they've been using the dagger ever since."

"How does that help us now?" Julianna asked.

"If my research is correct, we should be in the right year when Reed Townsend is ascending to Alpha."

Julianna's face brightened. "That means the dagger is here!"

"And Townsend is also the first son of the two Alphas, about to ascend himself." Cross added. "We could potentially be able to recreate what happened at Lucas's ceremony."

"But how can we be sure?" Elise asked. "It's not like we intended to come here in the first place."

"I'd like to believe we were brought here for a reason," Cross said. "The dagger and another child of two Alphas are right here, where we are now. It can't be a coincidence that we were brought here. With the dagger, Reed Townsend's blood, and Elise's power, we have a way home."

She didn't want to say aloud what they were all probably

thinking: that it might not work. But then again, what else could they lose? "I suppose ... we should give it a shot."

"Great!" Julianna looked much more positive about the whole thing than Elise felt. "So, how do we get close to that dagger?"

Cross stood up. "I need to gather intel."

"We can help," Julianna offered.

He shook his head. "It will be easier if I go alone for now."

"But—"

"At least for now. We don't know what to expect out there." he said. "I've taken precautions and put protection spells around this house. But, don't try to leave until I've come back."

"Where are you going?" Elise asked.

"I have to learn more about Reed Townsend."

"And how do you plan to do that?"

"I've picked up a few tricks here and there," he said cryptically. "I'll be back in the morning."

And once again, he disappeared.

Elise stared at the empty spot where Cross had been, wondering where he had gone to. A heavy silence crept over them.

"We'll be home in no time. Right?" But Julianna sounded like she had lost some of the confidence she had earlier.

"Of course." Elise slipped into her sleeping bag. This had to work. Otherwise, she didn't know what else to do.

———

Dawn was breaking by the time Elise was awakened by the

heavy footsteps walking across the wooden floor. Her wolf didn't sense any danger, which meant it knew who was in the house with them. She sat up immediately. Rubbing the sleep from her eyes, she looked up at the tall figure by the fireplace.

"It's me," came the reply.

Cross.

Her vision came into focus in the darkened room, and she sighed in relief. "What did you find out?"

"And what are you wearing?" Julianna's sleep-rasped voice piped up from the sleeping bag beside her.

Cross grinned. "I had to blend in while I gathered intel." Dressed in skin-tight pants, boots, and a loose white shirt, he looked more like a pirate than a Viking.

"You wouldn't have happened to gather some coffee, did you?" Julianna sat up and brushed her hair back with her fingers.

With a wave of his hand, two mugs of steaming hot coffee appeared on the floor next to the sleeping bags. "My father insisted that coffee was the first thing I learn to make, after water."

"Oh. My. God." Julianna's eyes widened as she took in a whiff of the rich aroma. "You can *make* coffee?" She took a sip of the liquid and let out a sigh. "Marry me, Cross. Right now."

Elise chuckled and to her surprise, Cross actually blushed. "Thank you, Cross," she said as she took sip from her own cup. "What did you find out?"

He sat down cross-legged next to them. "As I suspected, Reed Townsend is about to ascend to Alpha sometime soon, possibly in the next week or two. His parents passed away over six months ago in an accident."

She didn't know why, but she felt a pang of sympathy for this Reed Townsend, despite never having met him. But she supposed anyone would be devastated if they lost both their parents suddenly.

"The Lycan High Council has approved his ascension," he continued. "They're ironing out some details, but as soon as they arrive, they'll proceed with the ceremony which could be any day now."

"How did you find this all out?" Julianna asked.

"I located his home," Cross explained. "It was surprisingly easy, given that he's also the duke of Huntington. I just asked around, and some people directed me to where he lived. I waited until everyone was asleep, then I went inside and read through his mail. It took a while, but that's what I was able to piece together, based on his correspondences with the Lycan High Council."

"Good job," Julianna said. "Did you find the dagger?"

He shook his head. "There was no time to search the entire house. I went to the office first, since I guessed that's where his most important papers and items might be, but no sign of the dagger."

"It might be in another home, especially if it's an heirloom." Elise said. "I mean, if he's a duke, he probably has several estates all over the country. You might have to check them all."

"How do you know that?" Julianna asked.

"Er, I mean ... I do read books." She felt her cheeks go hot. "Jane Austen and uh, some of those romance novels Aunt Jade used to lend me."

She thought Julianna would mock her, but instead, the other woman clapped her hands together. "Great! Maybe you can figure out what clothes are appropriate for me to wear."

"Clothes?" she asked. "Why?"

"Julianna," Cross began. "You should leave things—"

"Oh, for God's sake, Cross!" Julianna got to her feet and placed her hands on her hips. "If you think I'm going to stand around and do nothing, you're mistaken."

"But Julianna, it can be dangerous out there for you two."

"Is it because I'm a girl?" Her voice raised by a decibel and a dark brow lifted. "Cross, I'm going to go crazy if I have to stay here another day. Besides, I've been a member of the Lycan Security Force for years. I can certainly protect myself, and I know how to lead investigations. With you and me searching together, we can cover more ground."

"It's not that I don't think you're capable." Cross shook his head. "I'm already taking a risk by talking and interacting with the people in this time period. Who knows what kind of damage we could cause to the future if we were at the wrong place at the wrong time?"

"But, if you have my help, we can find the dagger faster and get home sooner, right?" Julianna reasoned. "Don't forget, finding the dagger is just the first part. After that we somehow need to get some of Townsend's blood on it and then have Elise use her power to zap us back home. How were you going to do that all by yourself?"

"I was going to do it clandestinely. Maybe place a sleeping potion on him and then take some of his blood." Cross said. "But I suppose you're right. If we wait too long and he dies during the ascension ceremony before we find the dagger and get his blood, we might lose our only way home."

"Hey, I'm not going to stay here if you guys are going off

to look for the dagger," Elise said. "I'm coming with you. Don't even think of saying no, Cross." And if she were truly honest with herself, although she was scared of going outside, part of her was curious. What would it be like walking around in Regency London? She'd really only seen it in movies and read about it in novels.

"All right," Cross said with a defeated sigh. "Looks like I'm outnumbered. But you both have to stick close to me when we're outside. And don't talk to anyone."

"Aye, aye, captain!" Julianna said. "Now, how do we get some clothes so Elise and I can go outside without causing a scandal or ripping the space-time continuum?"

Acquiring the necessary clothing for the two females was harder than it seemed. For one thing, it would take Cross too long to learn how to recreate the fabrics and then how to construct the clothes. So, they decided he would have to steal the necessary clothes instead, popping in and out of some of London's finest dressmakers' salons without being detected.

Even then, it took him several trips, because he forgot the three or four layers of underthings that ladies wore in Regency times, plus a few other accessories and personal things they needed to look presentable to the outside world. "I never realized how hard it was to be a woman," Cross said with much humor.

Elise was actually glad to be wearing real clothes and happy in the fact that she could wear gloves without looking weird. From the piles of outfits Cross had provided them, she chose a light-blue empire-cut gown in a rich satin fabric and gloves that went up to her elbows. "I'm just glad we didn't get transported someplace where corsets were necessary."

"Hey, this actually isn't too bad," Julianna said as she

twirled around in a gold and white silk gown. "I'd rather wear something like that," she indicated with her chin at Cross's buckskin pants, shirt, and boots with her chin, "but I might make the stuffy London ladies faint."

"You look great, Julianna." Elise tapped her finger on her chin. "There's just something it needs ..."

"The hair," Cross gestured to Julianna's short bob. "You have the wrong hair."

Julianna ran her hands through her cropped locks defensively. "What's wrong with my hair?"

"From what I've observed while I was outside, ladies have long hair in these times."

The look of horror on Julianna's face was unmissable. "Don't you dare!"

But it was too late. As Cross waved his hand over Julianna's head, her short dark hair began to grow and lengthen until it reached down to her waist.

"No!"

"It's not that bad," Elise said as she pinned her own long red hair up. "I can help you fix it."

"Ugh!" Julianna gave a strand a tug. "It's so heavy."

Elise thought the long hair actually suited Julianna as it softened some of the more angular lines of her face. Not that Julianna wasn't pretty, but Elise suspected she often got compared to her mother and her two other sisters. They were beautiful in that exotic, sensuous way of the petite and curvy, while Julianna was more on the tall and athletic side like her older brother and father.

Reaching for the hairbrush, she ran it through Julianna's now-lengthy locks until they gleamed, then used the leftover pins to put them up. "There," she said. "Now it looks perfect." The thick, ebony curls were piled on top of her head artfully.

"I can't wait until we get home," Julianna grumbled. "I'm going to take a nice, long hot shower, then I'm going to chop all this off."

Elise smothered a laugh. "I think we should be all good." Both of them certainly were wearing enough layers of clothing. "What's the plan?"

"I'll take us to Hunter House," Cross said. "That's where he lives. From what I've read, the ascension ceremony is set to take place there."

"We won't get too close, will we?" Elise asked.

"No," he answered. "We'll observe from the outside across the street but no closer."

"Good thinking," Julianna said. "It'll give us an idea of what the house is like, then maybe we can figure out how to infiltrate it or possibly observe Townsend's daily routine. We'll need to know the best time we can nab him and get some of his blood."

"The street where he lives isn't too busy, but we'll have to be careful no one notices us. I'll transport us a block away, in an empty alley I've been using. From there, we can walk by the house." His voice turned serious. "For now, we'll take one lap around. That's it. Don't talk to anyone, and try to blend in."

"We'll do our best." Julianna winked at Elise. "Right?"

"Right." Elise tried to sound as confident as Julianna. But in truth, she was nervous as a lamb. What would the outside be like?

"Ready?"

She looked at Cross's outstretched hands, her heart

beating like a drum in her chest. "Ready." As his fingers closed over her gloved hands, she took a deep breath and closed her eyes. A cold sensation washed over her, and after a split second, she opened her eyes.

"Fucking hell." Julianna let out a gagging sound. "What is that smell?"

As they stood in the shadowed, narrow alley, the stench hit Elise's nostrils. "I guess romance novels tend to gloss over what history smelled like." She pinched her nose.

"How do people stand it?" Julianna moaned.

"They probably get used to it," Cross said with a grin. "Come on, it's better out there, I promise."

They each took an arm he offered and walked beside him as he guided them out of the alley. A fresh breeze greeted them as they turned the corner, and Elise took big gulps into her lungs.

"We're close," Cross whispered as they continued their stroll into the busy pedestrian street. They passed a few shops as well as people milling about. A few of them glanced their way as they walked by.

"Why are they looking at us?" Julianna's eyes darted around. "God, I'm so tempted to tell these people to fuck off."

While no one was outright staring at them, Elise could definitely feel eyes on them as they passed by. "Do you think they know?" Her wolf didn't seem alarmed by anything. In fact, it had been oddly calm this entire time. Still, the looks they were getting from the people around them were disconcerting and she did her best to ignore them.

"The house is around the corner."

Cross directed them to turn right, and as soon as Elise saw the building, she held her breath. *So this was Hunter*

House. "House" was a misnomer—it was more of a grand mansion, taking up the entire block. It was imposing, but not garish, and done in a neoclassical style. It kind of reminded her of the house she grew up in, though this building was at least twice as big.

Julianna let out a low whistle. "Wow. It's gonna take us a while to search the entire place."

"I'm told it has at least ten bedrooms." Cross slowed down as Julianna tugged on his arm, and they stopped right across the street from the house.

"That might be a problem." Julianna pursed her lips. "Ideally, we could wait until everyone's asleep and search one section each night."

"But if we don't find it in here, we'd have to search all his other estates," Cross said. "That could take weeks."

"How about if we get jobs inside the house? I could be a maid or something," Julianna said. "Like undercover work. As a maid, I could probably access all the rooms easily."

"Good idea," Cross said. "Now...."

A small movement from the corner of her sight made Elise snap her head back toward the house. Cross and Julianna were so deep in conversation that they didn't seem to notice that the large gate was ajar.

"Guys," she said. "There's someone …"

It happened so fast Elise barely blinked when she spied the small figure slipping out between the gates. Her wolf instantly went on alert, and she suddenly became aware of her surroundings. The small footsteps across the cobblestones. The pounding of hooves, and the rattle of wheels. When she turned her head, she saw where the thunderous sound was coming from. A coach was speeding down the road heading straight for the child.

Her wolf's instincts kicked in, and she wrenched free of Cross's arm. Her Lycan speed allowed her to reach the center of the street and grab the young boy frozen like a deer in headlights before he was run over by hooves and wheels. The momentum was too much, however, and she and the boy were sent sprawling across the sidewalk. He screamed and she held his tiny body to her, shielding it as best she could as they rolled several feet until her back hit the metal gates.

"*Oomph!*" she groaned as she lay sprawled out on the sidewalk. Good thing for Lycan healing; her bruises would heal by tomorrow, but she was still going to be black and blue for a couple of hours. But at least the boy was safe. She peered down. "Are you all right?" she whispered.

"Y-y-yes," said the small voice. "I just wanted to ..." He let out a sob.

"There, there," she soothed. "You're fine. Just—" She stiffened as she took a whiff of the boy's scent. It was undeveloped, but distinct enough that she knew he wasn't human. *A pup.*

"*Ahem.*"

She startled at the low baritone. A shiver ran through her, but instead of being afraid or defensive, her wolf's ears perked up, and it stood very still as if waiting for something. When she looked up from where she was sitting on the ground, she found herself staring into the darkest ebony eyes she'd ever seen.

CHAPTER THREE

For the last decade, order, routine, and schedules ran Reed's life. He woke up at precisely seven fifteen in the morning, dressed by eight, and sat down to breakfast by eight fifteen. His solicitor, Percy Whittleby, walked into his office by nine o'clock, where they could discuss the day's business dealings.

If there weren't too many things on their agenda, they would finish by lunch, and Reed would have a peaceful meal by himself in the dining room. If they ran later, then he and Whittleby had cold sandwiches and refreshments from twelve o'clock to twelve thirty before proceeding with business. In the afternoon, if he had the time, he would go to White's for a drink or two or a round of fencing at Angelo's before getting ready for the evening's activities. While he preferred to go to the theater or ballet with his latest female companion, he sometimes had to attend some boring dinner party or ball at the insistence of his mother—

"Your Grace?"

Whittleby's nasal voice was a welcome intrusion, and

Reed allowed the cold numb feeling to smother the other emotions threatening to surface, along with the distinct yowl from his inner wolf. His head snapped back to the other man. "What's next on the agenda?"

"Well, uh, there is the matter of the rental of the house on Barber Street."

"Barber Street?"

Whittleby coughed delicately. "Yes, Barber Street. You had it rented for Miss Boudreaux, but it's been three months since she ... she left the premises."

Ah, Anaïs. His mistress—former mistress, that is. The ballerina had been hysterical, threatening to leave him when he stopped visiting and paying attention to her. He didn't really know why she was so vexed, not when he allowed her to stay in the house and maintained her allowance even though he had no need of her amorous attention. One would think she'd be grateful to have a patron who left her alone most of the time. *French women were so temperamental.* Last he'd heard, she'd taken up with a viscount from Yorkshire. "So, what about it?"

"The owner would like to know if you plan to ... continue with the rental contract."

"I see. Well—"

The sound of the door crashing against the wall as it opened and a delighted squeal stopped Reed short. "What the—"

"Uncle Reed, Uncle Reed!" a high-pitched voice cried, as a small blur dashed into the room.

Despite the interruption, Reed couldn't hold back the small smile that was forming on his lips. William Lowell James Griffiths charged into his uncle's office with the exuberance that only five-year-old children seemed to possess. He darted past Whittleby, sped around the large oak desk taller than him, and ran straight into his uncle's legs.

"Hello, little pup." He got to his feet and hoisted William into his arms. "What are you doing here?"

William's blue eyes twinkled as he giggled. "Mama and I wanted to surprise you."

"Is that so?"

"William? William!" Another figure—this one older, taller, and female—came rushing into the room. "I told you to wait for me so Neville could announce us."

For a moment, Reed felt his heart stop. Eleanor was the spitting image of their mother with her reddish blonde locks, petite frame, and bright blue eyes. They looked so much alike it made his chest constrict. Maybe that was one of the reasons he'd seen less and less of her over the past months. He knew it was unfair, but he just didn't want to be reminded of the tragedy of their parents' sudden death.

Eleanor Amanda Griffiths, Countess of Winford walked in, stopping halfway when she saw William in his uncle's arms. "Apologies for the interruption," she nodded to Whittleby, "my son can be a handful."

"Good morning, my lady." Whittleby shot to his feet. "And no apologies needed."

"Still, we interrupted your chat." She walked over to Reed and then reached out for William. The young boy seemed reluctant, but when his mother raised a brow, he scrambled into her arms. "Please, go on and continue your discussion. You can pretend we're not here."

Whittleby's eyes bulged, and he sent a pleading look to Reed. Of course, matters such as mistresses were not discussed before delicate ladies, so he decided to spare the other man. "Actually, Whittleby was just about to leave. But, to answer your last question, no I will not be continuing that contract."

Whittleby looked relieved as he took a handkerchief out of his pocket and wiped his brow. "I'll take care of that matter then, Your Grace." He bowed and then looked to Eleanor and William. "My lady. Lord William." After a deep nod, he turned on his heel and walked out the door.

Reed turned to his sister. "To what do I owe this surprise visit?"

Eleanor looked at him innocently. "What, I can't miss my only brother and want to see him?"

That comment hit its mark and he winced inwardly. "You know you're always welcome to stop by."

William began to squirm. "Mama, can I please go and play?"

She sighed and set him to his feet. "Do you promise to behave?"

His little head bobbed up and down. "Yes, Mama."

"All right, off you go." She had barely finished the sentence when he broke free of her grasp and scampered toward the door. "And stay in the house!" she called after him. With a shake of her head, she turned back to Reed. "How have you been?"

"I'm fine." That was his standard answer whenever Eleanor asked him how he was. What else could he say?

"I would ask you if inheriting the dukedom has made you any busier, but then you've always been obsessed with work."

He tried not to let her tone irritate him. "I have seven

estates and half a dozen businesses in England, plus more abroad to oversee and run."

"And I know that you were able to expand the family estates and holdings because you've worked nonstop for the last ten years," she said. "And now ... with mother and father gone—"

"My responsibilities have tripled in the last six months." He didn't want to hear the words. Yes, he knew mother and father were gone, but hearing it out loud was another thing. "And soon I'll be Alpha of London." The ceremony would be held sometime in the next two weeks, once the Lycan High Council finished arrangements for their trip to London.

"But surely you can find some time to relax? Enjoy the season?"

"Surely you're joking," Reed said in an incredulous tone. "Why would I want to be out now, of all times? All of London's mamas will be looking at me like some prized stallion to breed with their debutant daughters."

"Reed Townsend!" Eleanor looked like she wanted to faint.

"Oh, come on now, Ellie," he said, using the childhood nickname he had for her. "You're a married woman."

"You're so full of yourself, just because you're young and handsome." She placed her hands on her hips. "If only those mamas and their daughters knew what a terrible husband you'd be, only living for work and business."

"Well, they don't want me for my winning personality, that's for sure." While it might seem egotistical, he was no fool. Reed knew he was a catch, not only because of his title but also for his wealth. The fact that he wasn't old and decrepit was a small plus, but he knew many women would do anything for a duchess's coronet. *Like Joanna.*

His wolf growled at the mention of the name. Indeed, he'd spent the last ten years drowning himself in work just so he didn't have to think of her.

"Reed?" Eleanor's brows were furrowed together. "Are you all right?"

His answer was automatic. "Like I said, I'm fine. Did you and William want to have lunch here with me? You know I can always ask Neville to tell the kitchen to prepare your favorites."

"That would be lovely, thank you, Reed. But there was something I needed to discuss with you."

"Of course." He motioned for her to sit on one of the chairs in front of his desk, then sat in his own leather seat. "What is it?"

"It's about our cousin, Bridget. Uncle Alec's daughter."

"Yes, I remember her." Bridget MacDonald was the daughter of their mother's cousin and Beta. *No*, he corrected himself. Technically, Alec MacDonald was now Alpha of Caelkirk, after Annabelle Townsend passed away.

While both entailment of the earldom and Alpha title of Caelkirk allowed the eldest child—regardless of sex—to inherit, it also limited it to the members of the clan. So, while Annabelle was Alpha, when she died, the only way Reed or Eleanor could inherit the Alpha role and title was to renounce their status in the London clan. Reed was already to be Alpha of London and Eleanor didn't want to give up her life in England, so they were happy to let their Uncle Alec inherit both titles. Indeed, as Annabelle's Beta while she lived in London, Alec MacDonald had been running the clan for the last thirty years anyway. He didn't have any sons, so both titles would eventually be passed on to Bridget.

Reed thought back to when he last saw her. "She's what ... fourteen? Fifteen?"

"Actually, she just turned twenty." Eleanor's lips pursed together. "You don't remember, do you?"

"Remember?"

She took a long, drawn-out breath. "Uncle Alec wrote a month ago and asked that we take her in and sponsor her for the season. I asked you if it was all right since it had been six months since Mother and Father passed away."

He quirked a brow. "And I said yes?"

"Yes."

"Ah, I see." Glancing at the half-written letter sitting on his desk, he realized that he had meant to continue that as soon as Whittleby left. The letter was for one of his lawyers in—

"Reed, are you listening to me?" Eleanor crossed her arms over her chest.

"What?" He shrugged. "If I said yes, then of course you should do it."

"Excellent." She clasped her hands together. "Grandmama and I will be meeting her and determining which balls and events we should take her to. You'll have to come to the major ones—"

"Me?" He asked in an incredulous tone. "Why do I have to go to balls with her?"

"She needs every bit of support behind her," Eleanor reasoned. "It's not that simple to launch her into society. She's not exactly ... I mean, you know ... she's ..."

"Scottish?" Reed finished. "She'll also be a countess in

her own right and an heiress. Surely between you and Grandmama, she'll be a smashing success in London."

"But she's not English, which means she'll most likely attract fortune hunters. But that's not the only thing." Eleanor let out a sigh. "Uncle Alec says she's already met most of the eligible bachelors in Scotland, and none of them are her True Mate."

"And how the devil is she supposed to know him?"

"You know how," Eleanor said in a serious tone.

He scoffed. "Right." The supposed legend that Lycans from his mother's clan knew their True Mates at first sight. "What nonsense—" He stopped when Eleanor narrowed her eyes at him.

"You know it's not nonsense."

"I wasn't going to call it anything," he said defensively. "Ellie, I'm sorry. I didn't mean ... that is ... I know you're very happy with Winford and I'm glad for you both."

Since Reed had never met his supposed True Mate before and even after Joanna, they had all thought that maybe the legend only applied to the Lycans who were pure Scottish. However, much to their surprise, Eleanor had recognized Jeremy Griffiths, Earl of Winford, as her True Mate.

Jeremy was fifteen years older than Eleanor and was just coming back from the war with Napoleon. Though he was part of the London clan, he hadn't been around since before the war began, so he'd decided to pay his respects to the Alpha. It was at her coming out ball that Eleanor had spied Winford and recognized him as her True Mate. Their mother had been excited, and though the then-duke of Huntington had his reservations, he couldn't deny his daughter or their True Mate pairing. Of course, they were married after an appropriate engagement period, and his nephew, William, arrived nine months to the day of their wedding. A year later, the clan's Beta had passed away and Winford was selected to be Beta, a position he still held today.

"Don't tell me you still don't believe, Reed," Eleanor said. "Maybe you just haven't met—"

"It's not that I don't believe." That was not quite a lie, but nor was it the truth. But how to explain to her? "I think ... maybe it's not everyone in our family that recognizes their True Mate right away. I mean, Grandfather and his father never did." In fact, according to their records, the only Alpha to have ever met his True Mate had been Lowell Townsend. "Maybe because it's only on mother's side of the family that only half the people on our side will have it."

"You mean, because I inherited it, maybe you didn't?" she asked skeptically.

"Perhaps." *Definitely.* That was it. Eleanor had the right idea.

"But ... it's just ..." A sigh escaped her. "When you meet your mate and you get this feeling ..." She blushed and clamped her mouth shut, her lashes lowering. Like their mother, Eleanor never talked about what it was like when she first met her True Mate, like it was some damned secret.

He mentally shook his head. Did he even want to know at this point in his life? Could he even recognize a True Mate? His emotions were so locked up, he didn't even think he'd recognize her if she lay sprawled out at his feet.

"Reed, you can't just stay unmarried forever."

He could barely stifle his chuckle. "Of course I can. I'm a *man*."

"But you need a wife. A duchess and a Lupa."

"There is no rule that says I *have* to," he reminded her. "Besides, I don't *want* a wife, a duchess, or a mate. I don't need one. I don't even need an heir. William will inherit the dukedom and the Alpha title." He had been contemplating it the last six months, and he had decided that that was the best course of action.

"But Reed, I—" Eleanor's hands gripped that arms of her chair and her body went stiff.

"Eleanor?" He cocked his head at her. "What's the matter?"

A loud scream pierced the air and Reed's senses went on full alert. His wolf's hackles rose, and its claws tore at his insides, warning him that something was *definitely* wrong.

"William!" Eleanor cried as her face twisted into a mask of concern. From the way his sister shot to her feet and called on her Lycan speed to propel herself out the office, she must have sensed real danger. A risk of course, considering half the staff wasn't Lycan. However, his wolf urged him to follow Eleanor, and so he did, all the way out the door and to the gate.

He spied the slightly ajar gate and his sister about to exit. With his instincts on full alert, he pushed forward, pulling her aside so he could be on the frontlines, in case there really was a threat. He stopped short as a bundle of blue silk sprawled at his feet. Much to his surprise, a figure unfurled in a flurry of fabric and startlingly blue eyes stared back up at him. The color of the sky when lightning struck the clouds.

And then he felt it.

Heat ran down his spine, followed by numbing cold. Then, it was like his head had been hit by a blunt object while a large fist slammed into his chest. All of this happened in a split second and without any pain.

His inner wolf let out a soul-piercing howl.

Mate, a voice inside him whispered.

Hell's bells.

"Oh, my Lord! William!"

His sister's voice cut through the chaos in his mind, and he blinked. Eleanor was by his feet, kneeling down as she gathered her son into her arms.

"Oh, William ... William, darling ..." she cooed as she soothed the boy. "I was so scared ..."

It was a feat to turn his gaze away from them. From *her*. He didn't want to look at her, really look at her.

"Elise!" another feminine voice called out. A woman in a gold ballgown was running across the street toward them. *What the devil was going on?* A third person—a rather imposing and tall man dressed like some kind of buccaneer—ran up behind her.

"Are you okay? Elise, this isn't what we—" The woman in gold looked up and locked eyes with him.

What strange eyes. One blue and one green. However, looking into this woman's eyes didn't give him the same reaction as the other one. Except that his wolf's claws extended, feeling the presence of an unknown wolf.

Lycan. She was a Lycan. And so was her male companion.

"Who are you?" he asked her. "And what are you doing in my territory?"

"Alpha," the man said in a reverent voice, his head dropping low and not meeting his gaze. "Forgive us for arriving unannounced in your territory."

Reed felt his anger rising. They knew they were in violation of the Constanta Agreement, the set of rules that governed Lycan kind and territorial matters. No Lycan was to cross into another's territory without permission. "You dare come here, into my territory and *my home*? How did you—"

"Reed!" Eleanor rose up to her full height and planted herself in front of him. "For goodness sake! She saved William! He could have been run over by that hackney coach." She glanced around. "Where is it?"

"The coachman has gone, ma'am," the man explained. "He didn't even see your son or my ... our ... Elise when she caught him."

His Elise? A pang of jealousy shot through him and he couldn't help but look to her to gauge her reaction. It was a move he regretted because his body instantly reacted to her again.

She was standing now, brushing the dirt from her skirts, then as she lifted her head, locked gazes with him. Her presence struck him like a bolt of lightning, and this time he could not turn away, not when she was staring up at him with those vivid blue eyes so big, they took up half her face. Her creamy skin was flushed and her pouty lips slightly parted.

And that hair—dark red curls that tumbled down her shoulders and back in an almost scandalous manner. No woman would leave the house with her hair in such disarray, and irrational anger surged through him, as if he wanted to keep such a sight to himself.

"Er, Elise?" the woman in gold said. "Are you okay?"

She blinked. "What?"

"Who are you?" Eleanor held William tight to her as her

eyes narrowed at the three strangers. "And which clan are you from?"

"We're from very far away," the man said. "America."

"Oh!" Eleanor exclaimed. "Americans! I've never met Americans before. Have you, Reed?"

"Only a handful," he answered, finally able to tear his gaze from the woman. *Elise.* Her name was burned into his brain. Did he dare say who she could be, what his wolf recognized? Was it really her?

This woman, who seemingly came from nowhere, wearing a ballgown in the middle of day, was his True Mate?

Did she feel it too? She didn't say anything, but instead, averted her gaze.

No. It couldn't be. This was all wrong.

"You seem to know who my brother is," Eleanor began. "At least, you acknowledged that he is Alpha, so you must know who he is."

"You're Reed Townsend, Duke of Huntington," the man finished.

Eleanor looked at him meaningfully, waiting to make an introduction. He cleared his throat. "This is my sister, Lady Eleanor Griffiths, Countess of Winford, and her son, Lord William Griffiths." He assessed the other man—quite tall, maybe as tall as his Scottish cousins, though he looked more like a tanned pirate with his long blond hair tied back and his buckskin pants, boots, and loose white shirt. He wore neither hat nor waistcoat. What the devil was he doing with two young women?

"You're probably wondering who we are," the man said.

Definitely not a gentleman, with those manners. But then again, they were Americans. Perhaps it was their first time in a civilized place like London. "Since you seem to already know who I am, I suppose you may introduce yourselves."

The young woman in gold opened her mouth but shut it when the man gave her a meaningful look, then turned back to him. "My lord—I mean, Your Grace," he began. "My name is Cross Alexander Jonasson of the New York clan. I am an ... envoy sent by the Alpha of New York City to meet with you and celebrate your ascension to Alpha."

"If you're an envoy, then why was I not informed beforehand?" There was something not quite right about Mr. Jonasson's story. "Our clans have no formal relations. There should have been a missive from your Alpha, and then a request for an introduction and meeting, which I would have had to approve with a letter of my own."

"We did send a letter, Your Grace," he said. "Did it not reach you?"

"Mail from the colonies gets lost all the time," Eleanor said. "Plus, with so much going on ... Did you address it to the right place?"

Mr. Jonasson shook his head. "I'm not sure, my lady. I mean, the Alpha just sent us ..." He turned to his companions. "Forgive me for failing to introduce you to my companions. This"—he nodded to the woman in gold—"is Miss Julianna Anderson, daughter of our Alpha. And ..." He hesitated for a moment. "Her cousin, Miss Elise Henney."

Both women gawked at him silently, not greeting him or even giving a curtsey. Were all Americans raised like wild animals?

"Reed." Eleanor placed a hand on his arm. "I think we should ... invite our guests *inside*."

He knew exactly what his sister was saying, of course—

get these strangely-dressed people inside the house before some nosy neighbor sees them and sent all of the ton's tongues wagging.

"Right. Let's sort this out inside." He led them to the front door which was now being held open by the faithful Neville. A Lycan himself, the normal unflappable butler frowned and his nostrils flared when his gaze landed on the newcomers.

"It's all right, Neville," he said in a low voice. "Would you please prepare some refreshments for our ... guests?"

The butler harrumphed, but said, "Of course, my lord."

"William." Eleanor put her son down. "Are you hurt?"

"No, Mama." William's voice was much quieter than it usually was. His little face scrunched up into a serious expression. "I'm fine."

Eleanor smirked at Reed. "My, that sounds awfully familiar. I wonder where he learned that?"

With all the excitement, Reed nearly forgot about his nephew. He bent down to William's level and then checked him over. He breathed a sigh of relief. Aside from his torn trousers, the boy looked unhurt. "William, you must never do that again, understand me?"

He nodded. "Yes, Uncle Reed."

"Excellent." He smiled at him and then ruffled his hair affectionately. "Now, why don't you go with Neville and he'll bring you a snack? Then you can go to the playroom."

His little head bobbed up and down, then walked toward Neville and tugged at his coattails. "Do you have some of those butter biscuits, Neville?"

"I believe Cook might have some hidden away somewhere, Lord William," Neville said. "Let's ask her, shall we?"

As his nephew followed the butler down the hall, Reed walked to his office, trying not to look back, despite his wolf's desperate desire to look at Elise and make sure she was still following. *Enough*, he said. It was undignified enough that he had to lead them into his own home like some servant, but he wasn't going to give in to his animal's whims. Because surely, this strange woman, this *American*, couldn't possibly be his True Mate. He was more convinced of it now. Maybe her reaction to him was because she was foreign.

"I hope Neville is brewing some strong tea." Eleanor sighed. "This excitement is too much." She turned to Elise. "Miss Henney, please forgive me for not thanking you right away for saving my son. You have my utmost gratitude."

"I-it was nothing, m-my lady." She curtseyed, and while Reed thought the move utterly strange, his sister seemed to be amused.

"Well, uh, they must do things very differently in America." Her eyes scanned Elise's evening gown. "Very different."

"Indeed," Reed muttered under his breath, then turned to Jonasson. "So, explain yourself and what you are doing here."

"As I said, Your Grace, we were just sent here by our Alpha. I believe ... he was first in contact with your late father, and he invited us to come here."

"My father told me no such thing." Surely Lowell would have at least mentioned it.

"We had heard he passed away," Jonasson continued. "And of course, our Alpha waited for the appropriate mourning period before contacting you and sending his condolences, along with an acceptance of your father's invitation to continue relations."

He could not erase that seed of doubt in his mind. "He would have discussed something like that with me."

"Reed, do you think it could have been right before the accident?" Eleanor said. "They'd been staying in Huntington Park for a few months and Father conducted most of his business from there."

A year before they died, Annabelle and Lowell had become tired of the London life and decided to live in the largest of their country estates "indefinitely."

"And you were always too busy to visit them regularly," Eleanor added.

Reed knew his sister had no malicious intent to her words; no, she was merely stating facts. His life revolved around their business in London and he had scarce little time to journey up to Huntington Park on a regular basis, so instead, he and his father relied on messengers who made the long trip. Reed had not seen his parents in two months when they passed away.

He did not say anything which his sister took as an affirmative. "See? It could be possible that's what happened right?"

"Perhaps Lady Winford has made a logical conclusion," Jonasson said. "Of course, you could confirm it with a letter to our Alpha. It will take a while, and the journey back will be long. Maybe we can come back next spring, should you still desire an alliance."

"Another year?" Eleanor said. "After you've journeyed for months to come here? Reed, surely you're not going to turn them away."

His wolf growled. *I should send them home,* he told his animal. *How can we trust them?* His every human instinct told him he should send them away. Yes, including *her*. The things she made him feel ... it unnerved him. But he had a feeling this was two against one: both his wolf and Eleanor would never give him peace. "I suppose you could stay in London. For now," he added in an ominous tone. As Alpha, he could ask them to leave at any time.

Eleanor clapped her hands together. "Splendid. Miss Anderson is the daughter of an Alpha, and I wouldn't want to offend their clan if we sent her away."

He frowned. That was the other thing that bothered him. "Why exactly did an Alpha send his daughter and niece without a proper chaperone across the sea?" The thought of Jonasson alone with Elise on board a ship with no one else for company made him want to break something. Even if the two women were not compromised, it simply wasn't proper.

Jonasson spoke. "I am their cousin as well," he explained. "Twice removed."

"And your chaperone? Surely your Alpha would have provided a duenna for the two young ladies. An older aunt or paid companion with impeccable reputation?" If they were lying, he would catch them now.

"She died," Julianna burst out.

"Miss ... Lucinda Jones passed away right before we docked," Elise said quickly.

"How awful!" Eleanor cried. "What did she die of?"

"Dysentery!" Julianna offered.

His sister looked like she needed her smelling salts. Dysentery? What proper young woman talked about such things in company? Elise, at least, had the decency to glare at the other woman.

"Truly terrible," Reed said. "Where did you intend to

stay in London?"

"We have just arrived from the port and will be looking for a suitable hotel," Jonasson said.

"Hotel?" Eleanor exclaimed. "No, you shan't be staying in some hotel! You'll stay with us," she declared.

"Eleanor—"

"If they had not traveled all the way here from America, William would be crushed under the hooves and wheels of that coach!" Eleanor got to her feet, her hands clasping together. "We have plenty of room and I will be an impeccable chaperone to the girls. It's no bother, since Bridget will be arriving soon, and so will Grandmama, so all three ladies will have two women of irreproachable reputations guarding their virtues." Her face brightened with recognition. "Oh, of course! Silly me. I've wondered why your Alpha would send two unmarried women across the pond. You're here for the season, aren't you?"

"Yeah, definitely. Totally. That's it. Whatever you say," Julianna nodded enthusiastically. "I—ow! Elise, why are you jabbing your elbow in my ribs?"

Elise's pretty face went pale. "It's not—"

"Oh, don't you ladies worry," Eleanor said, excitement tinging her tone. "I've already made a list of eligible Lycan bachelors since my cousin is also here for the season. This is so exciting. We've always made matches with nearby clans, but we might be making the first trans-continent alliance through marriage."

"M-m-marriage?" Now it was Julianna's face that drained of blood.

"Yes, Julianna," Elise said wryly. "Like you said, we're here for the season. London's marriage mart."

While the thought of Elise surrounded by a gaggle of beaux vying for attention made him feel like he'd been punched in the gut, the distaste in her voice made Reed's anger lessen. Still, the emotions inside him were in chaos, a state his normally controlled self did not enjoy.

Eleanor's lips pursed, and she tapped a finger on her chin. "Of course, you both are a little ... older than most of the girls coming out for the season. You're probably what ... twenty-four? Not fresh out of the schoolroom, but not quite ... of debutant age. Still, you're both quite the catch, especially if you're related to the Alpha of New York."

Julianna opened her mouth, but Elise hooked her arm around her waist and pulled her back. "Thank you, my lady, you're too kind."

"I can have someone fetch your things," Eleanor offered. "Are they still at the port?"

"We don't have any luggage, my lady," Jonasson said. "They were stolen."

"Stolen?" Eleanor gasped. "By whom?"

"Pirates!" Julianna said.

"Robbers!" Elise added at the same instant. The two girls looked at each other in bewilderment.

"Well, which is it?" Reed asked impatiently.

"Both," Jonasson said. "We were beset by pirates on the sea and then robbers had stolen our things when we landed."

"How terrible!" Eleanor's cheeks puffed up. "But it makes sense now," she said with a laugh.

"Sense?" Julianna asked.

"Why, yes," his sister tutted. "Why you're dressed up in evening gowns and why Mr. Jonasson doesn't have his coat. I thought it was a colonial quirk."

"We're dressed in ... evening gowns." Julianna sounded like she was asking a question and stating the obvious at the same time.

"You poor things. These gowns must be what those ... those brigands left you with. You certainly couldn't go out naked." She shook her head. "Don't worry, I have a few gowns you can borrow in the meantime. Good thing I'm such an 'unfashionable height' as Grandmama says," she said with a chuckle. "My gowns will easily fit Miss Anderson and we can always shorten them for Miss Henney."

"Gowns for the season will cost you a fortune," Reed commented. "Perhaps you may need to wait a while until you get some funds."

"We'll be fine," Elise snapped. "We aren't paupers."

That she seemed upset in turn made his wolf agitated. "I didn't mean—"

"We have the means, I assure you," Jonasson interrupted. "The er, pirates and robbers only managed to steal our luggage while I had our money stored safely away."

Reed looked the other man up and down, wondering where in the world he could possibly have a substantial amount of money hidden on his person.

"Excellent," Eleanor said.

There was a soft knock on the door before it opened. "Your tea is here, Your Grace," Neville then turned to Eleanor. "Lord William is in the playroom, enjoying his biscuits."

"Thank you, Neville," Reed said. "Actually, if you wouldn't mind, could you arrange for tea in the library instead? And show our guests there please."

"Yes, Your Grace."

"My sister and I will follow in a moment," he said.

"We will see you there, Your Grace." Jonasson and the two ladies followed Neville out. Once he was sure that they were far enough away, Reed turned to his sister.

"What the devil are you thinking, inviting them to stay with you and offering to sponsor them for the season?" His hands clenched at his sides. "We don't know them or if they're telling the truth about their Alpha and our father."

"Reed, don't be silly. Who could make up such a wild story?" Eleanor reached out and placed a soothing hand on his arm. "It all fits, right? You know Father and Mother were always very forward thinking when it came to alliances. Maybe this was their plan, right before they—"

"Still, it's all very strange. They're very strange." And, he did not like how Elise Henney caused so much chaos in both himself and his wolf.

"They're foreigners, of course they're going to be a little ... odd." Eleanor wrinkled her nose. "Think of poor Mother when she first moved to England. You know she must have had a terrible time, and Grandmama—and I love her dearly—couldn't have made it easy on her. I won't have those girls suffer like her."

That comment really hit him in the gut. He'd seen it over the years, of course—the dowager duchess never really got along with her daughter-in-law, and the two were often at odds with each other. "It is very odd that an Alpha would let his daughter and niece travel all the way here for an alliance."

"Maybe their customs are a bit more permissive." She narrowed her eyes at him. "You don't suppose he ..."

"He what?"

She shook her head. "No, preposterous. Neither of them would suit you."

"Not suit me?" Well, they were both American and untitled.

"Of course not," she chuckled. "I know you too well. Miss Anderson is too exuberant, you'd squash her spirit, and Miss Henney seems so shy, you'd scare her to death."

"Perhaps you're right." His wolf, on the other hand, yowled in protest at the latter of Eleanor's suggestion.

"Unless you're interested—"

"We've been gone a long time," Reed said. "Let us join our guests before they think we're talking about them.

"We *are* talking about them," Eleanor pointed out. "But I suppose you're right." She took Reed's offered arm and they strolled out of the office.

As they walked toward the library, Reed contemplated what he was going to do about Mr. Jonasson, Miss Anderson, and of course, Miss Henney. While Eleanor may have been convinced by their tale, he was not. There was something the three of them were hiding and he was determined to find out the truth.

In the meantime, he vowed to ignore Elise Henney as much as he could. He did not want or need a wife, not even a True Mate. Women were not to be trusted, as he had learned in the past. Besides, he couldn't even be sure they were True Mates, and there was no way he was going to confirm it by getting her with child.

The thought of Elise growing large with his pup made his wolf growl in approval. And while it brought out a primal feeling inside him, he quashed it, like he did with every emotion he'd felt for the last decade.

CHAPTER FOUR

Having tea with Reed Townsend and his sister was no less strained than their confrontation in the office. While Eleanor seemed to be doing her best to put them at ease, it was obvious to Elise that Reed was still highly suspicious of their story, if the way his dark, brooding eyes bore into her were any indication.

Just thinking of them made her shiver, the way his onyx eyes made her feel naked and stripped. It didn't help that he was handsome and imposing, so much so that her inner wolf went very still at his mere presence.

As the tea wore on, she tried not to glance at Julianna and Cross, as if any passing look between them would betray them even more. When finally Eleanor declared that they were to head to her home, which was conveniently located next door, she wanted to weep in relief, knowing she wouldn't have to endure Reed's oppressive stare much longer, and she would have some privacy to gather her own thoughts.

Eleanor's house, though not much smaller than Reed's,

was much more inviting. It was obvious that the cheerful young countess had put much love and care into decorating her home. As she and William bid them goodbye, they went to their own wing, the butler showed her, Julianna, and Cross to the guest wing. They first stopped by her room, and as soon as she entered, she sprawled out on the comfy four-poster bed and closed her eyes. She wondered what her companions were thinking. The only way out of this, as she figured, would be to leave right away. Yes, that was it. Cross could whisk them back to their hiding place and they could regroup and find another way to get the dagger. For now, she could close her eyes and enjoy being in this luxurious room for now. *Maybe Cross could whip up or steal some mattresses—*

"Oh. My. Fucking. God." Julianna seemed in a fury as she burst though the room, the door slamming behind her. "What the hell have we gotten ourselves into? Why didn't you tell me what a 'season' was?" Julianna stormed across the plush carpet, hands gesturing wildly. "A marriage mart? How does that happen? Are we going to be put on display and have men bid on us?"

"Uh—"

"This is insane. Barbaric. And she insinuated I was *old*! Like a wrinkly grape dying at the end of the vine! I'm not even twenty-four. I'm twenty-six."

Elise bit her lip, glad that at least to Eleanor, she looked much younger than her real age—which was thirty. In truth, she probably would have been considered a spinster in this age.

"I hope we find that damned dagger soon—" A knock on the door interrupted Julianna's rant. "Come in," she barked.

The door opened and Cross strode inside, his fingers on his lips to signal them to be quiet. He shut the door behind him slowly. "Under the circumstances, I probably shouldn't be in here, but now it'll be easier for me come and go." Cross's powers to transport himself and others across long distances had one caveat: He had to have been to a place before or at least have seen a picture and a satellite map of the area so he knew where to go.

"Cross, what are we going to do?" Julianna moaned.

He turned to Elise, his golden brows drawn together. "You shouldn't have done that, Elise."

"I know." She bit her lip. "But what was I supposed to do? Let that kid be run over? He could have died."

Juliana's mismatched eyes widened. "Fucking hell, did we just change the future?"

Cross thought for a moment. "Hmmm ... history might be okay. I do remember that when Townsend died, his nephew William inherited it which means he should have survived the accident."

Elise's chest tightened at the thought of Reed dying, and her inner wolf growled. *I hardly know him.* Yet that feeling of loss made a pit in her stomach form.

"Then maybe we're still safe." Julianna blew out a breath. "And when we go back, it won't be some weird post-apocalyptic future." Placing her hands on her hips, she trained her gaze at them. "But the question is, what do we do now?"

"I've thought about this," Cross began. "We might actually have a better chance at finding the dagger now."

"How so?" Elise asked.

"We now have direct access to Townsend for one thing."

Juliann's face brightened. "That's right. We can use this

to our advantage. We might even be able to figure out where the dagger is if we ask the right questions."

"Wait a minute." Elise shot up from the bed. "You guys can't mean to stay here? With them?" With *him*. "We should stick to our original plan. Cross, you can transport us back to the safe house, right?"

"Yes, but that would mean we would have to be even more careful. Townsend and his sister know our faces."

Julianna's face was grim. "While I don't want to be on some kind of auction block, I also agree. The sooner we can get Reed or his sister to give up the location of the dagger, then the sooner we can go home."

She knew they were right. But she just wished there was some other way.

"We must be careful," Cross said. "I think Townsend doesn't believe us. He knows something is up."

"Of course he does." Julianna gestured to her outfit. "They must think we're lunatics."

"Er, sorry about that." He scratched his head. "I just picked the two dresses that were easiest to steal. I'm not exactly a fashion expert."

"Well, hopefully Eleanor can help us blend in," Julianna said. "We have to stay inconspicuous. Good thing we're not English, and we can always pass off our faux pas as a *colonial quirk*." She did the air quotes when she said the last two words while copying Eleanor's posh accent, then promptly put her hands down. "I probably shouldn't do that, huh?"

"And you should probably control your cursing too," Cross added as a smile tugged up the corner of his lips.

"Fucking hell."

Elise chuckled, because what else could she do? She was going to be trapped here, at least until they found out where the dagger was. *At least we'll be sleeping in beds.*

CHAPTER FIVE

Their hosts left them alone for most of the afternoon which allowed Cross to make a few clandestine trips to gather more information, as well as money and bank drafts to fund their stay. While he didn't explain where he got the cash, Elise trusted that he got them from sources that wouldn't miss them.

Meanwhile, she taught Julianna all her knowledge—albeit limited to what she'd read in Aunt Jade's historical romances and *Pride and Prejudice*—about Regency England.

"So, let me see if I remember this." Julianna sat cross-legged on top of Elise's bed, scratching her head. "I have to call dukes and duchesses 'Your Grace' while everyone else is 'my lord' and 'my lady.'"

"Yes," Elise said. She remembered one particular novel where a dowager duchess—the title given to the 'old' duchess once a new one came into the picture—was teaching a young woman from America all about the peerage. She remembered loving that particular one, and often pictured the handsome hero in her head—tall, dark hair, broad shoulders, eyes black as coal and—

"How about people without titles?"

Knowing where—or to whom—her thoughts were going she was glad for the intrusion. "I think everyone else is just Miss, Mrs., or Mr. unless you're a servant. The higher-ranked ones are called by their last name and lower-ranked are called by their first names."

"How classist," Julianna sneered.

Not really wanting to have some sort of politico-socio-economic debate with her, Elise continued. She did her best, trying to recall what she knew, hoping that the authors she read did enough historical research. One particular author she read was a real professor of history, so she tried to remember those books. Julianna absorbed as much as she could and was greatly relieved to learn that the 'marriage mart' wasn't some barbaric ritual where they lined up ladies on an auction block and had men purchase them. It did, however, involve a lot of balls and receiving offers of marriage.

"When you think about it, it's probably simpler these days." Julianna's lips pursed together. "No dating apps, no texting, no going to bars, dealing with assholes who hit on you and then ghost you because they're too neurotic or cowardly to actually make any commitment. I mean, if marriage was your goal, then just get it over with, right? And you can just get to know someone after the wedding."

"Would you want to get married first before really knowing your groom?" Elise thought that part was barbaric. She knew enough that these days, divorce was difficult to obtain and often left a woman without prospects.

"Hell no. I mean," she stretched her legs out in front of her, "I don't want to get married *at all*."

"You don't?"

"Ugh, I'm a modern woman. I prefer to keep things casual." She grimaced. "I don't like the way guys can be so clingy either. I have my job, my apartment, my life, and I'm fine with that. I don't need a man to come in and mess it all up. You don't have a boyfriend either, right? So, you must know how freeing it is."

"Yeah," she said with a weak chuckle. In many ways, Elise admired Julianna because she actually *wanted* to be alone.

A knock on the door made them both freeze. "Come in," Elise called.

The door swung open and Eleanor strode inside. "Oh, you're together, excellent." She clapped her hands together, then stepped aside as two young women strode in. "I've had some gowns readied for you both so you can have something to wear for dinner. Melinda and Jane"—she gestured to the women—"shall help you dress."

"You're too kind, my lady," Elise said.

"We can dress ourselves," Julianna added. "No need to bother."

"Nonsense," Eleanor insisted. "I've taken them in so they can train as ladies' maids. You'll be helping them get some practice." Her face softened. "Please, this is the least I can do for what you've done. I don't even know what I would do ..." Her voice choked as her eyes became shiny with tears. She turned to Elise. "You saved my boy. Let me do this for you."

A flush of embarrassment crept up Elise's cheeks. "Anyone would have done it, my lady."

"I don't believe that." Eleanor took a deep breath. "You were at the right time and the right place for a reason."

"My lady—"

"And stop with this 'my lady' nonsense." Eleanor placed a hand on each of their shoulders. "I should like it if we become friends. Please, call me Eleanor."

Julianna nodded. "Then you should call us by our first names as well."

"Splendid." She signaled at the two maids. "Have the baths sent up for our guests. And make sure we at least have the morning gowns ready for breakfast tomorrow."

"You're too generous," Elise said.

"I have so many unused gowns from when my own season was cut short. Believe me, I'd rather they be worn then left rotting in the closet since they're more suitable for debutantes rather than married countesses. I would have liked to have finished the season but ..." Her eyes sparkled and a smile tugged at her lips. "But when I saw Jeremy at my coming out ball ... well, I instantly knew he was my True Mate, and that was that."

"You what?" Julianna and Elise said at the same time, their mouths opened in what was probably an unladylike manner.

Eleanor tittered. "Yes, it's a quirk in my family. We almost always instantly know our True Mate when we see them. Well, most of us anyway." She shrugged. "I'll leave you ladies to get ready. Dinner is served at seven o'clock, but we have drinks in the library at half past six." With a quick wave, she left the room.

"A bath sounds fuck—" Julianna covered her mouth

when she realized the two maids were still in there, albeit silent and stony-faced. "It sounds heavenly." She turned to one of the maids. "Er, which one of you will be helping me?"

"Me, miss," the blonde with the pixie-like face said. "I'm Jane."

"Nice to meet you. I'm Julianna." She stuck her hand out at the maid, who gave her a horrified look and then glanced nervously at her companion. "Er, right." She muttered something under her breath. "All right, Jane, I'm in your hands. Let's go."

"Melinda, right?" Elise asked the other maid after Jane and Julianna left.

"Yes, miss." She bobbed her head up and down, her dark curls bouncing around her cherubic cheeks. "If you excuse me, miss, I'll have Florence bring the tub up and get the bath ready." She curtsied and scurried out of the room.

The bath was as heavenly as Julianna said, and though she felt bad about all the labor that went into providing her with one—that is, the maids bringing up the buckets of water and supplies, plus the cleanup after—Elise felt a hundred times better afterwards.

Plus, while she felt weird having another person wait on her and help her dress, she had to admit it was necessary, seeing as it was so difficult to get all those layers of clothing on. Melinda had to do up all the tiny buttons on the back of her evening gown, a task she probably would have done poorly.

But Melinda was not just great at helping her get dressed, she was amazing at styling hair as well. She was somehow able to tame Elise's locks into a sophisticated updo. When she thanked the maid, she had blushed. "Yer hair's already so pretty and unusual, miss. I didn't have to do much." When Melinda reached for her hand to help her with the gloves, Elise suddenly pulled away. "Beggin' yer pardon, miss," she said in a timid voice. "Them gloves can be hard to put on by yerself."

"I'm used to it." She hoped she didn't traumatize the young maid by practically yanking her hands away, but if she had touched her bare hands, it would have been an even bigger disaster. "Um, Melinda, thank you so much. Would you mind giving me some privacy?"

"Of course, miss." The maid stepped back, gave her a small curtsy and then hurried out the room.

Elise sighed and turned back to the mirror. She really didn't look half bad. A wave of mortification swept through her again thinking about what she and Julianna were wearing as they paraded down the street. *The people around here must have thought we escaped from the insane asylum.* The dress she wore now—a dark blue silky gown—was much more subdued than her previous outfit, but just as lovely.

You can do this, she told herself. All she had to do was smile and look pretty. That was what most women in this era did, right? She had to remind herself this wasn't a Regency romance novel. This was real life. The best thing she could do was blend in and not get caught. Cross and Julianna would do the heavy lifting, all she had to do was not give them away. She'd already done that today, and hopefully she didn't ruin their chances of getting the dagger.

Smile and look pretty.

And definitely don't gawk at Reed Townsend.

I can totally do that.

Tucking back a loose strand of hair behind her ear, she walked out of the room. Much to her surprise, her companions were already walking down the hallway. Julianna looked absolutely gorgeous in her champagne evening gown, tucked into the right places to show off curves she usually hid in her pantsuits. Jane must have been an even better hairstylist, because she somehow managed to pile and tame Julianna's hair into a mass of curls and braids that made her seem feminine and alluring. Cross, on the other hand, looked incredibly handsome in his claret jacket, waistcoat, dark trousers, and boots.

"Don't you both look stunning," she commented as they met in the middle of the hall.

"I had to go find my own clothes," Cross said. "Since no one here was as tall as me. I hope this is okay."

"You look hot," Julianna commented. "Trust me."

Although Cross's cheeks colored again, he ignored the comment. "We should head downstairs."

They went downstairs on Cross's arm, and the footman showed them the way to the library. When she saw the occupants—Eleanor and an older man—she told herself she was relieved that Reed wasn't here.

Eleanor greeted them enthusiastically as they entered and introduced her husband, Jeremy Griffiths, Earl of Winford and Beta of the London clan, to each of them.

"Miss Henney," Winford began. "My dear Eleanor has not stopped talking about your brave deed and how you put your own life on the line to save our dear William. It is a debt we can never repay you."

"It was nothing, my lord." Elise lowered her lashes.

"Oh no, Miss Henney, for a parent, it was everything."

Being the perfect hostess, Eleanor must have sensed the lull in the room. "Holden," she called to the butler. "Why don't you serve some refreshments and—oh, good. You're here."

Elise didn't have to turn around to know who had just entered the room. Her wolf stood at attention, its ears perking up. She moved stiffly to face the newcomer.

Reed stood at the threshold, dressed in all black, save for the snowy white shirt. While on most people, black had a slimming, sobering effect, it seemed to do the opposite on him—it made his powerful shoulders seem broader, and the trousers molded to his legs showed off the muscles as he walked toward them. His hair, which had the tendency to curl at his nape, was brushed back perfectly to show off his tanned, handsome face. And those ebony eyes—though they only glanced at her briefly before greeting his brother-in-law and sister—seemed to bore into her. She tore her eyes away, suddenly finding the wallpaper interesting.

"Nice to see you finally socializing, Hunter," Winford said as he gave Reed a pat on the back.

"You make it sound like I'm some monk locked up in an abbey, Winford."

Reed's low baritone held a tinge of mockery in it, and while Elise usually thought arrogant men were a turn off, something about the quality of his voice sent shivers through her.

Winford didn't seem to mind as he continued good-naturedly. "In any case, I'm glad to finally see you outside our meetings. And of course, thankful for our guests from across the pond."

"Indeed." Reed's dark gaze narrowed. "Speaking of which, I've searched what correspondences and records I have from my father's office. There was no mention of America or New York. Tell me. Who is your Alpha again? What's his name?"

"George," Julianna offered.

"Michael," Cross blurted out at the same time.

"George Michael?" Reed frowned. "What a strange name."

"It actually sounds like a very English name to me," Julianna said wryly.

"Excuse me?" Reed's dark brow rose to his hairline. "I've never heard of an Englishman with that name."

"You'll have to take it on faith," Julianna quipped then added, "Your Grace."

Elise began choking on her drink which was a good distraction. Julianna patted her back and handed her a handkerchief while flashing her a tiny smirk.

Cross gave her a reproachful look before turning to Reed. "Are you looking forward to your ascension ceremony, Your Grace?"

Reed shrugged. "I suppose."

"Reed has been acting as Alpha for the last six months," Winford explained. "It's more of a formality at this point."

"Are you having the ceremony here?" Julianna piped in.

"Yes, but it will be a small affair," Reed answered. "I only want my grandmother, Eleanor, Jeremy, and William there."

"Family only," Eleanor said. "No need for fuss."

Elise could see where Cross was trying to push the

conversation, so she joined in. "I was recently a witness to another ascension ceremony in San Francisco," she lied. "The future Alpha used a ceremonial sword to seal the vow." She turned to Reed, though she was afraid to look him in the eye, so she focused on the spot just above his head. "Will you be using something similar, Your Grace?"

"I actually haven't thought about it," he answered.

"You could use Mother's dagger," Eleanor said. "It's a beautiful piece. She gave it to me a few years ago, and I've kept it with me in my jewelry case."

"She meant for you to have it." Reed's voice took on a surprisingly gentle tone. "I suppose I could use whatever heirloom Father used. I imagine it's gathering dust somewhere in Huntington Park."

"Oh!" Eleanor suddenly exclaimed. "Speaking of Huntington Park, I never got to tell you about my plan with Bridget. As I said, as she is arriving in England tomorrow, I've actually set it up for her to go to Huntington Park." She quickly explained to their guests who Bridget was. "Poor girl's never been outside Scotland or even Caelkirk. I thought it would be a soft landing, plus it will be a chance to get to know her. I've already sent a note to Grandmama about Elise and Julianna, and she's agreed to meet them there. Now that we have three ladies to launch into society, it would be best if we had a few days to get them ready."

Reed's face turned inscrutable, but before he could say anything, Holden entered the room announcing that dinner was to be served.

Though the meal was formal, Elise was glad that it went off without a hitch. For one thing, Eleanor was a good hostess and gave them directions on who was to be seated where.

Jeremy was seated at the head of the table with Eleanor at the other end. Reed sat on her right and Cross on her left. Julianna sat next to Cross while Elise found herself being directed to sit right next to Reed. *At least I won't have to worry about staring into his eyes*, she thought as she sat down on the plush chair.

The rest of the meal proceeded normally, and although the atmosphere was light, she couldn't help but feel awkward. Though she was sitting next to Reed, he didn't engage her in any conversation. She tried not to take it personally since he didn't seem to like to talk, period. If Jeremy or Eleanor asked him a question, he answered in monosyllables.

Of course, based on his attitude the entire time they were here, it could be that he thought them beneath them. He had that haughty, bored air about him that made it seem like he'd rather be elsewhere.

"So, to continue our conversation from earlier," Eleanor began. "We shall leave for Huntington Park in the morning. We should be there by luncheon, and Bridget should arrive at the same time. We shall stay for a few days, while Grandmama and I decide which balls and social events we can attend. I do hope you don't mind another day of travel?"

"Not at all, my lady," Cross said. "We look forward to it."

"Will you be joining us, Hunter?" Jeremy asked.

Reed shook his head. "I'm far too busy. Besides, I have an important meeting with a prospective partner in a few days."

She glanced at Julianna and Cross, their eyes briefly meeting. They were probably thinking the same thing: Without him around, it would be easier to search the premises.

Dessert was served, and once the plates were cleared

away, Eleanor stood up and declared they should have a nightcap in the library. As they all got up, Julianna stumbled back.

"Ooohhh!" She pressed the back of her hand to her forehead. "Oh my ..."

"Are you all right, Miss Anderson?" Jeremy looked at her with concern on his face.

"Yes, Lord Winford." She made an exaggerated sigh. "I'm afraid our ... trials for today have made me lightheaded and ..." She staggered back, and Elise managed to catch her before she bumped into the poor footman who was holding the back of her chair.

"You poor dear," Eleanor said. "Well, why don't you go upstairs and get some rest?"

"Thank you, my lady." Julianna turned to Elise. "I'm feeling so weak, would you mind helping me up the stairs?"

"Of course."

They excused themselves as they left the dining room, Elise holding on to Julianna's elbow to support her. As soon as they were at the foot of the staircase, she shrugged off Elise's hand. "Finally, I thought that dinner would never end."

Elise raised a brow. "What's going on?"

"I hoped I wasn't too obvious." She scratched at her head and muttered a curse. "Why the hell do I need so much damned hair? Anyway, I figured this would be our only chance to check Eleanor's room for her mother's dagger."

"What?" She couldn't believe Julianna had been faking it. "You want us to search her room?"

"Well, I'm going to sneak into her room. You just have to

stand watch outside and make sure no one comes in while I'm searching."

"You can't mean ..." Her heart pounded in her chest. "Why not let Cross do it?"

"Because he can't go in there without having seen the room first, and if he gets caught in Eleanor's room, who knows what Lord Winford would do? Besides, this is our last chance."

She had to admit that Julianna had a point. Julianna could simply claim she had been lost, not trying to seduce the earl's young countess. "All right, tell me what to do."

They climbed up the stairs and turned left into the family wing of the house. "I snuck around before dinner to scope out the floor and that"—she pointed to the second to last door —"is her room. I'll go in, and you stay out here. If any of the servants come, just tell them to go away."

"Go away?"

"Yeah. Just scare them off." She glanced around, then picked up the skirts of her dress. "All right, wish me luck."

Elise watched as Julianna snuck off and disappeared into the room. *Oh God.* Maybe they shouldn't have taken such a risk. It was one thing if a servant was around. But what if Eleanor or Jeremy came upstairs? It wasn't like she could just tell them to leave. What if—

"What are you doing here?"

There was no mistaking who said those words. Even her wolf knew who it was, and it let out a pathetic whine. Her heartbeat stopped for a split second, then began to race. Slowly, she pivoted and found herself staring up into the ebony darkness of Reed Townsend's eyes. "Y-Your Grace?"

His stare was menacing. "I said, what are you doing here?"

God, she wanted to run away. But Julianna—and their only way home—was depending on her. "I brought Julianna back to her room and I was going to go back downstairs but I got ... lost."

His mouth thinned into a grim line. "Really? Perhaps I should escort you back downstairs." He made a grab for her arm. She was too fast however, with her Lycan reflexes and her natural aversion to touch, and evaded his grasp. He didn't seem to like that, and he took a step forward to crowd her personal space.

He was taller than her, but here in the dim hallway illuminated only by candles, he seemed even more imposing. Shadows cut his face into sharp lines, but for some reason, he looked even more handsome and attractive. As if to prove a point, a sudden heat surged straight to her stomach.

"What are you really doing here, skulking about like some thief? Are you hoping to find some jewels or silver you can hock for some coins?"

The heat of sexual attraction suddenly turned into anger. Okay, technically, they were going to *steal* something, but once they used the dagger to get back home, it would be left behind. But that wasn't the point.

Maybe it was the homesickness, the fear of never getting back to her time, or just generally feeling helpless in this strange place, but something in her snapped.

"How. Dare. You." She took a step forward and looked him straight in the eyes. "I don't know what I've done to you personally, *Your Grace,* but I don't think I deserved to be treated with such contempt and dislike. You've been nothing but a jerk this whole time, from the moment we arrived through to dinner tonight." A spark of electricity crackled at her fingertips, but she didn't care.

"Miss Henney—"

"I'm not done!" She held up a hand. "Furthermore, I get that perhaps you're unconvinced of our motives, but I assure you we do not mean to harm you or anyone under your protection. Believe me, if you were our enemies, we wouldn't attack you from behind like cowards!" Her tirade made her run out of breath, like she had run a mile in ten seconds, so she heaved great big gulps of air into her lungs, trying to get oxygen into them again.

Reed's face was stony, but the power from him practically vibrated. She resisted the urge to shrink back. He reached for her again, and this time, she let him touch her. His hands wrapped around her upper arms, and despite the cover of his gloves and hers, the heat from his palms branded her. He stepped forward, and she staggered backwards until she found herself trapped against the wall.

"Elise." Her name on his lips was a raw, low growl that made her shiver.

As he was lowering his head, horror shot through her. *No!* If he touched her bare mouth with his—

A loud cough made him let go of her and step back. He turned around. "Mr. Jonasson."

She peered around his large frame and saw Cross at the top of the stairs staring at them. She let out a breath of relief and stepped around Reed. "Cross," she began. "What are you doing here?"

"I was going to bed," he explained. "The earl and countess stayed downstairs to give the servants some last-minute instructions as Lady Winford wanted to leave first thing tomorrow." His blue-green gaze narrowed at Reed. "Your Grace? I thought you said you wanted to say goodnight to your nephew."

"Yes, of course." He gave them a curt nod. "Mr. Jonasson. Miss Henney." Pivoting on his heel, he walked away from them and then entered the first door on the left.

"Cross," she urgently whispered as she closed the distance behind them. "Julianna—she's in the countess's bedroom. That door."

He didn't waste any time and instead dashed toward the direction she pointed him. As soon as he entered, her heart stopped banging into her chest like a wrecking ball. Cross could whisk Julianna away with no one the wiser.

She turned on her heel and sprinted down the hallway. It was only when she was in the safety of her own room that she allowed her body to relax.

What the hell was she thinking? Talking to Reed that way? Sure, he couldn't send her to jail, but he could probably insist that they leave his territory. And then they would never get close to the dagger.

She desperately wanted to get away from him. But at the same time, that small touch—not even bare skin—was branded into her brain. Her wolf seemed to relish his touch, rolling around like some dog in heat.

Now's not the time to be attracted to anyone! Especially not that ass! She was scolding her wolf, but really, she was telling that to herself too. Perhaps Julianna would find the dagger tonight and that would be that.

"I just dropped Julianna off at her room."

She nearly jumped out of her skin as Cross materialized

in front of her. Would she ever get used to it? Probably never. "Did you find it?"

He shook his head. "It's not the same dagger. Julianna confirmed it as she had seen the artifact during Adrianna's ceremony."

Damn.

He cocked his head at her. "Are you all right? Did Reed suspect anything?"

She swallowed. "I'm fine." She quickly explained to him what Julianna had planned.

"She and I came to an agreement. No more going rogue missions," he said wryly. "But at least we eliminated the mother's dagger. So, it's definitely the one at Huntington Park."

"I guess we're not going home tonight."

His smile was sad. "No, not tonight." He grabbed her hand and squeezed it. "Don't worry, Elise, we'll find it. We're much closer now than we were yesterday."

She was glad he was feeling positive. Someone had to be in this situation. "You're right." She squeezed his hand back.

"Only one hundred and eighty rooms to search."

She laughed. "One hundred and eighty?"

"That's what Reed said. Huntington Park has one hundred and eighty rooms."

"Well, we better get started soon," she said wryly.

"Elise, if Reed tries to get too close—"

"He won't," she bit out. "I mean, he's not going to be there, remember?"

"True." He let go of her hand and stepped back. "I'll see you in the morning."

"See you."

As she watched him dematerialize, fatigue began to set in. She was so tired. All she wanted was to go home to her own bed and her own time where things made sense. And, if she were really honest, she was eager to put as much space and time between her and Reed Townsend, before he made her feel things she had no right to feel.

CHAPTER SIX

Elise hadn't dreamt of *the incident* in years.

She thought it was all behind her by now. But maybe it was all the years of bottling it up inside her that now it was threatening to explode.

He'd been her first crush. Her first love.

It was in first grade that she had first met Chris Lopez, when he scared away some bully trying to steal her lunch money. Since that day, she never left his side. Lara and his mom thought it was cute the way Elise would follow him around with that puppy-dog look in her eyes. They became best friends in second grade and were inseparable until they turned sixteen. She confessed her love for him the night of prom.

And then she nearly killed him.

It was so clear that it was like she was living it again and it wasn't a dream. The sequence of events was captured in her mind so fully, it was like it was yesterday and not fourteen years ago.

His car stopping just outside the gates of her house.

Telling Chris that she loved him.

Him, leaning down to give her her first kiss.

Her hands going up to cup his jaw.

The white-hot shock of electricity that shot through her lips and hands as a thousand volts of electricity flowed into Chris.

His body going limp.

"Miss, miss!" Came the frantic cry that woke her up from the nightmare.

Elise sat up in bed, her vision still blurry. "Sorry, what time is it?"

The indistinct shape beside her bed came into focus. "It's still early, miss," Melinda said. "But it sounded like you were havin' a nightmare."

"I was," she confessed. "Thank you for waking me up."

"I have some breakfast for you," she gestured at the tray on the bedside table. "After you finish eating, I can help you get ready for travelin' today. I have your gown all pressed and ready."

"That would be lovely."

Her hands were still shaking from the vivid dream, but she pushed those thoughts aside. *Food might help*, she thought as she reached for the tray.

Despite the fact that the toast tasted like ash in her mouth and the tea was like dank water, she gulped it all down. Then Melinda helped her put on the fine cream muslin gown and traveling jacket plus the matching boots. By the time she came down, everyone was already downstairs and ready.

"The coach is ready, my lady," Holden informed them.

"Excellent, thank you, Holden," Eleanor said.

The trip to Huntington Park wasn't bad, Elise supposed,

and Eleanor said it would only take three hours, and riding inside the comfortable coach was a treat she'd only read about in novels. The inside was spacious and luxurious, large enough to hold Eleanor, William, Cross, Julianna, and herself. William seemed shy and curious at the same time, giving her glances as she sat across from the young boy, which didn't escape Eleanor's notice.

"William," she began. "You didn't properly thank Miss Henney for yesterday. Would you like to say something?"

The young boy nodded. "Miss Henney, th-thank you."

Elise thought he was adorable, the way he was so formal. "You're welcome, Lord William."

He then turned to his mother. "Are we nearly there yet?"

"Almost," Eleanor assured him.

She nearly burst out laughing as it seemed being impatient during family trips was a universal thing. "Lord William, would you like to play a game?"

"What game?" His eyes widened.

"Julianna and Cross should know this one," she said, looking at her companions. "It's called 'I Spy' and it goes like this...."

The rest of the trip breezed by as they played the game, and Eleanor even participated. When they arrived, the household staff was lined up in front to greet them. After all the formalities, Eleanor led them to the drawing room. "Edwards, the butler, informed me that Bridget is already there and that Grandmama's coach should be arriving shortly. If you don't mind, I think it best we all get acquainted."

When they entered the drawing room, there was a young woman seated in one of the couches, facing away from them.

"Cousin Bridget," Eleanor greeted. "It's nice to see you again. Oh my, you have grown up!"

The young woman stood up and curtsied. "Lady Winford—"

"Eleanor," she insisted. "You've always called me Eleanor, remember? Though you were so young then, you probably shortened it to Ellie."

Bridget's pretty face broke into a smile and her blue eyes sparkled as her shoulders relaxed. "Ellie, yes. I remember. You were always so nice to me, even though I was a bit of a rambunctious child, always running around and getting my dress dirty." The lovely lilt of her Scottish accent made her sound like she was singing.

"I remember, all right," Eleanor chuckled. "But I recall being jealous of you because you could do all those things. Oh! Excuse me, I haven't introduced our guests." She introduced Cross, Julianna, and Elise to Bridget and briefly told her about them.

Bridget looked relieved. "I'm glad I won't be alone going to my first season." A frown crossed her face. "I had hoped my True Mate would be someone back in Scotland, but my da's been waiting for two years, and I've met every eligible Lycan and human in the county and still nothing."

That was the second time someone mentioned about knowing their True Mate, and although Elise was dying to ask what that was all about, she refrained.

But apparently, Julianna didn't have such restraints. "Hold on a minute!" Julianna held her hands up. "Can you explain to me about this knowing your True Mates thing?"

Bridget opened her mouth to speak, but was interrupted

when the butler entered and announced, "Her Grace, the Dowager Duchess of Huntington."

The tension in the room suddenly thickened and Eleanor quickly turned toward the entrance. Though she hadn't instructed them to do the same, they all seemed to naturally follow her and faced the woman standing at the threshold.

As the dowager duchess strode in, Elise knew why she commanded such respect. Despite her age, the power emanating from her was difficult to ignore. Elise felt her own wolf—and the others around her—cower and shrink back. It almost reminded her of Reed's presence which made sense. She was technically Lupa of the clan and Reed's grandmother, after all.

"Your Grace," Eleanor began. "Allow me to introduce our guests to you."

The duchess said nothing but raised a brow. She was the picture of matronly restraint and calm in her dark brown traveling outfit, but the power brewing in her was there, simmering at the surface.

"Mr. Cross Jonasson, envoy of the Alpha of New York, and his cousins, Miss Elise Henney, and Miss Julianna Anderson who is daughter to their Alpha. Mr. Jonasson, this is my grandmother, Miranda Townsend, the Dowager Duchess of Huntington."

"How do you do, Your Grace?" Cross gave a smooth bow. "It is an honor to be here, and we thank you for welcoming us into your territory." Elise and Julianna followed with deep curtseys.

"And of course, you know my cousin, Bridget MacDonald, daughter of Lord Alec MacDonald, Earl of Caelkirk and the Alpha."

"Thank you for welcoming me into your territory, Your Grace." Bridget did the same deep curtsey.

The silence as Miranda Townsend's hawk-like eyes roamed over them was deafening. She addressed Bridget first. "You have excellent coloring, very fashionable. But then again, blonde and blue-eyed girls always are."

Bridget's eyes widened, but she didn't say anything.

The duchess then turned to Elise. "I almost thought *you* were Bridget, with those brazen tresses." She wrinkled her nose. "No pink for you, it would look dreadful with your complexion and hair. You're pretty enough to turn heads, though."

Elise was so shocked at the older woman's rudeness she didn't know what to say.

Finally, she turned to Julianna, and her face twisted in horror. "Oh my." The duchess's nose wrinkled. "You'll need the most work. Far too tall. You have a good face, but those eyes destroy the symmetry. And that skin." She tutted. "Did your mother let you run around the fields?"

Julianna looked dumbstruck. "E-excuse me?"

"You're far too tanned," the dowager duchess remarked. "From now on, you will not be permitted out in the sun."

"I'm not *tanned*," Julianna exclaimed. "I'm Italian."

From the look on the duchess's face, one would have thought she said "serial killer."

"Italian?" came a voice from behind the duchess. The dowager's presence was so arresting that no one had noticed the man who crept in behind her.

The man who stepped out from the duchess's shadow was older with white hair and a beard, and he wore a rich red velvet coat and trousers. "You are Italian?"

The dowager's face remained impassive. "I almost forgot. I have a guest as well. This is Signore Franceso Rossi, an envoy sent by Prince Giovanni, the Alpha of Florence. He's my guest."

"I am not just a guest," Signore Rossi said with a deep, flamboyant bow to the ladies. "I am also a gift."

"A gift?" Eleanor asked.

"Prince Giovanni is not just my Alpha, but my patron as well," Rossi explained. "I am an artist. He has sent me here to paint the portrait of your family, as a gift and to strengthen relations with your clan."

"I've not decided if I shall accept the prince's *generous* offer." From the tone of disdain from the duchess's voice, it was obvious what she thought of the offer. "But I have allowed Signore Rossi to accompany me here and perhaps he may be inspired to paint the landscape ... or something else."

"It is very different, England," Rossi remarked. "But, *bella.*" He turned back to Julianna. "You said you are Italian?" He spoke a few words of Italian.

Julianna nodded. "On my mother's side." She replied with a few words and from the way her eyes darted at the duchess, Elise could only guess what she was saying.

"English, please," the duchess demanded. "Signore Rossi, if you are to stay with us, then you must speak in English, at least in our presence."

"Of course, Your Grace." He bowed to the duchess. "My deepest apologies. It has been many weeks since I have spoken my native language and to speak with such a beauty as Miss Anderson"—he smiled brightly at Julianna—"is a rare treat for me in this land."

"You're forgiven, Signore." The duchess turned to Cross. "Do the ladies have a dowry?"

"A substantial one, Your Grace," Cross assured her.

"Grandmama!" Eleanor exclaimed, clearly embarrassed at her grandmother's behavior. "Can we not speak of such things later?"

"Of course," the duchess said. "We have far too much work ahead of us." Her eyes trained on the three women again. "And we don't have much time if we are to launch these women into society. I insist we begin immediately. Madame Marie is already in the parlor, where she can take their measurements for their gowns. They will need many outfits."

"I've brought my own gowns, Your Grace," Bridget said.

The duchess's head snapped back to the young girl. "I'm sure you have." She pivoted on her heel. "Come. We have no time to waste."

"Maybe you'd like to check my teeth too," Julianna grumbled.

"What was that?" The duchess didn't even bother to turn her head.

"Nothing, Your Grace," Elise offered and grabbed Julianna by the elbow.

"Good," the duchess barked as she walked out the door. "Men don't like women who talk back."

If they were in a cartoon, steam would have been coming out of Julianna's ears, but Elise yanked her elbow in the form of a warning.

"Do not be fooled by the duchess's demeanor," Rossi said in a reassuring tone. "I've spent some time in her company in the last week. I know she means well."

"I think she was rather disappointed I never got my own launch," Eleanor said with a laugh. "And she didn't have any daughters. She wants you all to make good matches."

Julianna grumbled again but said nothing.

"All right then." Eleanor clasped her hands together. "As Grandmama said, we don't have much time, and there's so much you have to learn. Let's get started, shall we?"

"Kill me now," Julianna stage-whispered. "Please. Or I'll do it myself."

"It's not that bad," Bridget giggled as she whirled past them in the arms of the dance instructor that the dowager duchess had employed. He had also brought along his own pianist, a Monsieur Delacroix, to accompany them.

"Surely you've gone through worse than this?" Elise asked.

"I've had to learn how to resist torture," Julianna said. "And believe me, this is worse."

The whole afternoon flew by in a whirl of activity as the duchess and Eleanor threw them into a gauntlet of preparations for their coming out. First was Madame Marie, an apparently well-known seamstress who did the gowns for only the most fashionable ladies of the ton. She spent most of their time complimenting each girl, but also bemoaning the lack of time and hands she had to prepare all their outfits—which was of course, soothed by promises of additional funds by Eleanor and Cross. When Madame was dismissed, they sat down to learn table manners which wasn't too bad as Elise and Julianna knew which fork to use with what, though the duchess scolded Bridget a few times for picking up the wrong spoon.

Finally, after tea, they were now moving on to dancing lessons. Elise wasn't terrible at it—she did learn to waltz, and she was thankful her mother had been insistent she and all her siblings take lessons when they were teens. But Julianna had been terrible, and the instructor, Monsieur Fermin, nearly walked out twice before Elise suggested Bridget ought to have a turn.

"A natural dancer," Monsieur Fermin said to the young Scot as he gave Julianna the side-eye. "Unlike others."

Julianna stuck her tongue out at Fermin; a bold move, but she must have dared it because the duchess and Eleanor were deep in conversation in the other corner of the dancing room.

"That's not the way a lady behaves," the duchess said without looking up at them.

"Jeez, she must have eyes on the back of her head," Julianna groaned.

Elise suppressed the giggle in her throat. She caught Cross's eye from across the room and wondered what he was thinking. Since he hadn't been dismissed by the duchess and he didn't have a reason to take his leave, he had no choice but to join the ladies in their "lessons." The duchess barely paid any attention to him though, except for asking him a question about Elise or Julianna or their fathers' supposed wealth. Cross had answered with half-truths here and there.

"I *had* heard that the Alpha of New York owns many properties in the colonies," the duchess stated. "How about Miss Henney's father?"

"He is in the ... food and medicinal business, Your Grace," Cross said.

"A merchant?" The duchess gave a delicate wrinkle of her nose.

"A wealthy one, Your Grace."

Elise supposed that was technically true. Her father had one of the most successful biotech companies in Silicon Valley, while her grandparents had started a grocery chain and restaurant supply company.

"Well," the duchess harrumphed, "as long as he can pay for her gowns and upkeep, I'm sure her background won't be a deterrent."

"I'm seriously going to deck her, I don't care if she's old," Julianna growled under her breath. "I really will."

"It's not worth it," Elise chided. "Besides, maybe we'll find the dagger and we'll be out of here soon. Just play along, okay?"

The dowager duchess turned to Monsieur Fermin. "How are your lessons going?"

Fermin stopped the dance and nodded to the pianist. "Splendid, Your Grace," he assured her. "I won't stop until these ladies are the belles of the ball. They will be the most graceful—" His eyes nearly bulged out of his sockets. "Your Grace!" He took a deep bow.

All eyes went to the entrance of the dance room. Elise felt that white-hot sensation in her belly as she saw Reed standing there, looking devilishly handsome in his dark traveling clothes. Everyone immediate got to their feet save for the dowager duchess.

"Reed," the dowager duchess's face turned surprisingly tender as she accepted a kiss on the cheek from her grandson. "I was told you weren't going to be here."

"I'm allowed to change my mind, aren't I?" he said. "It *is* my house." He turned to the other occupants of the room and nodded at them so they could take their seats. "Cousin Bridget, you're all grown up now."

Bridget curtseyed. "Thank you, Your Grace."

"And, Monsieur Fermin, is that you?"

The dance instructor's face brightened. "I'm glad you recognized me, Your Grace."

"How could I not?" Reed's mouth quirked into a smile, making him look less severe. "I spent hours under your torture—er, tutelage."

Instead of being offended, the dance instructor merely laughed. "And you turned out so splendidly, did you not? His Grace has been the best student I've ever had."

"Maybe he can give us a demonstration," Eleanor cackled.

"I don't think—"

"Oh, Your Grace!" Monsieur Fermin's voice pitched higher with excitement. "That would please me so much." He looked at the three women. "And the ladies would benefit from dancing with a gentleman. If you please, Lady Bridget."

"Oh no." Bridget waved her hand as she plopped down in a chair next to Julianna. "I just finished dancing. My feet need a wee bit of a rest."

Monsieur Fermin grimaced when his gaze landed on Julianna. "Miss Henney," he said as his eyes trained on Elise. "If you please."

Her heart jumped to her throat. "I couldn't possibly—" Her protests died as Reed stepped in front of her and offered his hand.

"Miss Henney, may I have this dance?"

His voice was like thick, smooth honey. She stared at his

hand until Julianna elbowed her, jolting her enough to make her shoot to her feet. "Leave room for Jesus," Julianna teased.

Elise had no choice but to take his hand. This time only she wore gloves, and his touch sent a shock of electricity across her skin. There was a flash of surprise in his eyes, but that stony mask returned so fast she thought she'd imagined it.

"The waltz, Your Grace?" Fermin asked.

Reed nodded as he placed a hand on her waist. As the pianist started a slow waltz, he began to lead her into the dance. Elise realized that with the exception of last night, this was the closest they'd ever been. At this distance, she allowed herself to breathe in his scent—and her senses were filled with something earthy and delicious, like the scent of fresh rain and strangely enough—sunscreen. It reminded her a lot of lazy summer days at the beach.

The other thing she realized was that Monsieur Fermin wasn't lying. Reed was an excellent dancer. When she danced with Fermin earlier, the instructor was precise, but at the same time, light on his feet and almost feminine.

Reed was the opposite. His presence was commanding, but he led her around the room with a sensuous and unmistakable masculinity that made her knees weak. Though her lashes were lowered, she could feel his hawk-like gaze on her, and she cursed herself silently when she felt the heat creep up her cheeks.

His hand tightened its grip on her waist as he pulled her to him. Her wolf reveled in the closeness—which was, by today's standards, nearly scandalous. She realized he had somehow drawn them to the farther end of the ballroom.

"Nothing to say today, she-wolf?"

Her head snapped up to meet his gaze. Oh God, why did she go off on him last night? But she couldn't help herself. He was just so infuriating. "We are in a room full of people, Your Grace," she said. "I wouldn't dare say anything."

"Maybe you can show me your claws again when we're alone."

The way he said those words made heat curl up in her stomach. *When* we're alone, he said. Not if.

"Maybe I won't make that same mistake again." She suddenly stopped, bringing their waltz to a halt. "Your Grace," she added.

"Is everything all right?" Monsieur Fermin called as he motioned for Devereux to stop playing.

"It's all fine," Reed said. "I just found the waltz too ... boring."

She fumed silently. *Boring?*

"Lady Bridget is an excellent dancer," Fermin offered. "Perhaps you can dance the *Quadrille* with her?"

"Of course." Reed turned away from Elise and toward Bridget. "May I have this honor, cousin?"

As Bridget took her place, Elise silently padded back to her chair next to Julianna. She avoided the other woman's gaze and kept her eyes down to her lap. When she tried to look up and saw Reed and Bridget dancing, a strange tightness in her chest began to form and her wolf growled softly. *Shut up*, she told her animal. Bridget and Reed were cousins. There was no need to feel ... weird just because he was touching her. And yet that feeling wouldn't go away.

Finally, after what seemed like hours—though it had only been a three-minute dance—Eleanor declared it was late, and they should all prepare for dinner. Elise was glad to be out of there—almost as glad as Julianna it seemed as the younger woman practically fled out of the dance room.

Elise was glad that Melinda was waiting in her room. The maid explained that they had traveled behind the earl's coach and she had spent the afternoon making sure her room was ready. Melinda helped her bathe and get dressed in a simple cream evening gown, cut in an empire style that was fashionable in these days.

Dinner wasn't as bad as yesterday. Since Reed and his grandmother were technically hosts, they sat on either end and Elise was in the middle, next to Signore Rossi. The charming Italian man had seemed to take a liking to Julianna, who kept extolling her beauty and virtues, much to the duchess's horror.

When dinner was over, all the men went to the library to partake in some drinks and cigars, while the women went to the parlor for coffee and some sweets. When the dowager duchess decided to retire, that meant the ladies could as well.

"I'll come to your room later tonight," Julianna whispered as they walked up the stairs while Bridget was behind them. "So we can start the search."

She nodded and then bid her and Bridget good night as she went to her own room. Melinda was already there, and the maid helped her undress, get freshened up, and change into her bedclothes. As soon as Melinda closed the door, she threw the covers aside and sat up.

Without a clock, she couldn't tell how much time had passed, but it seemed to crawl by. She nearly jumped out of her skin when the soft knock came at the door.

"It's me," came Julianna's soft whisper.

Elise released the breath she was holding and opened the

door. Julianna put a finger to her lips and then gestured for Elise to follow her. They walked down the long corridor, then down the stairs to the main foyer.

"Cross should be here any minute." Julianna glanced around. The foyer was dark and empty. "Are you sure you want to join us, Elise?"

"Of course, I'm not going to let you do all the work," she said. "And with three of us working at the same time, we can cover more ground. What's the plan?"

"Cross did some exploring this afternoon," Julianna began. "We've eliminated places where the dagger can't possibly be—like the servant's areas, the gardens, and stables —and mapped out the main house."

"Any luck in getting Reed to talk about where the dagger is?" Elise asked.

She shook her head. "According to Cross, Reed genuinely doesn't seem to know." Her brows wrinkled. "He thinks the dowager duchess might know so he wants me to work that angle." Julianna made a face. "Ugh. So, it's possible that old bat is the only thing standing between me, a shower, and a cheeseburger."

Elise smiled. "Seems like it."

Julianna crossed her arms over her chest. "You'll have to help stop me from wringing her neck."

"It shouldn't be too—" Elise suddenly stopped and held a finger up. "I think someone's coming." Elise's keen hearing could pick up sounds from upstairs. Footsteps. And from her position at the end of the alcove, she could see exactly who it was.

Reed.

He was dressed casually in a loose white shirt, tight

breeches, and knee-high boots. As shafts of moonlight hit his face, her heart hammered in her chest. He looked handsomely dangerous, but even more than that, they would be in real danger if he discovered them sneaking around in the dark. *Again*. And this was his home, so he could throw them out this time.

Biting her lip, she knew there was only one thing she could do. She caught Julianna's eyes and pointed to herself, then nodded her head.

Julianna's mismatched eyes widened, and she shook her head to disagree, but it was too late. Reed was nearing the bottom of the stairs, and he would see them. With a deep breath, Elise ran as fast as she could—away from Julianna and toward the long hallway on the other side of the foyer.

Her heart slammed over and over again against her ribcage as she made a run for it. She used her Lycan speed, but since he was a Lycan too, he surely saw her as she ran across the foyer. He was so close she could feel his presence at her back. And that was her intention, to draw him away from Julianna.

"Where do you think you're going?" The hand that wrapped around her arm was firm and she found herself pushed up against the wall. "Are you lost again, little she-wolf?" His face was so close to hers she could feel his breath on her skin.

"Y-Your Grace," she whispered. "I-I couldn't sleep. I was just trying to f-f-find a book or something to read."

"Is that so? Then why did you run away from me?"

"I don't—I'm sorry," she stammered and tried to squirm away from him, but his grip tightened.

"Do you know what could happen to young, innocent

women who creep around other people's homes in nothing but their nightgowns?"

She could see his eyes glowing in the dark. A sign that his wolf was near the surface. Despite being a Lycan herself, she couldn't help but feel like Little Red Riding Hood, about to be eaten by the Big Bad Wolf. When she opened her mouth, no sound came out, so she shook her head instead.

"No?" He cocked his head. "Let me show you."

Elise barely had time to protest as his head descended toward her. It happened in a split second, but it was like time slowed down, and scenes from her past flashed through her mind.

Her body froze, waiting for the uncontrollable surge of power to course through her and shock Reed into a coma, just like it did to Chris.

But it didn't come. In fact, though her body hummed with electricity, it stayed contained within her.

Oh.

And Reed ... his lips molded against hers in a sensuous assault, teasing her at first. Her heart beat with an erratic staccato, pounding madly against her chest as he continued to kiss her. She found herself pressing her bare hands against the front of his chest. His muscles jumped at her touch, but he didn't stop kissing her. If anything, his kisses became more insistent, and feeling bold, she slid her hands higher, stopping at the nape of his neck to tangle with the errant curls of his hair.

The feel of his bare skin against her fingers made her moan—not only did the heat shoot desire all the way to her core, but she realized this was the first time she'd ever touched a man's bare skin. When she felt the brush of something hard against her hip, she gasped, but pressed herself up against him.

Reed pushed her back against the wall, pinning her. With nothing but her thin nightgown and his breeches between them, she could feel every hard plane of his muscled body. She wantonly opened her mouth to let his tongue slip between her lips and touch hers. Another shock of electricity spread through her body, but again, it didn't seem to affect him.

A hand slid under her nightgown, pushing it up until it was above her knees. When his fingers moved higher, she felt her knees go weak.

The loss of his lips made her whimper, and as he raised his head, the naked desire on his face was unmistakable.

"You kiss like a virgin, but your body says otherwise." The flare of his nostrils told her that he could smell her arousal.

He raised an eyebrow at her as if waiting for her to say something. She gasped in horror and pushed him away. *I should slap him. Tell him that he should stay away from me and this wasn't proper. That this was a mistake.* But the words weren't coming out of her mouth. Her wolf, on the other hand, rolled around in delight at the thought that he wanted them so bad.

The conflict between herself and her animal paralyzed her. And so, she did the only thing she could think of.

She pushed past him and ran like a coward.

CHAPTER SEVEN

Reed had every intention of staying in London and letting Eleanor and his grandmother take care of the crazy Americans. His sister was the one who insisted on being their champions, despite his objections, so she could deal with them. He didn't have to see them if he didn't want to.

Yes, he was decided on staying in town.

That is, until Elise Henney showed her claws after dinner.

He was never one to play games with women. Many of those he dallied with or took on as his mistress tried to manipulate him emotionally. Except few of them realized that when you had no emotions, you couldn't be manipulated. Anaïs was the most recent one to make that mistake, and she probably wouldn't be the last.

Elise wasn't playing games with him, but somehow, that made him want to know more. She was so passionate in her defense—and her fury at him—that anyone would have believed her. But he still wasn't convinced she was telling the truth. He had to know what was going on.

And he had to have another whiff of her delicious scent. His wolf had howled possessively when it smelled her last night—like strawberries and lemons mixed together reminding him of summer days of his childhood. It was enchanting and he couldn't get enough.

His damn obsession with her made him act impulsively. Before he knew it, he was heading to Huntington Park instead of spending the week in London attending to business.

Dancing was not part of his plan, but he took advantage of it. Holding her close had brought up emotions in him he didn't want to name—desire, yes, but something else too. And so, during dinner, he did his best to avoid looking at her, but he failed miserably as he kept being drawn to her beautiful face and the expanse of creamy skin exposed by her dress. Sure, he had seen many more daring outfits on other women, but even in the plain gown, her beauty shone even more and incited his lust.

He tried to forget her, but his damn animal kept him up. The wolf was restless knowing she was nearby and under the same roof. He thought some brandy would help, but when he saw the shadow crossing the foyer, he just *knew* it was her. Seeing her run had made his Lycan instincts flare up, and he chased after her.

In the moonlight, she seemed even more beautiful, and her scent overpowered him. Bewitched him, really, and he could no longer fight it and he had to taste her.

And she turned out to be everything he could ever want. All his erotic dreams rolled into one package.

This was pure madness.

But at the same time, not. She was perfect in his arms.

Although her kisses seemed tentative, her hands and body were bold. She was following her instinct, the desire to be one with him.

Her True Mate.

Now, *that* was the part that was madness.

Because although he wanted her in his bed, he still didn't trust her. The fact that she was once again prowling around the house in the middle of the night showed that she was hiding something.

No, he was not going to fall into this trap again. Elise Henney was a woman, and he would not allow himself to be in that situation again.

And so, he avoided her for the next day and a half. He worked in his office or went about on a tour of the estate, giving excuses to his grandmother and Eleanor that there were many things that needed his attention. Not that he could avoid her.

Just now, he thought he heard her laughing and giggling, and when he looked out the window, he saw Elise and Julianna with William. They were running around in the garden—probably playing tag— and Elise looked carefree, her cheeks were flushed with exertion, and she was more beautiful than ever.

His every thought was consumed with Elise. Wanting her, and at the same time, wanting nothing to do with her.

"Your Grace." Edwards walked into his office as he was meeting with Whittleby. "Apologies for the interruption, but your guests have arrived."

"Guests?" Reed asked. "I have guests?"

"Viscount Daly, Your Grace," Edwards said. "He says you are expecting him and his children. They're already unpacking their coach. Shall I prepare some rooms for them?"

"Unpacking?" He and the viscount had been trying to meet in order to talk business about a new shipping venture to the Caribbean. They were supposed to have a formal meeting yesterday at Hunter House, and he knew it was rude to cancel last minute. So, instead of outright canceling the meeting, he had sent Daly a note offering to host the meeting at Huntington Park instead at his convenience. Still, he didn't mean for Daly to stay or to bring his children.

"Your Grace?" Edwards asked.

He let out a drawn-out sigh. It wasn't like he could toss them out now. "Show them in and get some guest rooms prepared for the viscount and his children." Eleanor and Grandmama were probably not going to like this seeing as the reason they came here was to keep Bridget, Elise, and Julianna away from the ton's prying eyes. However, Daly wasn't exactly one of the elite members of society, though he was well-respected enough. Because of his large holdings in the Caribbean, the viscount had spent considerable time there and only returned recently with his children. He had heard that the viscountess had died when the children were younger, contracting some terrible tropical disease.

After giving last-minute instructions to Whittleby and dismissing him, Reed prepared himself for his unexpected guests.

"Your Grace," Edwards began as he re-entered the office. "His lordship, Viscount Daly, the Honorable Simon Richardson and the Honorable Beatrice Richardson."

Edwards ushered in the three newcomers. Hugh Richardson, Viscount Daly, came in first. They had only met twice before, first after being introduced by a mutual friend at White's, and the second after the viscount called on him and proposed the business venture. The viscount was a tall, thin man with snowy white hair and a thin mustache.

The two people behind him, however, he had never met, though the viscount had spoken of his children before. Simon and Beatrice were twins, apparently, both with blond hair and green eyes, and dressed fashionably in the London style.

"Your Grace," Daly began as he took a deep bow, "we are utterly honored by your invitation to your magnificent home." Simon followed suit, while Beatrice made a deep curtsey.

"Your invitation came as a pleasant surprise, Your Grace," Simon said.

It was definitely a surprise, Reed thought to himself, but bit his tongue. "Thank you for making the trip here."

"I've heard many great things about Huntington Park, Your Grace." Beatrice looked up at him from lowered lashes. "And I must say, words do not do it justice."

"Thank you, Miss Richardson." He cleared his throat. "Your messenger must have gotten lost on the way here to announce your arrival," he said in a careful tone. "So, you must forgive me if your rooms are not ready. I'll have Cook prepare some refreshments in the drawing room."

"You're too kind, Your Grace," Simon said.

He led them out of his office toward the drawing room down the hall. However, as they made their way, a small figure darted down the hallway.

"Uncle Reed!" came William's boisterous laugh. "She's coming after me! Help!"

He bent down to catch his nephew before he bumped

into him or his guests, but as he looked up, his gaze crashed into brilliant blue eyes.

Elise seemed just as surprised to see him, and she suddenly stopped to a halt a few inches from him. Her chest rose and fell from exertion, and she let out a series of quick breaths. "Your ... Grace." She curtseyed. "We were playing and—"

"Elise is so good at tag," William declared. "She's caught me twice already, and I thought if I ran inside, she wouldn't be able to find me. I'm sorry to bother you, Uncle Reed."

"You're not a bother at all, William. But young lords shouldn't run inside the house," he said as he put William down, though he couldn't help but smile and ruffle his hair. He glanced up at Elise again, but she averted his gaze. He couldn't blame her but couldn't stop himself from admiring her in her light blue morning gown which clung to her curves. A rope of her brazen red hair had escaped her coiffure and curled around her delicate, swan-like neck.

A cough from behind made him startle. "Your Grace," Viscount Daly began. "Why don't you introduce us to your nephew and his, uh, friend?"

Reed straightened his spine. "Of course." He introduced William to the three before turning to Elise. "And this is Miss Elise Henney. She's our ... guest from America."

"How do you do?" Elise said.

"An honor, Miss Henney." Viscount Daly took her gloved hand and kissed it.

"Lovely to meet you," Elise greeted back.

"A pleasure to meet you," Simon said.

Reed's wolf suddenly began to growl at him and he was glad the Richardsons weren't Lycan. But why his wolf was acting that way, he didn't know. Perhaps it was the way Viscount Daly's lips seemed to linger too long on her hand or Simon's eyes quickly darted down her décolletage.

"We should be off." Reed patted William on the head. "Run along now, William. Miss Henney." With a quick nod, he sidestepped them and proceeded down the hallway to the drawing room, ignoring his wolf's protests.

Since Reed's unexpected guests had decided to stay for two days, he couldn't avoid joining the evening's dinner. Eleanor was not too pleased with newcomers, but she could hardly say anything since it was his home. Grandmama, on the other hand, welcomed their presence. "He's the perfect test," she had said. "A member of the ton, so he knows how to act in society, yet he's been away long enough that he doesn't hold too much influence if any of the girls have any missteps."

After his valet helped him dress in his customary evening formalwear, he headed down to the library for drinks. Everyone was already there, even Jeremy, who had arrived sometime in the afternoon. He was chatting with the dowager duchess, while Signore Rossi, Eleanor, Cross, Bridget, and Julianna were sitting on the settee by the fireplace listening to Viscount Daly talk about his home in the West Indies. However, his gaze was once again drawn toward Elise who looked stunning in a green satin evening gown. A dark, unknown feeling stabbed through him when he saw Simon Richardson talking to her, which only grew when Elise laughed at something he must have said.

Ignoring his own family—and all propriety—his strode toward them, hands clenched at his sides.

"And so, while I was chasing the puppy—" Simon's blue eyes widened when he saw Reed approach. "Your Grace." He dipped his head. "Good evening."

Elise's mouth parted, and even as she curtseyed, he couldn't stop himself from thinking about how soft and delicious it was the other night when he kissed her. That night seemed like it was a long time ago. "Good evening. I trust your rooms are comfortable, Mr. Richardson?" He wasn't above reminding the young fop who owned this house.

"They are, Your Grace," he answered. "Thank you."

His eyes darted toward Elise. She was doing that thing again where she was looking right through him. It damn well irritated him. "It seems I've interrupted your story. Please, go on."

"It wasn't important, Your Grace," Simon said.

"Your Grace." Beatrice Richardson seemingly popped up from nowhere. "Good evening." She gave a low curtsey, bending forward slightly so he could see the daring neckline of her silver evening dress. "Thank you for being such a generous host to us."

"My pleasure," he said, giving her a bright smile. From the corner of his eyes, he noticed Elise's narrowed gaze and flared nostrils at the arrival of the other woman. *Interesting.*

"Dinner is served," came Edwards's announcement.

"Miss Richardson, may I have the honor?" He offered his arm to her.

Her face lit up. "Thank you, Your Grace." She took his arm, her smile wide.

As they walked out, he heard Simon offer his arm to Elise

and while he felt a flash of anger, he buried it deep inside along with his wolf's yowls. When they arrived at the dining room, he escorted Beatrice to her chair which was in the middle of the table seeing as she wasn't one of the higher ranking ladies. He took his seat at the head, while Grandmama took the opposite end. Much to his dismay, Simon was seated next to Elise and he had to watch him charm her—and the other ladies around him—through most of the dinner.

"You know, that veal is already dead," Eleanor remarked.

"Excuse me?"

She looked at his plate. "Your veal. It's already cooked and dead, you don't have to torture it."

He froze and realized that he was holding his knife and fork with a vice-like grip and had viciously cut the meat into tiny pieces without eating a single morsel. "Very funny, Ellie."

"Your Grace," Viscount Daly said. "Is it true you're having some unseasonably warm weather lately?"

"That's what my gardeners told me," Reed answered.

"Maybe we could have a tour of the estate?" Daly continued. "I've heard that Huntington Park is the most splendid estate in England. Even grander than the royal palace."

"I wouldn't quite say that," Reed said. "But it had been expanded and kept up well."

"How about a picnic?" Beatrice suggested. "It would be a shame not to take advantage of the weather."

Reed snorted. "I don't—"

Eleanor placed a firm hand on his arm. "It will be a nice break for everybody." She glanced at Bridget, Julianna, and Elise. "I'm sure we would all enjoy it."

He was about to protest when his grandmother chimed it.

"What a splendid idea." The dowager duchess waved away the footman who moved closer to refill her wine. "We should definitely have a picnic."

"It must be so beautiful this time of year," Signore Rossi said. "I'm eager to see the beauty of the English countryside, and perhaps I shall be inspired to paint."

"There's nothing more beautiful," the duchess said. "I've always loved the grounds of Huntington Park, though I didn't agree with all the newer additions."

Though she hid her smile behind her napkin, Eleanor's grin reached her eyes and he knew exactly what she was thinking and what their grandmother was referring to.

Their parents' passion for each other was no secret, and they expressed it in many different ways. One way was a private garden they had built on the estate filled with erotic statues they had collected from all over the continent. "Lovemaking is a beautiful thing," his father had said when he showed Reed the private area when he was coming of age. "Especially with your mate. You shouldn't be ashamed of it."

Try as he might, he couldn't stop himself from looking at Elise again. Her head was turned to her right, chatting with Julianna, and his eyes immediately went to her exposed neck. Maybe he shouldn't have just stopped so soon the other night. He would have liked to nuzzle down all the way to her—

"Reed." Eleanor's voice was firm. "How about it? A picnic tomorrow?"

He focused his attention back to his meal. "A picnic it is." If everyone was going, he supposed it wouldn't be too bad. And he could always talk business with Lord Daly and head back to the house if things got too boring which picnics often did.

"Excellent, I'll have Mrs. Jameson arrange it," Eleanor said.

Reed took a sip of his wine, contemplating leaving the picnic after an hour or so. Yes, that was a good plan. He would show up as he didn't want to offend his guests, especially Viscount Daly, then he would make his excuses.

Beatrice sent him a knowing glance and a small smile, lifting her glass of wine toward him boldly. He wasn't stupid, he knew that she was trying to flirt with him and normally he wouldn't have entertained such thoughts, especially from a young miss and the daughter of a future partner in a lucrative business deal. However, it didn't escape his notice that Elise was currently shooting daggers at Miss Richardson.

Maybe tomorrow wouldn't be boring at all.

CHAPTER EIGHT

"You look lovely, miss," Melinda said as she gave Elise a final inspection.

"This riding habit is lovely," she corrected, frowning at her reflection in the mirror. Despite what the maid said, she could only see the dark circles under her eyes and the sallow color of her skin, which was the result of long, sleepless nights.

Despite the fact that they spent two nights here, they still only had time to search twenty rooms so far. It was difficult to get into the more private rooms—such as the east wing where Reed, Eleanor and Jeremy, and the dowager duchess were staying because during the day there were dozens of servants milling about and at night, the family was there. They had tried their best to get more information out of Eleanor, but it sounded like she didn't know anything either, while the duchess barely spoke to them unless it was to correct whatever mistake she and Julianna had made during their "lessons."

It was frustrating to say the least, but Elise was glad that between her days with the dowager and nights searching for the dagger, she didn't have time to think about Reed.

Except maybe right before she fell into bed, exhausted.

Or as soon as she woke up.

Or when she was dazing off into space while the dowager was giving some lecture about appropriate topics for small talk.

Ugh.

Damn Reed. Why did he have to go and kiss her? And, more important, why wasn't he shocked into a coma?

Not all witches and warlocks had a power, but as her mother was one of those "blessed" with one, it wasn't far off that she would be, too. It manifested itself when she was four years old, and she had shorted their entire house's electrical system when she touched a power outlet. Uncle Daric had bound her powers after that, and while he unbound them when she was fourteen, she never could control it, no matter how many lessons she got from Lara or Daric.

And of course, her cursed power malfunctioned at the worst time and hurt the last person she kissed—the love of her life and best friend.

To this day, no one knows how or why it happened. One moment Chris had his lips on her and then the next, electricity was coursing through his body. They were just outside the house, so she ran into the house, calling her mother and father for help and brought Chris to the hospital.

While they were able to help cover up the whole incident, they couldn't help Chris. He was in a coma for three months, and when he woke up, he couldn't remember what happened. While he was asleep, her parents had whisked her away, sending her to live in upstate New York with her grandmother until she went to college. Chris had tried getting in contact with her, but she couldn't bear to see him again and told him to forget about her. She knew she hurt him, but it was for his own good. Last she heard he was married with a kid on the way.

And here she was. Still stuck with a power she couldn't control or want. The gloves helped keep the electricity from harming anyone else, and she didn't dare get too close to anyone ever again, afraid that the touch of her bare skin would send someone else into a coma.

That is, until Reed Townsend.

"Miss?" Melinda's voice was full of concern. "Are ye all right? Ye seem like a million miles away."

Over two hundred years away, she corrected mentally. "I'm fine. Just tired." She wished she had some concealer. "The outfit really is lovely." It was lemon yellow, perfect for a picnic on a sunny day and had sturdy leather boots to match.

"I'm sure Mr. Richardson will like it," the maid said with a grin.

She laughed. "Simon? What makes you say that?"

"Oh, you know ..." Melinda raised a brow. "Us downstairs people, we talk. And the footmen said that handsome devil was payin' ye particular attention, out of all the lovely ladies during dinner."

"He was sitting beside me, so that could be why he was giving me all his attention." Simon really was handsome—exactly what she thought a hero in a regency romance would be like. But there was something about him ... or rather, something that just wasn't there.

"Whatever you say, miss." Melinda gave her a wink before asking to be excused.

Was Simon really into her? Well, maybe she would have noticed if that sister of his wasn't making cow eyes at Reed the whole night. *"Thank you for being such a generous host to us,"* she mocked into the mirror, copying Beatrice's high-pitched, posh tone and twirling a lock of hair with her finger while cocking her hip like some high-school girl.

Stop it. She righted her posture and smoothed her hands down her gown. It was just a stupid kiss, and soon they would find the dagger and be back home and Reed would be far away.

A thought made her chest ache. In the future, Reed would not be around *at all*. He would be *gone*.

"Elise! C'mon."

Turning her head, she saw Julianna's head poking through the door. "You're running late. We were supposed to meet everyone in the stables five minutes ago."

"The stables?" She hoped Julianna was joking.

But she was not.

"Don't ye worry, miss," the groom said as he led a mare to her. They didn't actually have to go into the stables as the grooms and stable hands were assisting everyone with their horses, but still, it was intimidating to be around the huge beasts. "This is one of my gentlest ones."

Looking over her shoulder, she saw everyone else seemed to be more relaxed around the horses. Even Julianna and Cross had mounted their rides with ease.

"I, uh ..." Nervousness made her hand shake as she accepted the reins. Sure, she worked at an animal shelter and was really good with animals, but she'd never actually ridden one before. And this horse seemed so huge.

"Miss Henney, may I be of some help?"

She turned around and saw Simon Richardson behind her, looking handsome and well put-together in a dark blue velvet riding jacket, brown breeches, and calfskin boots. He held a hat under one arm. If she really was a miss from this era, she probably would have swooned.

"Um, I've actually never ridden before." And certainly not side-saddle.

"Don't worry, Miss Henney." He fixed his hat on his head. "Please. Allow me." Simon linked his hands together and lowered them. "Place your left foot here and then hold on to my right shoulder."

While she thought a ladder would have been a better idea, the groom didn't seem to object. With a shrug, she followed his instructions.

"All right, straighten your knee ... that's it." Slowly, he raised his cupped hands and lifted her up. Her body brushed against his, a fact that he seemed fully aware of as his lips curled into a lazy smile. A shiver ran through her—and not the good kind.

"There now," he said as she settled into the saddle. "That wasn't too bad, was it?"

"Not at all." She tried not to think of how close he was and how his hand was on her mare's flank which meant it was only inches from her thigh.

Suddenly, a thunderous sound came from behind the stables. A large black horse galloped toward them, stopping short just a few feet from Simon. Of course it was *him*.

Dressed in all black and sitting atop the huge black stallion, Reed looked like he had ridden from hell itself. "Mr. Richardson," he began, his voice flat and his expression looked like he was ready to bite someone's head off. "Perhaps you should get on your own horse, so we may proceed. You're the only one not mounted yet."

"I was just helping Miss Henney get on her horse." Simon cocked his head at her. "She's never ridden a horse. I was thinking I could guide her mare alongside mine."

"Benton will assist her from now on." Reed signaled to the groom, who took the reins from Simon. "You needn't bother."

"Of course." Simon nodded to Elise. "I'll see you at the picnic then."

"I'll see you there," she said to Simon sweetly, then glared at Reed. But she didn't have time to retort to him as the groom began to lead her away.

The nerve of that man! Simon was only helping her. Sure, he was getting fresh, at least it was for this time, but Reed didn't have to dismiss him like he was nothing. But then again, was she surprised? The man treated anyone he didn't deem his equal with contempt.

Deciding not to let him ruin the one day she didn't have to worry about dancing, table manners, or suitable dinner conversation subjects, Elise found herself admiring the beautiful countryside. Huntington Park really was breathtaking. Everything was so green and smelled so fresh. The rolling hills seemed to go on forever, and for a moment, she forgot all about her troubles and what brought her here as she just basked in the wonders of Mother Nature. Maybe it was the witch side of her—but she felt so much more connected to it out here where there was no pollution, no cars, no technology.

"We're here, miss," Benton the groom announced. "Let me help you down."

"Thank you."

Glancing around, she saw everyone making their way to what was probably the picnic spot—a table set up under a giant oak tree.

"You know," Julianna said as she sidled up next to Elise. "When they said picnic, I was thinking of soggy sandwiches and potato salad. Not this."

"They certainly do things with flair."

Elise guessed that the servants had been sent ahead to make sure the elaborate setup was ready. A large table covered in fine linen was heaped with food and drinks, along with a huge floral centerpiece. Three footmen stood on the sides ready to serve guests. They also had blankets spread out around the table, as well as comfy-looking cushions to rest on.

"The food looks good though," Elise commented.

"I'm just glad to eat food without having hawk-eyes"—she cocked her head at the dowager duchess, who was already seated on one of the blankets with Signore Rossi—"watching every move I make and telling me I'm doing it wrong. Now, let's get some grub!"

They both grabbed a plate and piled it with food. The kitchen staff really went all out as there was a wide variety, from cold sandwiches to delicate pastries to delicious sweets and cookies.

"Miss Henney, Miss Anderson." Simon had popped up from behind and positioned himself between them. "If you have yet to secure a spot, I would like it if you would sit with me."

Julianna made a face, but before either could say anything, he guided them over to an empty blanket which was, thankfully, next to Eleanor, Jeremy, and William. The little boy's eyes lit up when he saw them approaching.

"Elise! Julianna!" William waved at them enthusiastically. "May I sit with them, please, Mother?"

Eleanor patted him on the head. "Only if there's space and they don't mind."

"Not at all," Julianna said as she sat down and gestured to the empty spot beside her. "Come here, squirt."

His face scrunched up. "What is a 'squirt'?"

"It means, a cheeky little boy like you." She ruffled his hair affectionately.

Since William had taken the spot next to Julianna, Elise had no choice but to sit beside Simon. "Thank you," she said as Simon helped her get comfortable.

"Of course." He gave her one of those bright-as-sunshine smiles. "I suppose we foreigners should stick together."

"Foreigners?"

"My sister and I grew up in the Caribbean," Simon explained as he sat beside her. "Our father's business was over there, so we grew up in his estate on a sugar plantation. We've only been back two years. Father wanted Beatrice to have a proper coming out and thought it was time for us to return to England."

"That must have been an interesting childhood," she remarked.

"It was." There was a tension in his jaw and his eyes darkened for a moment. "But we had servants and tutors from here and France. Father wanted us to be brought up like a proper English gentleman and lady."

"And your mother?"

He swallowed audibly. "Died."

"I'm so sorry." She placed a hand over his.

"It was a long time ago," he said.

She decided to change the subject. "So, your parents are English, and they gave you a real English upbringing. Why do you say you're foreigners?"

"Because, try as we might, we don't fit in here. Sure, my father's title and money can open certain doors, but some things remain ... unreachable to us." He turned to her, his blue eyes pinning her. "And they still treat us differently."

She felt a sudden pang of sympathy for him. "I know what you mean." And she really did. This place was so different. She had never felt more out of place in her whole life.

The silence between them hung in the air until he spoke. "I've heard America is an interesting place as well."

"Have you been?"

"No, but my father has." He signaled for the footman to bring them over some wine, then handed a glass to her. "Will you tell me about your home?"

"I—" she faltered then cleared her throat. *I could give him some vague details.* And so, she spoke a little bit about her home and her family, without giving too much away. Mostly half-truths, stuff that she didn't have to make up so it didn't bite her in the ass later. Simon seemed interested in every word she said, even asking her a few questions and asking for her opinion on what she thought of England so far.

"I've only been here a few days," she said. "But—"

A loud, high-pitched laugh pierced the air. When she

turned to the source, she saw it was Beatrice, who was seated next to Reed. Jealousy knifed through her as she watched the younger woman place a hand on his arm and look up at him invitingly. The only satisfaction she got was seeing the dowager duchess—who was sitting beside Reed—flash a disapproving look at the young woman.

"My sister can be boisterous," Simon commented with a wry smile. "It's part of her charm."

I'm sure it is. "She's very, er, friendly."

"Thank you for sugarcoating it," he joked. "Maybe it was the years locked away in our lonely little schoolroom, but she enjoys company now. She loves being surrounded by her adoring beaux." He lowered his voice. "Although I should probably warn her that she's no match for His Grace."

She blinked at him. "Excuse me?"

"I've only heard about his reputation," Simon leaned toward her. "You do know why his nickname is Hunter, don't you? And it's not because of his grand London home."

"No, I don't." And she wasn't sure she wanted to know.

"Because apparently he has a reputation for being focused when hunting down his prey."

She followed his gaze back to Beatrice and Reed. He was offering her a pastry, which she took from him, their fingers brushing. She forced herself to turn away. "His prey?"

"Yes, prey. Whatever he wants, he gets. Business deals, valuable assets, artwork …" He turned so his face was inches from hers. "Even women. There was a story about his last mistress, Anaïs Boudreaux, the famous ballerina. She was actually under the Earl of Abernathy's protection, but Hunter wanted her. And so, he took her."

"Took her?"

He chuckled. "Not that he spirited her away in the middle of the night. But he offered her a larger house and a bigger allowance, so she left Abernathy that very day."

Of course Reed would have a mistress. All rich men of this era did. Even the heroes in her most favorite novels had them, though they were dismissed once the hero met his true love. But still, the idea of him keeping a woman somewhere ... he probably visited her all the time. Hell, he could have visited her anytime in the past days. Even after their kiss in the hallway.

Her stomach churned at the thought, and even though hot rage was ready to spill out of her, she couldn't help but look back at Reed and Beatrice who were now deep in conversation, their heads bent together. *Well, if she wanted him, she could have him.* She would rather be alone forever than be with a ruthless man like Reed.

God, I'm going insane. She shook her head. What the heck was she thinking? This was the past. She was from the future. In her world, Reed didn't even exist anymore. He was dust and—

"Miss Henney, you look pale," Simon said, concern in his tone. "Are you all right? Would you like some water?"

"I-I-I'm fine," she croaked, then pasted a smile on her face. Reed Townsend had no bearing in her life, past or present. She was better off focusing her energies on trying to get home. But for the meantime, she could have some fun too, right? "And please, do call me Elise."

He returned her smile. "Then you must call me Simon."

"Simon it is. So, why don't you tell me what it's like to come back to England after all these years?"

"This was much more fun than I thought it would be," Julianna said as she plopped on the grass next to Elise. "Thank God Eleanor put William down for a nap. I thought that boy would never get tired." She and William had chased each other around the field of wildflowers not far from the picnic area. Elise had joined them earlier, but she grew fatigued herself and declared she would sit down for a few minutes. "I'm sweating like a pig."

"Don't let the duchess hear you," Elise teased. "She'll probably say something like, *Miss Anderson, sweating is so very unladylike!*"

Julianna sat up straight and placed her hand on her lap. "*And then you'll never find a suitable husband,*" she said, mocking the dowager's severe tone. "*By the way, could you find my maid so she can take this stick out of my ass?*"

Elise covered her mouth, but not before a loud guffaw escaped her lips. "Julianna, you're terrible."

"That old bat's driving me crazy." She stretched her arms over her head, then lay back on the grass.

"And what about Signore Rossi?" she teased. The old Italian had really taken a shine to Julianna.

"He's old enough to be my dad," Julianna retorted. "Besides, he's just like any flirty Italian. Goes after anything in a skirt. But I'm not getting any pervy vibes. I think I remind him of his home, that's all."

Her expression changed and Elise knew what she was thinking. "I miss home, too."

Julianna sighed. "I just want to go lock myself up in my

apartment and put on my sweats and binge-watch Netflix for a week."

"That sounds like fun." A wave of homesickness hit her. She was already missing her family, her bed, her home, and her job. "I—" She stopped when she felt something wet hit her cheek.

"Oops." Julianna sat up and brushed a drop from her forehead. "It was pretty clear for a while." A frown marred her face as she pointed at the ominous clouds with her chin. "Where did those come from?"

"Weird English weather." Elise got up and helped Julianna to her feet. When she looked back toward the picnic area, she saw that the footmen were starting to pack up the table and food. "Looks like our picnic's going to be cut short. Where's Cross?"

"He went back to the house to do more searching while everyone's gone." Julianna brushed the blades of grass off her riding habit. "He said he'd come back in an hour."

"I just hope no one notices he's gone."

The rain picked up, and thunder rumbled overhead. Julianna grabbed her hand. "C'mon, we should go."

As they walked back, it seemed everyone else was headed back to the picnic area too. That is, everyone except Reed and Beatrice. Elise ignored the stab of jealousy in her stomach.

"Uh, this dreadful weather!" Eleanor scowled. "Looks like we'll have to head back to the house. We don't want anyone getting sick. I already had the groom escort Grandmama first, so we'll be on our own."

The rain began to really pour from the gloomy skies sending everyone rushing to their mounts. Jeremy and Simon all helped the ladies get onto their horses and then began to lead their party back toward the house. If anyone noticed that Reed and Beatrice were missing, no one commented on it.

"Father, I'm frightened," William cried when thunder rumbled overhead. He was riding in front of Jeremy, his small body tucked into his father's chest.

"Don't worry, William, it's just a little rain and thunder." Jeremy was the one leading Elise's horse, so he switched her reins over to one hand as he tried to soothe William.

The next peal of thunder was so loud, Elise thought her eardrums would crack. A second later, a jagged streak of lightning lit up the sky. William let out a scream, which frightened their horse. Jeremy dropped the reins trying to comfort the boy and calm their horse at the same time.

Elise grabbed them just in time and steadied her horse as she felt its nervous energy. "It's all right." She rubbed the mare's neck. "Nothing to be—"

An even louder crack of thunder boomed overhead, and this time, the lightning streaked right in front of them, a few feet away. Her horse reared back, but her fast reflexes had her holding onto the creature's mane which prevented her from falling. However, the mare's distress caused it to turn around and run like mad, and Elise could do nothing but hold on as tight as she could as the horse galloped farther and farther away from everyone else.

The rain pelted at her like tiny icy knives. It also made it difficult to keep her hold on the horse's mane and the gloves she wore were not helping. Her fingers slipped out of the gloves, and she felt herself falling. In a desperate move, she made a grab for the reins but got only air.

As she fell, she landed on her right foot, then tumbled down the wet grass. She let out a cry as pain shot up her leg.

When her body stopped rolling, she pushed herself to her back and stared up at the gloomy skies.

Rain continued to pelt her, and her habit was now soaked and muddy. She wiggled her toes. It was like razor-sharp claws were digging into her ankle, but it didn't seem to be broken. As a Lycan, a sprain would heal in an hour or two, so she wasn't too worried. However, she couldn't very well just sit in the rain, especially not when lightning could strike her in an open field like this.

Gritting her teeth, she hauled herself upright resting her weight on her left foot. Not sure what else to do, she dragged herself across the field trying to find any kind of shelter. The rain and fog made it difficult to see anything, but if she walked long enough and far enough, she'd find something. Tears pooled in her eyes as the pain became unbearable, but she soldiered on.

As she walked in the rain, her keen ears picked up another rumble from far away. But it wasn't thunder. No, this sound was rhythmic and pounding, making the ground shake. She turned her head toward the sound, blinking the mixture of tears and rain away from her vision. In the distance, she saw a dark shape advancing toward her, emerging from the fog. It was growing bigger and bigger until ...

Oh, crap.

The mounted rider stopped just inches from her, the horse coming to a halt expertly with little resistance. Reed looked down at her from atop his stallion, his face practically murderous. "What the hell did you do?"

It took her a second to realize that he was somehow mad at her! "What did I do?" she cried. "What did I do?" Oh, this damned man! Without another word, she turned around and began to limp away from him.

Boots thumped on the ground. "Elise, wait. Wait!" He cursed a blue streak.

Though she tried to walk faster, it was no use because her injury wasn't healing fast enough, and he was much taller than her. He caught up with her in a few steps. "You're hurt."

She ignored the way his voice sounded surprisingly gentle. "Ya think?" she shouted.

He ran his fingers through his hair, then reached for her. "Let me help."

She evaded his grasp. "I'd rather walk!"

"Well that makes you a damned fool!" he shot back. "Do you even know which way to go?"

She looked around, then pointed to her left. "There."

"Try again." He crossed his arms over his chest.

"There?" She pointed to the opposite way.

He gave her an arrogant smirk and shook his head.

"Ugh!" She raised her hands in frustration. "I don't even care where I'm going, as long as it's far away from you."

"Me?" He stepped closer to her. "I'm the one who almost broke my neck riding here to come after you."

"I'm sure Beatrice would be sad if that happened."

"Miss—" His face changed from angry frustration to confusion and then to something else she couldn't name. "Well, if you're waiting for Simon to come after you, then you'd be waiting a long time. He's probably already back at Huntington Park with everyone else by now."

She pursed her lips together, not knowing what to say.

"Let's continue this conversation when we're somewhere dry."

He began to stalk toward her, and she couldn't move away, not with her ankle. "Where are you—what the heck!"

Reed bent down and slipped his other arm behind her knees, then hoisted her up against his chest. Her cheek pressed against his shoulder, and when she got a whiff of his scent, she felt oddly comforted. "Your Grace ... please, you shouldn't ..."

"You can't very well walk with that injury." He walked them all the way back to his horse and then gently put her on the saddle. "The house is too far away for Thor to carry us both, plus I don't want him injured if he slips." He grabbed the reins and began to lead the horse forward.

"Where are we going?"

A tick in his jaw pulsed. "I know ... a place not too far away where we can take shelter until the rain stops and your ankle heals."

He walked ahead, gently tugging on the reins to make Thor follow his directions. A few minutes later as they rounded a hill, she saw what looked like a large, manicured hedge. "What is that?"

"A private garden," he explained. "Or rather, a statuary my parents built. There's a little roof inside where were can wait out the rain." They turned, following the hedge until they came to a small metal gate. He didn't even bother asking her permission, but instead, lifted her off his horse. "Can you stand for a moment while I secure Thor?"

His surprisingly gentle tone shocked her into silence. So, she nodded instead, then watched as he tied the reins around a post next to the hedge. After checking that Thor was all right, he opened the gate. "Please, allow me to help you." He offered her his arm in a gallant manner and there was no hint of mockery or disdain in his voice.

Gingerly, she took it, though this time, he made no move to lift her up. Instead, he led her inside the garden. When they got through the small opening through the hedge, he stopped just at the entrance as there was a thatched roof awning right above them, sheltering them from the rain.

With the fog and rain, she could only make out the outlines of the various statues inside the enclosed garden. To her, they looked like big globs of marble. *Hmm...I wonder what they're supposed to be?*

"How is your ankle?" he said, breaking the thick tension of silence between them.

"It's getting better," she answered. "It should be healed in an hour or so."

"What happened?" There was genuine concern in his voice. When she didn't answer, he continued. "I was riding back when I saw Eleanor and Jeremy. They said your horse had run away."

"She got scared by the lightning and ran off." She'd never seen lightning strike so close. It was almost unnatural. "I couldn't hold on, and I fell."

"We can head back as soon as the rain stops. So we won't be suffering each other's company for too long," he said.

He sounded almost sorry and repentant. And she didn't like the things she was feeling right now. In the last couple of minutes, he actually sounded like he was worried about her.

Reed Townsend was such a conundrum. One moment he was cutting her down with his stares and the next, he was acting like some hero in a romantic novel. Of course, it didn't help that he was handsome. And that he was actually nice to his grandmother and sister. And he was a good uncle to William. Or—

Stop it.

She couldn't start having these feelings for him. So instead, she thought about what Simon told her earlier, about his reputation and his mistresses, and reminded herself that he was a cold, unfeeling brute. "I'm sorry to have inconvenienced you, Your Grace," she said, using the chilliest tone she could. "I'll try to keep out of your way from now on."

"Elise, I didn't mean it that way." He raked his fingers through his damp hair. "And I doubt you'll be able to keep out of my way."

"And why is that, Your Grace?" And she made the mistake of looking at him. His dark eyes drew her to him like a moth to a flame.

"Because I can't seem to stay away from you."

The words made her jerk back. Quickly, she pivoted away from him. "The rain has slowed down." With a careful gait, she stepped forward. The pain in her ankle was less pronounced now. "This sure is an interesting collection." She moved closer to the white statue on her right. "What is this—"

"Elise," he began in a warning tone. "You probably should know something about this place—"

"Now that's weird ..." She blinked. There wasn't just one figure, but two. A male and female. And they were both nude, kneeling in front of each other on a slab of marble. The man was between the woman's thighs, his mouth pressed between her breasts.

Heat crept up her cheeks and she swallowed hard. Then she looked at the other statues. All around them were couples in marble, entwined in passionate embraces. The one just opposite from her had a man standing behind a woman, his hands covering her breasts. Another had a woman tied up with ropes against a column, while her lover knelt in front of her, his face buried between her thighs. All the statues were expertly sculpted that they almost seemed alive, their expressions frozen at the height of pure ecstasy.

Where the heck had he taken her?

CHAPTER NINE

When Reed imagined the first time he would take a woman to his parents' secret erotic statuary, he didn't think it would be because he was performing a chivalrous act for a virginal miss. In fact, he imagined that it would have been a *very* unchivalrous act.

"Where are we?"

Elise was staring up at him, big blue eyes wide, her moist, plump lips parted, and her wet riding habit clinging to every curve. Standing amongst the erotic imagery, she looked even more tantalizing than any of the statues around them.

"I told you. It's a private garden." He took a step forward, which prompted her to step back. "My parents' private collection."

Her eyes grew impossibly wider. "Collection?"

"Yes. They ... let's just say their passion for one another was legendary. And this was one place where they demonstrated it." That didn't sound at all right, and from the way she crept back away from him even further, she must have misunderstood. "What I mean is, they didn't think there was anything wrong about passion or ... relations between a man and a woman." The last thing he wanted to do was frighten her, so he tried to find words that she might understand. "They were True Mates, and so they were madly in love with each other. This," he gestured around them, "was one way they expressed it. Most of the statues were imported from the Continent."

Her eyes grew dark, and she lowered her lashes to the ground.

"Don't, Elise." He moved toward her, and with nowhere else to go, he had her trapped against the marble base of the statue behind her. He placed a finger on her chin and tipped her head up to face him. "Do *not* turn away from me."

Blue eyes suddenly turned fierce, and he could see the fire in them again. "Don't tell me what to do. I'm not some simpering miss you can direct and bend to your will."

"Not like Miss Richardson?"

There it was again, the flaring of her nostrils and the contempt on her face. He'd seen it during dinner the night before and he wanted to test her reaction again. So, he made sure to pay particular attention to Beatrice today.

However, that plan backfired because she had been occupied with Simon, and not only did that enrage him, but now Miss Richardson seemed to think that he was interested in her. She had been like an irritating little gnat the entire morning and the only way to escape was to take Thor for a ride, claiming his horse needed the exercise since it had been a while since he'd come to Huntington Park.

When it began to rain, he joined the party again, only to find his sister in a panic and Elise gone. After Eleanor had calmed enough to tell him what happened, she pointed toward the direction where her horse went. His heart had stopped in his chest when he saw Elise was alive—hurt, but alive—as a million terrible scenarios had gone through his mind while he searched for her. Unfortunately, the closest place they could take shelter in was here, a private garden surrounded by erotic imagery.

She swatted his hand away. "I don't care about her. Or what you do with her or any of your mistresses!" A small gasp escaped her lips, like she was just as surprised as he was by her own words. He noticed her body tense as if ready to run away like the other night, and he knew he had to stop her. So, he did the only thing he could think of: pin her against the base of the statue with his body and hold her delicate wrists in his hands.

"No!" True fear crossed her face and she winced as if anticipating something bad to happen.

"I would never hurt you," he said in a calming tone. "But I can't let you believe ..." Did someone tell her about Anais? "I can only guess that the Honorable Simon Richardson has been feeding you lies—don't deny it, you've only been in England a few days so you haven't heard any gossip, and neither Eleanor nor Grandmama would feed you such salacious details." She struggled to get away from him, but he held her in place. Unfortunately, her sensuous curves rubbing up against him only fed his desire and his shaft went completely hard. "But you must believe me. I have no interest in Beatrice and I no longer have a mistress. It's been six months since I've even looked at a woman."

Her body went rigid. "Your Grace, I don't need to know—"

"Of course you do, otherwise you wouldn't have brought

it up." In a completely impulsive move, he leaned down and pressed his nose to the soft spot just below her ear. Her pulse jumped and he could hear her heart hammering in her chest. When her exotic scent filled his nostrils, he let out a groan. God, he wanted her. Damn all propriety.

He trailed his lips up her neck, across her jaw, waiting for her to protest. When she didn't, he kissed that damn teasing plump mouth. Just like before, she stood there, unmoving as the statues around them. Again, it was like she was waiting for something, but when whatever it was didn't come, her lips began to move against his.

He let go of her hands, but instead of falling limp to her sides, she slid them up his chest. *There was the sweet temptress from the other night.* She obviously wasn't very skilled at kissing, but her natural reactions drove him wild just the same. He slid a hand up her waist, to her ribcage, under her jacket, then higher to cup a breast. When she didn't cry out or push him away, he unbuttoned her shirt.

She gasped when his hand covered her naked breast and he used that chance to slide his tongue inside her mouth. Lord, she tasted sweet, like ripe peaches. Her tongue touched his tentatively, sending his body aflame. Her nipple puckered between his fingers and when the scent of her arousal hit his nose, he pressed the bulge between his legs against her. As if on instinct, her legs parted, allowing him to brush his erection against her core.

This was madness. He had to stop before he compromised her. But his wolf urged him on. Wanted him to make her theirs and bind her to them. Watch her belly grow large with their pup and—

No. Not again. He would not make the same mistake again. Of giving his trust and his heart to another woman.

He pulled away from her, cursing himself silently for letting things get too out of hand. Elise was a proper young woman. Related to the Alpha of another powerful clan. She was looking for a husband, not a romp between the sheets. The latter was the only thing he could give her.

"Elise, I'm—"

"No!" She screamed as she pushed him to the ground and threw herself on top of him. Before he could figure out what was going on, a bright light exploded above him. Heat seared the air as a fireball launched over them, hitting the statue of the kneeling man and woman.

He rolled her over, protecting her from the debris as the sculpture exploded, sending bits of marble and mortar around them. "What the hell?"

She mumbled something he couldn't hear as another ball of fire shot toward them. His Lycan instincts took over as he quickly wrapped an arm around her waist and pulled them away to a safe distance. Another sculpture shattered behind them as the fireball missed its mark.

Rage poured through him and he called on his wolf. There was no time to remove his clothes as his animal burst from his skin in a burst of fur, claws, and teeth. It was furious that anyone would dare attack their mate.

Like most Lycans, his animal form was bigger than ordinary wolves, its fur a mixture of brown and gray. Its keen senses picked up something *other* nearby, and as its massive head swung around, it found its target. Standing by the entrance of the garden was a figure in a red robe, his face hidden by the hood over his head. The robed man raised a hand toward him as a ball of fire formed in his hand.

The wolf sprang into action, leaping into the air toward the robed man. It landed on top of him and immediately set its sights on the man's throat. As its large maw opened to take a bite, a hot, searing pain made it yelp and roll away from its intended victim.

A stinging burst of pain shot through his wolf, and because they shared a body, Reed felt it too. Singed fur burned at his nostrils and he realized the man must have burned them. The fur was gone from his wolf's flank and the exposed flesh was red and angry. *Goddammit!*

"No!"

Elise's cry made him forget the pain. He looked around frantically searching for her, and to his horror, he saw the robed man approaching her, hands aflame.

Damn you!

He forced his wolf to get up, to reach her before—

Another burst of light blinded him temporarily. When his vision came back, he wasn't sure if he was hallucinating because of the pain or if what he was seeing was real. Elise stood firmly her arms outstretched as something white streaked out of her hand—was that lightning? Whatever it was, it hit the robed man straight in the chest and sent him flying halfway across the garden. Her mouth open in shock, she stood there, staring down at her hands. With a shake of her head, she seemed to snap back to her senses.

"Reed!" She called. "Where—oh!" As soon as she spotted him, she picked up her skirts and ran toward him.

"Oh no!" she cried and knelt beside him. "You're—oh God!"

He wanted to tell her that he would be fine. The pain was intense, but he would heal. But they had to get out of here before the robed man tried to hurt them again. He urged his wolf to stand.

"No," she protested when his wolf tried to get up. "Don't move. You'll just hurt yourself more."

His burned flesh was still stinging, but it would start to heal soon. He had to talk to her and convince her to leave now. *Rest and get well*, he told his wolf. Slowly, he tucked away his wolf, pushing it deep inside him as he took control of their body and turned back into his human form. A pained groan escaped his mouth as another fresh bout of pain shot through him.

"I told you not to move," she chastised.

"Where ... is ..."

Her body went stiff, then her eyes narrowed with steely determination. "Wait here." She stood up and began to walk toward the direction where she had sent the man flying.

"Elise, I—" When he tried to stand, a wave of pain forced him back to his knees, and he collapsed onto the wet grass. A few moments later she came back, her pretty face drawn into a frown. "He's gone. Burned through the hedge."

She removed her riding jacket and placed it over his torso —whether to help with the healing or for modesty, he didn't know. But he didn't question it as she sat by him, then lifted his head gently and placed it on her lap. She began to run her fingers through his hair in a soothing manner.

"What the hell happened?" He looked up at her. "What are you?"

Her fingers stopped midway. "I ... I'm what they call a hybrid."

"A hybrid?"

"I suppose ... you don't have them here in England." She bit into her lip. "My father is a Lycan and my mother is a witch."

"A witch?" Witches and warlocks didn't mingle with Lycans. In fact, the magical beings hated their kind. Every few generations or so, war would break out between the two factions. But still, he couldn't discount what he had seen with his own eyes. Maybe things really were different in America.

"Yes," she continued. "She's a blessed witch—meaning she has additional powers—and so do I."

"You can create lightning."

"Lightning?" Her expression changed. "Oh. Right. Lightning."

"But you're also a Lycan."

She nodded. "Yes. I can shift as well, and I share my body with a wolf."

"But that man ... he wasn't a hybrid, was he?" He didn't sense a wolf inside the man in the robe. "Was he a warlock?"

"I ... I don't think so," she said.

"Then what is he?"

"I believe he's something else ... a perversion of Mother Nature. He's what our—my mother's kind—call a mage."

"A—"

"Bloody hell, what in God's name happened in here, Hunter?"

He turned his head toward the direction of the voice. Jeremy stood in the entrance of the garden, his expression shocked as he surveyed the ruined statuary and Reed's obvious naked state. Behind him, looking oddly calm, was Cross Jonasson. His blue-green eyes were also surveying their surroundings, and Reed didn't know if he was happy or furious that the man didn't call him out for a duel immediately for being naked in the presence of his cousin.

"He's been hurt," Elise explained. "The lower half of his torso's all burned and bloody."

Jeremy walked toward them and then offered a hand to Elise. "Miss Henney, I think it's best if you, uh, let me take care of my Alpha's injuries."

Her face went red. "Of course, my lord." Gently, she eased his head from her lap and got to her feet.

Jeremy knelt down beside him and clucked his tongue. "Are you all right?"

"I could use a bottle of whiskey or two," he joked. "But I'm already healing."

"I've brought dry clothes." He glanced down at the riding jacket covering his lap. "When you two didn't return right away, Eleanor and Grandmama insisted I come after you for, uh, propriety's sake."

"Right."

"I brought Mr. Jonasson of course, since he's her guardian." In a low voice, he added, "Shall I get your pistols out and be ready to act as your second?"

He glanced over at Jonasson, who seemed to be more interested in examining what was left of the marble statue than defending his cousin's honor. "If you check the extent of the burn injuries on my torso, you'll see that there's no way I could have compromised Miss Henney."

"Which begs my earlier question: What the bloody hell happened?"

He sighed. "I don't really know myself, but I'm going to find out."

CHAPTER TEN

Once Reed's injuries had healed enough so he could get dressed and ride Thor, they made their way back to the house. He instructed Jeremy to ride ahead and summon Miss Anderson to his office, then make sure the human servants, Lord Daly, Simon, and Beatrice were kept far away while they interrogated their guests. Much to his consternation, Miss Anderson wasn't alone when they entered his office; Grandmama and Eleanor were also there waiting for them. The exasperated look on Jeremy's face told him that the two women had somehow browbeaten his Beta into telling them what he knew and now refused to leave the matter to the men.

"I was worried that you—my own grandson—was going to sabotage all my work with Miss Henney," the dowager duchess began. "Going after her by yourself like that—you could have ruined her, you know." She tutted at him. "But thankfully, Mr. Jonasson doesn't seem to want your head, which leads me to believe that nothing inappropriate happened."

He almost wanted to laugh, but stopped himself. "Forgive me, Grandmama. I was worried for Miss Henney. I was told she had never ridden a horse before. No one knows the grounds better than I, so I thought I would have the best chance in finding her."

"You just about scared me half to death," Eleanor exclaimed. "And—Reed! You're bleeding!"

He glanced down at the shirt Jeremy had brought him. The bleeding had stopped long ago, but not before some of the blood transferred to the fabric. "It's nothing, I'm fine—for goodness sake Ellie, stop with your hysterics! Winford, get your wife some smelling salts before she faints." With a deep sigh, he limped over to the leather chair behind his desk, then sat down to face everyone. Jeremy had taken a hold of his wife and was helping her sit on one of the armchairs. Cross stood off to the side, leaning against the fireplace as Elise and Julianna huddled together in one of the settees.

Meanwhile, his grandmother sat in one of the plush chairs, back ramrod straight. "Explain," she said knowing that the single-word command was enough.

"I found Miss Henney after she'd been thrown off by her horse," he began. "We took shelter from the rain and then we were attacked."

"Attacked?" Julianna looked at Cross and then Elise.

"A man in a red robe appeared and he used magic on us. He burned me before Elise fought him off." He hesitated, wondering if he should mention what Elise had told him. Did her cousins know? They must. Still, he decided that was her secret to keep. He was still trying to come to terms with it himself.

"Magic?" The dowager duchess's brow rose all the way to

her hairline. "Dear Lord, are those evil witches starting a war again?"

Elise let out a low growl. "Witches are not—"

Cross cleared his throat. "I'm afraid we are dealing with something else entirely."

"Mages," Julianna supplied.

"Mages?" Jeremy repeated. "What's a mage?"

"A mage is—*was* a witch or a warlock," Elise continued. "Magical beings use natural magic and only for good. However, when a witch or warlock breaks the laws of nature to further their own desires, they become something else entirely. They use blood magic—evil, dark magic that comes at the cost of hurting life. Not like pure nature magic which all *good* witches and warlocks use."

"We've never heard of such things," the duchess crowed. "How do we know you're telling the truth?"

"The New York Lycans have recently tangled with them," Cross said. "Twice now they've tried to hurt our Alpha and his family."

"They tried to murder me, my sister, and my mother." Julianna's face was red with anger. "And they tried again with my brother before we came to be here."

"How did they get to England?" Eleanor asked.

"I don't know, my lady." Cross shook his head. "But their influence has been growing for decades now. It's not unlikely that they have made their way here to London and perhaps the rest of the Continent."

"What do they want?" Jeremy stood up. "Why attack us?"

"They hate all Lycans," Julianna said. "They want to destroy all of us."

"What can we do to stop them?" Reed finally asked. This ... mage was a threat to him, to his family, his clan. And he almost killed Elise.

"We must be vigilant," Cross said. "If our history with them tells us anything, it is that they could strike again."

"Could there be more of them?" Reed asked.

"I don't know." Cross faced him, looking at him with those strange eyes. "Maybe, maybe not. It takes decades for a warlock to fully transform into a mage."

Jeremy harrumphed. "Then how do we stop them?"

"I think we should head back to London," Reed interjected. "Out here, there are too many factors ... too many things can happen. We can all stay at Hunter House so it'll be easier to watch out for each other."

"Your Grace, is that wise?" Julianna shifted in her seat uncomfortably. "I mean ... well ... London has so many people."

"And out here with no one else around, it's easier to attack us," Reed snapped. "We'll be like sitting ducks just waiting to be sniped off one by one."

"I have an idea, Your Grace," Cross said. "I believe ... well, the mages in America seemed to be drawn by power. Twice now they have attacked our ascending Alphas. Perhaps we could draw him out during your ceremony."

Reed contemplated his words. "You mean, set a trap?"

"Exactly."

He didn't like the prospect of confronting the mage once more, but then again, this might be their only chance. Unless the mage struck again before that, which could happen at any time. "I suppose we could do that." Better to be prepared and take out the bastard before he hurt anyone again. "You have a plan for defeating this mage?"

Cross nodded. "We have dealt with them in the past, and we can tell you what we know, if you agree."

"Do we really have a choice?" Jeremy asked. "Aside from waiting for him to attack us again."

Reed knew the answer to that. "All right then. I'll send a message to the high council and tell them we want to do the ceremony sooner rather than later."

"Instead of a small ceremony, we should have a big one," Jeremy added. "I know you didn't want to make a fuss, Hunter."

He sighed, knowing what Jeremy was suggesting. He was a good Beta, after all, plus a seasoned veteran of war. "No, you're right. We need all of the clan around us. Maybe we can even call on our Scottish allies for help."

"We'll be there too, of course," Julianna said. "I mean, after all, we have the most experience with the mages."

"I think it would be best if the ladies were somewhere safe," Jeremy suggested.

"No way." Elise got to her feet. "We are not sitting back while you fight him."

"Eli—Miss Henney." It took all of his power to stay calm. Her life was in danger! There was no way he was going to let her near that murderous mage. "Between the London clan and the Caelkirk clan, we should be able to round up a good thirty able-bodied male Lycans."

"But wouldn't that seem strange?" Elise shot back. "Mages are smart. He'll know something is up when he sees that only the men are attending your ceremony."

"Elise is right," Eleanor said. "Just because we're women doesn't mean we can't fight. We're Lycans too."

"Darling." Jeremy put a hand on her arm. "Please—"

"Don't patronize me, Jeremy." She brushed his hand away. "If that mage got to William ..." He had never seen his sister look so fierce. Lady or not, a she-wolf showed her claws if there was any threat to her pups.

"They're right," the dowager said, much to Reed's surprise. "Reed, we must make everything look authentic, if we are to draw this despicable mage out."

"Grandmama—"

"A ball." The duchess paused dramatically. "Yes, we shall have a ball. It will not only be a good way to get the clan and our allies together, but that way, you can finally take your place as Alpha in a grand way."

"But—"

"No buts, Reed." She raised a hand to stop his protests. "Your ascension ceremony may be the last I'll ever witness, and so we must make it a splendid one. Not a very big one, of course. Just the clan and our allies. Say, one hundred people?"

Reed knew it was useless to argue with his grandmother once she made up her mind, so he allowed her to continue.

"I'll take care of the arrangements. The invitations, the decorations, the musicians, the food—I even know where your father kept the dagger he used. It was your grandfather's, you know." She stood up, and every male in the room got to their feet. "I'll have my work cut out for me, between the ball and making sure these ladies are properly launched into society. I've already decided that they will be having their debut at the Marquess of Finnerly's ball. So, if you'll excuse me, I'll have to get started. Ladies," she turned to the women in the room. "Come. There's no time to waste. We shall have to leave for London in the morning."

Eleanor stood up. "Let's go, Elise, Julianna." She shot them a look that said, *don't even try*. The two women looked at each other and then followed Eleanor and the dowager out the door.

"I bet if your Grandmother was at the front lines, we would have defeated Napoleon within the first year," Jeremy joked.

"I'd have given her six months," he answered wryly.

"But seriously, we must speak about the ladies." Jeremy ran his fingers through his hair. "You're not really going to let them be there, are you, Hunter? If that madman even got near Eleanor—"

"I won't let that happen." Reed ground his teeth together. "But we should come up with a plan. Any ideas, Jonasson?"

The other man crossed his arms over his chest. "I have a few. But we should not exclude the women. We need all the help we can get."

He was obviously talking about Elise's powers. Did Julianna have them too? Did Cross? "All right, we can discuss this over the next few days." Hopefully, they'd come up with an acceptable plan that wouldn't involve anyone getting hurt.

Though he hated that they now had an enemy to worry about, focusing their energies on trying to defeat the mage at least gave him something to think about other than Elise Henney.

CHAPTER ELEVEN

Elise didn't know what excuses Reed made to their guests, but the very next day, everyone left Huntington Park to go back to London. With all the excitement of the packing up and heading back to town, there had been no time to speak privately with Julianna or Cross. Neither of them had come to her room for their usual late-night searches, but she supposed that with everything that had happened, they had to change tactics.

It wasn't until that afternoon that she saw a note slipped under her door from Cross, telling her to come down fifteen minutes earlier than usual for tea with the duchess. By the time she reached the parlor, Julianna and Cross were already there.

"We don't have much time, so I'll try to be brief," Cross began. "I'm working with Reed and Jeremy to come up with a plan to entrap the mage. He's already sent letters to the Lycan High Council, all his clan members, plus his uncle in Scotland for assistance. Lycan messengers have been dispatched, and with minimum stops to rest, it should take them three days to arrive in Scotland. He's sure that he'll get a positive response from the Alpha of Caelkirk, so their forces should be here in five or six days."

"What have you told him about us?" Elise asked.

"I haven't told him anything about where we came from, but I did tell him what we knew of the mages."

"We know where the dagger is. The old bat has it," Julianna said. "Let's just grab it and go home."

Cross's face turned bleak. "We could."

Julianna raised a dark brow. "I sense a 'but' coming along."

Cross's face turned serious. "I haven't been completely honest with you both. I was sworn never to tell anyone this, but I think it's important you know."

"You've been keeping something from us?" Julianna's face flushed with anger. "Cross, I thought we were in this together!"

"It's not my secret to tell." He took a deep breath. "It wasn't my father or my grandmother who was having the premonitions about the mages. It was my brother, Gunnar."

Elise sucked in a breath. "I thought he could only do some limited transmogrification, like the way Astrid has a short range when moving from place to place?"

"Yes." His mouth set into a hard line. "But his premonitions are so clear and vivid that it would drive him crazy and send him into seizures. My father tried to bind it permanently to help him, but the binding somehow damaged his wolf. Then one day, he lost control and ... there was an accident at a club. Over a hundred people were knocked unconscious."

Daric's words came back to Elise. *I do not know what a*

permanent binding would do to your wolf in the long term or your ability to shift. But he did. Daric bound his son's powers and it harmed his wolf and other people. She had to laugh at the irony of being called a blessed witch. *More like a curse.*

"Okay, so it was your brother who had the premonition?" Julianna asked. "Why keep it a secret?"

"Because the Lycan High Council would have ordered him put down," Elise concluded.

He didn't say anything, but Cross's silence confirmed the reason why.

Julianna went pale. "My father wouldn't have let anything happen to him."

"I know," Cross assured her. "But if the high council insisted, he would have been caught between a rock and hard place and my father didn't want to put the Alpha through that."

"I ..." Julianna shook her head. "So, what did he see?"

"Gunnar only told us what he thought was necessary." His ocean-colored eyes shifted. "But one thing I can tell you is that we go back to our time. He's seen all of us in a future event. And all of his premonitions have come true so far."

"Okay, so let's go back!" Juliana waved her hands in the air for emphasis. "We can be home in no time."

"My father and I have had many discussions of the future and the past. I've come to the conclusion that our coming here wasn't an accident. Or perhaps it was what set things in motion here. In our time, I read that Reed was killed by 'evil forces.' I believe that when we came here, we brought that evil force." He paused, as if searching for the right words. "I think the mage who attacked Elise and Reed is the same mage who brought us here. He might have traveled back with us, too."

"Wait, hold on!" Julianna exclaimed. "So, we came to the past, brought the mage with us, and now he's going to kill Reed, which is what will be written in the history books, which you will then read in the future ... er, you've read in the past?" She sank down on the nearest chair. "I'm getting a headache thinking about it."

"I know it's a paradox, but that's the only explanation." His jaw hardened into a straight line. "As sure as I am that we're going back to the future, I'm also certain that means we set things in motion in the past."

"At least it means we'll be going home," Julianna sighed.

"The mage might have figured out the same thing which is why he's going to attack on the night of the ascension ceremony." Cross said. "Somehow, he knows that the dagger is the only way back. Or, since they've been doing research on the artifacts for decades now, he might know the way back."

"Which is all the more reason we should use it now," Julianna insisted.

"And then when we strand him here, what happens?" Cross said. "He could wreak havoc on the timeline. Change history as we know it. He could even kill all of the London clan. No, I think when we go back, we're meant to take him with us. After all, if we're trying to recreate the events that brought us here, then he needs to be there too."

Elise's stomach churned at his words. But she knew it was a real possibility.

"I didn't even think of that." Julianna's mouth thinned into a grim line. "Oh my God. What if we go back home and we're in some weird alternate timeline where the mages are our overlords?"

"Which is why when we leave, we also have to take him with us." Cross's tone was dead serious.

"You're right," Elise conceded. She didn't want to be near that mage again—what was his name? Malachi—but they might not have a choice.

"What are we going to do then?" Julianna's brows drew together. "What's the new plan?"

"We must continue as we are doing—playing along," Cross said. "It'll allow us to stay close to the family, and during the ceremony we'll be near the dagger. Should the mage attack, we'll be ready."

"And if he doesn't?" Julianna asked. "Can we just take the dagger and go home?"

"He'll come," Cross said with certainty. "We already know that. But until that time, we can't let any harm come to the dowager, Eleanor, Jeremy, and especially William. History must happen the way it was intended to happen."

A dark, foreboding feeling came over her. It became difficult to breathe as her ribs seemed to contract into her chest when a question popped into her mind: *What about Reed?*

History must happen the way it intended to happen. According to history, Reed Townsend was supposed to die on the night of his ascension ceremony. And *they* were the reason why.

"Elise, are you okay?" Julianna's face was full of concern.

"I—I'm fine." Her throat tightened at the tears she couldn't shed. She hadn't even had time to process what happened between them yesterday in the statuary. She'd spent a sleepless night thinking of his kisses and his touch …

and now all she could think of was his body being burned alive by that mage.

"Are you sure?"

"Yes," she insisted. "I'm just tired."

"Don't you know showing up early is just as rude as being late?" came the dowager duchess's rebuke as she entered the room. Signore Rossi came in behind her and greeted them a good afternoon. Bridget, too, was not far behind, and she flashed them a bright smile as she entered.

Elise was glad for the interruption. "Apologies, Your Grace," she said. "We've been idle and anxious all day."

"If you excuse me, Your Grace," Cross said as he took a deep bow, "Lord Townsend is waiting for me."

The dowager duchess gave him his leave, and he left the parlor. "Neville will be serving tea in a moment, but before he does, I have an important announcement."

"Announcement?" Julianna echoed.

The older woman's nose twitched. "I have not yet decided if Signore Rossi," she nodded to the Italian, "should paint the Townsend family portraits, but since he doesn't want to remain idle, I've permitted him to paint one portrait." Her gaze went laser-like toward Julianna. "Yours, my dear."

"Mine?"

"*Si, signorina.*" Rossi placed a hand on his chest. "It would truly be my honor to paint such a beauty as you. I can only hope to give your enchanting face some justice."

Elise smothered a laugh at Julianna's horrified look.

"I can't possibly—"

"It will be a test," the dowager interrupted. "If I like the portrait, I shall commission Signore Rossi to do all of ours."

"It would truly make me happy," Rossi said.

And probably line his pockets, Elise thought. After all, these days, artists needed a patron to survive.

"Of course, sitting with Signore Rossi for a few hours a day will cut down on your lessons with me—"

"Hold on." Julianna held up a hand. "If I sit for this portrait, I don't have to do dancing lessons, learn etiquette, and brush up on my knowledge of *Debrett's*? Count me in!"

"You'll still be expected to know those things for your debut in three days," the duchess countered. "But yes, you'll have to sit and smile as Signore Rossi paints your portrait."

"Doesn't sound like a bad deal," Julianna whispered to Elise. "I can sit and smile."

"I'd pay a lot to see that," Elise whispered back. And it seemed, at least for the time being, there wouldn't be much to do except sit and smile until the ascension ceremony.

Elise couldn't decide if the next three days went by quickly or slowly. Sometimes it felt quick as she went through the whirlwind of events that came with the preparations for their debut—dress fittings, more dancing lessons, etiquette lessons, and learning all about the most important families in England.

But then, it also felt slow as she had not seen Reed at all. When she did have idle time, all she could think about was him. His arrogant, handsome face and the way it softened in the garden when they were alone. His kisses and his touch setting her body on fire.

However, whenever she replayed the scene in the statuary in her head, whenever she got to the ending, she came to realize something: Even before the mage attacked them, he was the one who pulled away from her first, who stopped the kiss and acted like they'd done something wrong.

And now he's avoiding me. It was that small voice inside her head talking. *He regrets what happened.* Or he was repulsed by the idea that she was a hybrid. During that meeting in the study, he didn't mention to anyone that he had seen her use her powers. Obviously, in this era, Lycans still very much hated witches.

Of course, there was that possibility that he was busy. The atmosphere in Hunter House was tense, and most of the time, it was just her, the dowager duchess, Eleanor, Julianna, Bridget, and Signore Rossi around during dinner. Cross updated them when he could, but he was busy with Reed and Jeremy all the time. She could see his patience was being tried as well as he seemed tense and spoke tersely. It probably killed him not to be able to use his powers to help, but they all agreed not to tell anyone more about hybrids and other information that could jeopardize the future.

So, there was a life and death situation, but she couldn't squash that tiny voice in her head telling her that Reed didn't want to see her anymore.

It was the afternoon of the ball when the duchess declared they rest before getting ready. They were in the parlor, finishing up tea. "There will be dancing until dawn," she declared. "And you ladies must be ready."

Bridget seemed the most excited out of all of them. "I can't wait." Her pretty blue eyes sparkled. "Perhaps I'll meet my True Mate tonight."

"You know," Julianna said as she turned her head toward

Bridget. "You never did tell us about this knowing your True Mate thing."

"*Signorina*, please!" Rossi stuck his head from behind the large canvass and waved a paintbrush in the air. "Do not move!"

"Oops! Sorry." Julianna returned to her original pose, seated with her hands on her lap, her head turned toward the artist.

"I suppose no one has told you about my family legend?" Bridget asked.

"No," Elise said.

"Well, how do I explain it?" She looked up thoughtfully. "The Lycans in my family always know their True Mates as soon as they meet them. We're supposed to get this feeling or reaction. I'm told it's difficult to describe, and it's not always the same for everyone. But, when you feel it, you *just know*."

"How does that work? And why only your family?" Julianna piped in, though she remained perfectly still.

"I don't know why, that's just the way it is," Bridget stated matter-of-factly. "It happened to my parents, to Eleanor's parents, Eleanor, and Reed too."

Elise felt like she'd been struck on the head with a blunt object. Reed already had a True Mate?

"No, not to Reed," the dowager duchess said in a scathing tone. "That ... woman he married was certainly *not* his True Mate."

Bridget covered her mouth in horror. "Oh, I'm sorry, Your Grace. I didn't realize."

"He's married?" Julianna said, her head snapping toward them which earned her another reprimand from Signore Rossi.

"*Was* married," the duchess corrected. The air seemed to grow colder, and the tension in the room became thick as molasses. "That *woman* is no longer with us. I would say God rest her soul, but ..." She stood up. "We will not speak of such things as it's not something one discusses in polite conversation." Without another word, she strode out of the room.

Elise let out a breath as soon as the air in the room felt normal. *Reed was married.* Had been married, apparently, but his wife died. What had happened to her? She scanned her memories of the past week, trying to remember if there had been any indication he'd had a wife. There were no portraits of her, no feminine touches in his home, and no one mentioned her at all. It was like she'd never existed.

"So, what's the story with the wife?" Julianna asked Bridget. So lost in her thoughts, Elise didn't realize that Signore Rossi had packed up and left, leaving the three of them alone.

"I'm afraid I was too young to know," Bridget said. "And no one will tell me the exact details. I only know that he was married, and she died a year or two after the wedding."

Julianna let out a snort. "You're not really serious, right? About the True Mate thing? Like, you're supposed to just know who he is? You lock eyes across the ballroom and bam! You're my True Mate?"

Bridget looked at her like Julianna had just told her that Santa Claus didn't exist. "Of course I'm serious. It's all true. At least for my family."

"Bull—I mean, I'm having a hard time believing it." She stretched her neck from side to side and rubbed a hand on her lower back. "Man, sitting for hours isn't easy work. I think I'll take the old bat's advice and get some rest. I'll see you guys tonight."

"I think I'll take a wee nap as well." Bridget bid Elise goodbye and followed Julianna out of the parlor.

Elise sank deeper into the couch, her emotions a whirlwind inside her. She wasn't sure what disturbed her more—the fact that Reed had been married to someone who wasn't his True Mate or that his real True Mate was somewhere out there, waiting for him to recognize her. She supposed she should feel sympathy for the poor woman seeing as Reed was such a cold-hearted snob who thought everyone was beneath him.

But no, there would be no True Mate for him.

Not now, and not ever. Her throat tightened again, thinking of what would happen to Reed. And all because of them.

You can't change the past, she chided herself. The future she knew depended on it.

Maybe it *was* better that Reed was avoiding her. She swallowed the tears forming in her throat and stood up, her fists at her side.

Protect the family. Get home. Keep the past intact.

Those were her main objectives, and she would focus on those for now, rather than trying to change things she had no control over or pine for a man who was, for all intents and purposes, already dead.

CHAPTER TWELVE

"Ah, so this is where you're hiding."

Though Reed cringed inwardly, his face remained impassive. Of course Jeremy would come to White's looking for him. He looked up at his brother-in-law's disapproving face, but didn't move.

"May I have a word, Your Grace?" Jeremy said in a terse tone.

"If you will excuse me, gentlemen," he said to the other men at the card table as he stood up. "I have some family business to attend to."

"Can't stand to lose another round, Hunter?" Hugh Montley, the Earl of Haughton, joked.

"You're not leaving now, are you?" Viscount Byron waved at him to try and get him to sit down. "In all my years here, I've never seen you lose this much."

"Which is why I should cut my losses short." He gave them an apologetic nod and then followed Jeremy out of the card room. "To what do I owe this visit?" he asked. "Did Grandmama send you after me?"

"You know what tonight is," Jeremy said.

"I do?"

"Stop playing games, Reed." Jeremy gritted his teeth. "It's the Finnerly's ball. Look, I know you've been occupied with all the planning with the *ascension* ball." He lowered his voice as they were out in the hallway, where any member could pass by and hear them. "And you do deserve some time to unwind. But you know how important tonight is to Eleanor and Grandmama."

"This was their idea," he stated.

"Look, Reed." He placed a hand on his shoulder. "Grandmama may not look it, but she's genuinely worried about the whole mage thing. Eleanor says ... well she thinks your grandmother is afraid of losing you, like she did your father. This ball, the three ladies, they give her a much needed distraction after months of mourning. A successful debut will make her immensely happy."

Reed went silent as guilt creeped in. Sometimes, he forgot that while he had lost his father in that accident, Miranda Townsend had lost her only son.

"You don't have to dance with anyone, not even the three women." Jeremy's tone turned lighthearted. "In fact, I'm sure Grandmama would prefer it if you didn't show any favoritism toward any of them."

"Then why show up at all?"

"You're the duke of Huntington, head of the Townsend family," Jeremy pointed out. "Your presence alone will ensure none of the ton dare say anything bad about our dear guests. But if you show an interest in any of them, no man would dare come near her. They'll think you're either interested in wedding her, which means no one will dare offer for her because they can't compete with the lure of a dukedom or that you've already sunk your claws into her and that would make them targets for every lecherous bastard."

"So, they just need me for my title?" he asked wryly.

"Your reputation precedes you, I'm afraid," Jeremy joked. "Besides, if you want to dance with any unattached young woman without sending tongues wagging, you'd have to partner with every respectable matron in the ballroom before even approaching anyone else."

"You mean, every unattractive, gossip-mongering, harridan in the room."

"Exactly." Jeremy patted his shoulder in a good-natured manner. "And you'd never do that. So, what do you say? All you have to do is stand and make nice conversation."

Reed had absolutely no objection to going to the Finnerly's ball. When Eleanor first brought up the subject of Bridget coming for the season, he knew that at some point, his sister and grandmother would coerce, guilt, or bribe him into coming to a ball or two. The only reason why he was hiding out at White's now was he had successfully avoided Elise for three whole days and he wasn't about to break his streak.

Knowing that she was under the same roof as him but not being around her was torture, but he had to bear it. It was too risky. If he were ever alone with her again, he'd throw out what little morals he had and take her to bed. Though she might not understand it herself, Elise wanted him too. It was obvious from their last encounter. But what happened in the statuary only cemented the fact that they truly couldn't be together. She was part witch—a fact that the clan would never approve of. Witches and warlocks were their natural enemy, and many of the older clan members would surely object as many still remembered the last few skirmishes they'd had with the magical beings.

But he supposed he couldn't hide from her forever. Besides, a ball was a public place, so there wouldn't be anything inappropriate happening there.

"I guess I have no choice," he conceded. *I'm doing it for Grandmama,* he convinced himself. It would make the old woman happy.

"Splendid," Jeremy said. "Good thing you're already dressed in proper attire. We should go now or Grandmama will have the constables of the Bow Street Runners looking for us."

They took his coach and made their way to the marquess and marchioness of Finnerly's stately manor on Upper Brook Street. James and Eleanora Williamson were one of the most respected couples of the ton, one of the few alliance families that knew about Lycans, and had been best friends with his parents. In fact, they were his godparents, and his mother had named Eleanor after the Marchioness. The dowager duchess had, indeed, made an excellent decision in choosing this as the three ladies' debut.

As soon as they alighted the coach, they headed straight to the entrance. The line of guests waiting to be announced wasn't too long, and soon they were up next.

"The Earl of Winford," the butler announced in a monotone drone. "His Grace, The Duke of Huntington!"

It seemed the very mention of his title was enough to bring the entire ballroom to a hush. But Reed didn't pay them any attention. In fact, he didn't even notice anyone else in the room, except for one person.

Elise was easily the most beautiful woman in the entire

ballroom. Madam Marie must be some kind of magician when it came to dressmaking, because the gown she had made for Elise was stunning, and so was Elise. The fabric was the exact shade of blue as her eyes, and much to his surprise, had delicate silver threads embroidered on the skirt which resembled streaks of lightning. Her flaming red hair was done up in braids rather than the more fashionable curls, but it only made her look like a Greek goddess. It seemed, however, that he wasn't the only one admiring her charms. Her current dance partner—Baron Wisely—was gazing so far down her décolletage that Reed thought his eyeballs would pop off.

"Are you all right, man?" Jeremy asked.

"I'm fine."

"Then why are you growling?"

He realized that his wolf's growls were so loud that his chest was vibrating. "Where's Eleanor and—never mind, I see them."

He made a beeline for the two women who he spotted standing by the dance floor with Signore Rossi and Cross. The beaming smile of his sister and the smug look on his grandmother's face told him the two women were extremely pleased.

Well good for them. He was decidedly *not* pleased at all.

"You're finally here." Eleanor smirked.

"Who chose that damned dress for her?" Though he didn't mention her name, it was obvious from the way his eyes never left Elise who he was talking about. "How could you let her leave the house in that?" he accused Cross. "She's on display for the world to see."

"It's a beautiful dress," Eleanor defended. "Madam Marie assured us it was the height of fashion these days."

"Every man in here is staring at her assets, and I don't mean her dowry," he snarled. The music's tempo began to decrease and the dancers started slowing their steps as the minuet came to a stop. Wisely had barely let go of Elise when he saw three more men approaching them, probably to claim her for a dance. Well, he was not going to let that happen.

"And where do you think you're going?" Eleanor asked as he took a step toward the dance floor. Her hand on his arm made him halt.

"I'm going to save her from those foolish fops." He gnashed his teeth as he recognized Sir Richard Gardner—a man twice her age and a known lech—got ahead of the other two men advancing toward Elise.

"You will not go near her."

His grandmother's words stunned him. "Excuse me?"

The dowager duchess's eyes narrowed at him and her nostrils flared. "If you approach her now and ask her to dance—your first dance not only for this ball, but in God knows how long—you'll be sending every single gossipmonger and flibbertigibbet's tongue wagging. With your reputation, who knows what they'll say? You'll ruin all mine and Eleanor's hard work for the past week with one single impulsive move."

Goddammit all to hell! His grandmother was right. Sure, he didn't care a whit for his own reputation, but Elise—who was not only untitled, but a foreigner—would suffer most. *Sometimes, I really hate this society.*

Jeremy caught his gaze and gave him a knowing smile. His brother-in-law's words from earlier in the evening at White's. *You'd have to dance with every respectable matron in the ballroom.*

"Bloody *hell*."

And so, he did.

He danced his first dance with their hostess, which was at least the easiest hurdle of them all seeing as she was an old friend of the family's. Lady Finnerly liked to remind him of all his childhood escapades, but that was perhaps the least embarrassing part of his evening.

The ton's most upright and virtuous women were also the most ancient. He smiled through the many times Lady Abernathy smashed his toes, and didn't bother correcting Lady Manderlay when she kept calling him "Wilbert" for some reason.

Reed estimated he danced with a dozen partners, and he would have bloody well danced with the housekeeper and the Devil himself if that's what it took so he could finally ask Elise. She could very well turn him down, which would probably happen considering his luck tonight.

After he downed a glass of champagne he grabbed from the tray of a passing waiter, the orchestra began to strike up a waltz. He dropped the glass onto the nearest flat surface and made his way to Elise who was chatting with his grandmother and their host and hostess. The sea of people parted as his determined strides brought him to her.

The marquess was in the middle of telling a funny joke Reed had heard about a million times when Elise's gaze landed on him. Her body went rigid as her laughter died before the marquess said the punchline.

"May I have this dance, Miss Henney?"

Her jaw dropped when he held out a hand to her. "I'm not sure—"

He lowered his voice so only she could hear him. "I've danced with every respectable woman over the age of sixty here so I could ask you. So please, dance with me before my reputation suffers any further."

The tension in her body broke and her shoulders relaxed. Her hand went to her mouth, but she nodded and offered her other hand. The breath he'd been holding slowly escaped his lungs. He led her to the dance floor and settled her into his arms for the dance.

He twirled her around in perfect rhythm with the music. Finally, he had her close, in a place where, ironically, men and women could have a real conversation. However, he found himself thoroughly annoyed because of the lack of privacy, and she was once again looking up at him without *really* looking at him, alternating looking at his forehead and over his shoulder.

"Didn't I tell you not to turn away from me?"

Her eyes blazed like blue fire. "Giving me orders again, Your Grace?"

"Like back in the statuary?"

She faltered in her step at the reminder, but he held her firm and perhaps just an inch or two closer than propriety deemed acceptable.

"Are you angry with me? For staying away from you?"

That question seemed to have caught her off guard, and she finally looked him in the eye. "So, you were doing it deliberately?"

"I—I was busy with preparations for the ascension. You know that."

"Of course, Your Grace."

The chilly, respectful tone made him want to scream. He wanted to see her passion and fury again. To defy him. To defend him the way she did against the mage. She was magnificent, never more so than now, in her lightning ballgown. Her skin glowed under the thousand candles overhead, and that sensuous scent of hers was like a siren song, calling to his senses and making his wolf crazy.

"You look beautiful tonight, Elise."

"Thank you, Your Grace," she said without missing a beat.

"Don't do that," he rasped.

Her head jerked back so she could look at him again. "Do you have any other orders, Your Grace?"

Frustration made him want to shake her. "Elise, just ... please. Don't act this way."

"Then what do you want with me?"

The dance was almost over, yet her question still hung in the air. He knew he could direct her away from the ballroom, maybe into some private alcove or to the balcony where they could pretend to want some fresh air. But her question stopped him short. What did he want with her?

The truth dawned on him. He didn't stay away from her because she was a half witch. She was off limits for any casual dalliance making marriage the only way to sate his lust, but that would mean doing the one thing he could never do: trust her. No, he wasn't giving that much power to any woman again.

The waltz finally stopped, and the other couples around them released each other. He followed suit, then led her back to his grandmother.

"Thank you for the dance, Miss Henney." He bowed to her. "Goodnight."

Turning on his heel, he walked across the ballroom and straight out the front door. His wolf growled in protest. It didn't understand what was happening with its human side. All it knew was that they were walking away from their mate, a fact that angered it. It wanted to take control of their body and turn back. Wrestling with his inner animal, he pushed it deep inside him.

He could feel the eyes on his back, hear the murmur of the crowd as he passed by, but he didn't care. If he didn't get out of here now, he couldn't be responsible for his or his wolf's actions.

CHAPTER THIRTEEN

As she watched Reed's retreating back, Elise told herself that this was for the best. Allowing herself to feel for Reed would only end up with her getting hurt once she lost him. It was better this way, wasn't it?

She really didn't expect him to show up at all. All the excitement of going to the ball actually distracted her, and she found herself actually looking forward to the evening. They did cause a stir when they arrived, and many of the single men had begged to be introduced to them. Elise remembered her lessons, accepting invitations to dance as etiquette required. Not that she had to worry, because the dowager duchess's attentions were all on Julianna, as it seemed she couldn't do anything right in the eyes of the elderly woman. During her first dance with Baron Redmond, she nearly tripped over and then bumped into another couple. The look the dowager gave her when she came back could have frozen a volcano. Elise had to physically hold on to Julianna before the younger woman did something scandalous.

Overall though, she was having a great time, distracted by the dancing and just the idea of being at the ball. Then, Reed showed and asked her to dance.

"What in the world happened?" Eleanor looked despondent as Elise approached them. "Why did he leave? Oh, my Lord, this is a disaster."

"He had an emergency," Elise said. "He said something about securing the perimeter of the house, in case the mage came back." Hopefully that lie wouldn't come to bite her in the ass, but what was she supposed to do?

The dowager duchess looked at her strangely, like she was trying to peer into her thoughts. And then she said something really odd. "Do not fret. All is not lost, and I believe we can still salvage the situation."

Elise didn't think there was anything to salvage, but she remained quiet. A few more men asked her to dance, which elated Eleanor, but she couldn't bring herself to care. *We're going home soon*, she told herself. It didn't matter what these people thought.

"Just let me at her," Julianna said through gritted teeth. "I swear, I can make it look like an accident."

"Julianna!" Bridget covered her mouth, but her smile lit up her eyes. "Her Grace means well."

"I don't see you excited with all your prospects," Julianna shot back.

The other woman's smile seemed to die. "It's just ... well, we've been here for hours and I still haven't felt *it*. I don't think my mate is in England."

Elise wanted to comfort her, so she reached out a hand. "Don't worry, this is only the first night." She really did hope

Bridget would find her True Mate. She made a mental note to check up on the Caelkirk clan history when she got home.

A knot in her stomach formed. Pretty soon, they would be home.

She should be happy that she would be able to go back to her house, her job, her own life. At least that's what she told herself.

———

The next day at breakfast, the dowager duchess and Eleanor were already receiving requests to call upon the three women.

"Which do we accept?" Eleanor asked. "I think Viscount Aster's really interested in you, Julianna."

Julianna choked on her tea, sputtering liquid all over the fine white linen and earning her a reproachful look from the duchess. "I, er ..."

"I've made a decision," the duchess said.

"Of course you have," Julianna muttered as she wiped her mouth with a napkin.

The dowager continued, as if she didn't hear Julianna. "Reed has informed me that the Caelkirk clan is arriving tomorrow, and so the ascension ceremony will proceed tomorrow evening. That said, we need to suspend any visits from gentlemen callers for now."

Julianna and Bridget both seemed to sigh in relief.

"But that doesn't mean we can't hold a soiree of our own," the duchess said. "So, I've taken it upon myself to arrange an impromptu musical concert here at Hunter House tonight."

"Is that wise, Grandmama?" Eleanor asked, concern marring her face. "Perhaps the timing isn't right."

"Seeing as what we are about to face tomorrow, I think the timing is splendid. A relaxing evening of music is what we need to prepare us for the coming storm."

And because she was the Lupa and dowager duchess, no one questioned her. Nor did they ask how she was able to organize a quartet at such a short notice or send out invitations, all the while still preparing for tomorrow's ascension ball and ceremony.

Melinda was amazing, as usual, and after an afternoon of primping, she declared Elise ready for the evening. As usual, she came downstairs with Cross and Julianna. He updated them briefly on what was happening and confirmed that a Lycan messenger from the Caelkirk clan had arrived ahead of the Alpha and his men to let them know they would be arriving at dawn the next day. They had also picked up more allies along the way from another clan closer to the English border. All in all, there would be around thirty-five male Lycans coming to the ball. It seemed everything was all set for tomorrow.

When they descended the stairs into the main foyer, Elise was surprised to see both Lycan and human guests, including Viscount Daly, Simon, and Beatrice, but she supposed that since tomorrow would be a Lycan-only affair, the dowager invited their human friends and acquaintances as well.

Reed, of course, was the last to arrive with his grandmother on his arm. Elise's heart gave a leap when her eyes landed on his tall, handsome form looking so elegant in his all-black formalwear. Whether he even knew that she was there, she didn't know as he didn't bother to look her way. Instead, he led the dowager duchess into the formal dining room, signaling that dinner would begin.

Since they had about two dozen guests that night, dinner was served in the formal dining room. It seemed the dowager had not pulled any stops as the long table was richly decorated with flowers, crystal centerpieces, and the finest linen and china she had ever seen. Elise also found herself seated next to Simon Richardson, who was as charming and attentive as ever. He was a good distraction, she supposed, as she was near enough the head of the table that she could definitely see Reed if she looked his way. She told herself it was better to not look at him.

And she also told herself that she didn't mind one bit that after dinner, Reed escorted Beatrice into the ballroom, which was set up for the performers and the audience. Her wolf yowled despondently, but she ignored it. She avoided Simon and sat between Cross and Julianna instead.

Elise was glad for the distraction of the music, but from where she was seated, she could clearly see Reed and Beatrice as they sat next to each other. Once in a while, Beatrice would lean toward him and whisper something in his ear, and he would give her a short nod.

Unable to look at them, she tried to focus her eyes elsewhere. On the movement of the cellist's fingers as he played Bach's *Cello Suite No. 1 in G Major*. On the candles burning above, on the outrageous peacock feathers on the Countess of Heath's coiffure, or even at her companions. Julianna looked bored out her mind, while Cross ... well, Cross looked odd. Instead of his usual guarded expression, he seemed almost forlorn. His mysterious blue-green eyes shifted colors as the candles flickered above, and she felt an overwhelming sense of sadness from him as the nurturing, empathic part of her reached out to him.

"Are you all right, Cross?" she whispered. "You seem sad."

Her question seemed to catch him off guard as ocean-colored eyes crashed into hers. "What makes you say that?"

She shrugged. "You look like you're a million miles away. Do you want to talk about it?"

Before he could answer, the cellist ended the prelude, and everyone began to clap. She followed suit and when she turned back to Cross, she found herself staring at an empty seat. *Weird*. Despite all this time they spent together, she realized that she still didn't know Cross that well. He'd always been a quiet person growing up, but it seemed that he'd withdrawn even more the last few years.

When the quartet began to play the next song, she turned her attention back to the music. In truth, she was glad the dowager had suggested this. Tomorrow's ball surely wouldn't be a lighthearted and carefree affair like this one. It would be a battle, one where she could lose everything.

When the first half of the concert was over and the butler announced a fifteen-minute interval, Elise shot to her feet and hurried out of the ballroom ahead of everyone. Where she was going, she wasn't sure, but she didn't want to have to watch Reed and Beatrice anymore. Thankfully, she spied a balcony door not too far from the room and made her way outside. The cool air was refreshing, especially after being indoors most of the day. Out here, overlooking the garden, she could feel closer to nature, something that was always difficult when she was in the big city. She could just concentrate on the air, the trees, the scent of the flowers. The minutes ticked by, and she wished that she didn't have to go back inside. But knowing that the night was not done, she knew there was no escaping the rest of the evening.

Reaching for the door, she opened it, but the voice coming from the inside made her stop.

"... splendid, truly splendid, Your Grace. You must tell me where you found these talented musicians." It was Lady Finnerly, the hostess from last night's ball.

"I'll send a note in the morning with their information," answered the dowager. She cleared her throat. "I am glad we had a good turnout, despite the last-minute invites."

"Speaking of guests," Lady Finnerly's voice lowered, "what do you think about the pretty young miss that seemed to have captured your grandson's eye? She's that girl who grew up in West Indies, right?"

The duchess gave a delicate snort. "I don't give a whit where she's from, but she's far too forward and lacking in grace."

"Well, Reed's late wife was all grace, wasn't she? I thought Joanna had the most splendid manners. And gorgeous too."

The mention of Reed's wife made Elise's heart stop. She glanced around, but unless she leapt off the balcony, there was no way to escape from overhearing this conversation.

"Bah, that woman."

"A tragedy."

"What happened to her was a tragedy," the duchess said. "But *she* was a *travesty*. A disgrace to our name. I was glad my grandson caught her in bed with her lover."

"Annabelle told me the story in confidence." Lady

Finnerly sounded like she wanted to faint. "But each time I hear it, it still makes my blood boil, what she did to that poor boy."

"And apparently, she was *enceinte* with her lover's child."

Lady Finnerly gasped. "And she would have let Reed claim the child? What would have happened if the child's wolf did not manifest?"

"She was not only vain but stupid too," the dowager said harshly. "The smartest thing she did was to drown on that ship with her lover."

"The scandal that it would have caused would have destroyed the Townsend name, not to mention that the clan would have been in an uproar."

"Still, I didn't wish her any harm. That ship sinking was the real tragedy and I'm afraid that only made this worse for Reed. I only wish he—" She stopped short. "It looks like the musicians are ready. Let's head back, Eleanora."

Elise remained rooted to the spot as she listened to the two women's footsteps move farther away. She opened her mouth trying to draw oxygen into her lungs, but it was like the air was too thick. Her heart twisted in her chest, and she had to brace herself against the door to steady her feet as her mind reeled with the information overload.

Reed's wife betrayed him. He caught her in bed with her lover, the same man who got her pregnant. Then she died ...

She bit the back of her hand to stop herself from crying out. *I wish tomorrow would just be here already so I could just go home.* But at the same time, that knot in her stomach grew at the thought of what would happen. Emotions like a violent storm churned inside her, knowing what was to come. She couldn't even bring herself to be jealous of Beatrice, because if she were truly honest with herself, she would rather the other woman have Reed. She would rather he find happiness again in the arms of another woman if that meant he was going to live.

And the thought struck her like lightning. *I love him.*

And she would lose him.

Tears swelled in her throat, and it took all her strength to keep them from spilling over. She took a deep breath and stepped back inside. If she were around other people, distracted, then she wouldn't cry.

The hallway was empty, and she saw the last of the guests pouring back into the ballroom. As she hurried back, she saw Cross about to head in. She rushed at him and grabbed his arm.

"Elise?" His eyes searched her face. "Are you all right?"

"Cross, I ..." She swallowed the lump forming in her throat. "Cross, isn't there another way?"

"Another way?"

"I mean ... we have all these Lycans here coming to fight the mage. And you ... you have so much power ..." Her hands were trembling as she clung to him. "Can't we save Reed?"

He shook his head. "No, that's unthinkable, Elise. We can't change the past. Reed's supposed to die tomorrow, and William will be Alpha someday. Elise," he gently pulled her hands away from his coat. "Elise, when we get back home, Reed would have been gone for over two hundred years. Just a few days ago, when we were in our own time, he was already dead to us."

He was right. Before they came to this place, she never even knew he'd existed. "I'm sorry, I just ... I feel bad. For ...

for the duchess and Eleanor. They've suffered a lot these last months."

"Elise," he began. "I'm sorry." The swell of music drifted out into the hallway. "They're starting up again. We should go back."

She allowed him to lead her inside the ballroom, and as soon as they sat down, her eyes darted straight toward Reed. Her stomach sank, and her heart lurched as she saw his elegant, severe profile. Her impression of the haughty and cold duke melted away, and instead, she felt his pain, thinking of the betrayal and loss he'd experienced in his life.

He must have felt her looking at him, because his head turned back and those obsidian eyes bore right into hers. She quickly turned away and focused her attention on the musicians, trying to keep her emotions at bay.

CHAPTER FOURTEEN

It felt like hours since Melinda had helped her undress and get into bed. Elise was staring up at the ceiling trying to sleep, but her mind wouldn't quiet down.

Also, that damned clock in the corner ticked so loudly, it might as well have been stuck to her eardrum, each tick reminding her of the coming day, of what was to come.

Tick.
Tick.
Tick.
Tick.

With a frustrated cry, she threw the covers off and ran to the mantle, reaching for the tiny pendulum in the back to make it stop. She wept with relief at the silence, but as the tears fell down her cheeks, she crumpled to the floor as the hopelessness of her situation washed over her.

If only there was a way to save him without changing the past.

If only she could stop time itself.

If only ...

Steely determination swept through her, and she got to her feet. Wiping her cheeks with the back of her hand, she headed for the door, opening it slowly in case anyone was around or awake.

She padded down the hallway, out of the guest wing, and headed for the main wing. Although Hunter House was large, it wasn't as gigantic as Huntington Park, and thus it was easy to guess which area the rest of the family was staying since the servants had already retired downstairs. Using her Lycan hearing, she tuned in to the sounds of people. The first room she passed by must have been William's, as she could hear the even sounds of his small heartbeat and breathing. The room next to his was his parents', and it was obvious Eleanor and Jeremy were still awake, talking softly. Then there was the room across from theirs, and she heard the sounds of pages turning, and she recalled the dowager duchess saying that she read in bed every night to help her sleep.

Heart banging in her chest like a drum, she soldiered on passing a few more rooms, all empty, until she came to the last door in the main hallway. Touching her palm to the wood, she closed her eyes, her hearing tuning in to the strong heartbeat inside. Her hand slid down to the knob and pushed it open.

The room wasn't dark, as the fireplace provided both heat and light. She had expected Reed to be in bed, so she was surprised to find he was by the fireplace. Wearing only his dressing robe, he leaned one elbow on the mantle as he held a glass of wine in the other. The light cast shadows on the angular lines of his face making them look harsher than usual. Yet, she could see past the ruthless, cold surface and just see *Reed*.

In a split second, his head snapped toward her. Those midnight eyes glittered when they landed on her, and shock registered on his face.

"Elise?"

She closed the door behind her and walked toward him. He seemed frozen, his face still.

"What are you doing here? You can't—"

She held up a hand to silence him, then took the glass from his hand and placed it on the mantle. Her mind whirled, trying to find the words. Wanting to tell him how sorry she was for trying to push him away and that she understood why he acted the way he did. And that she loved him, and if they only had tonight, then she would rather have that than have nothing at all.

Tick.

Tick.

Tick.

Tick.

Without saying a word, she stopped his clock too, then took a step closer until she was a hair's breadth away from him. Heat from his body radiated toward her, and she reached up and placed a hand on his firm jaw.

"Elise," he rasped as he snaked a hand around her waist and pulled her to him, his lips pressing firmly against hers in a move that was more caress than kiss. His scent threatened to overwhelm her, and he held her tighter.

She trembled in his arms, her body thrumming with a

desire she had never felt before him or ever. That she would give her body for the first time to the man she loved seemed fitting, and if he were the only man she ever knew, that was fine.

Her feet lifted off the ground, and she realized he was carrying her to his bed. He lay her down gently on top of the covers, then positioned himself at her feet. Reaching for the hem of her nightgown, he lifted it up and over her head. Onyx eyes blazed his desire as his gaze feasted on her naked body.

He growled and then swooped down again to take her lips, his mouth devouring hers. He tasted like sweet wine and she found herself getting drunk and heady from his kisses.

A hand cupped her breast teasing the nipple to hardness. A gasp left her lips when he pulled away and lowered his head to tease her other breast, leaving kisses around the soft flesh before sucking the nipple deep into his warm, wet mouth.

"Reed!" She cried out as pleasure unfurled from her belly spreading out like licking flames all over her body. A small cry left her lips when he pushed her body up, and his breath tickled the soft mound of curls between her legs. When his mouth pressed up against her core, she bucked up against him. Large hands held her hips down, and he used his shoulder to nudge her thighs apart baring even more of her to his feasting tongue. When his mouth found her clit, she moaned aloud, moving her hips up at him eagerly. That only made him suck on her nub harder, and when he slipped one finger inside her, she thought she was going to expire from the sensations of pure pleasure.

She fisted her fingers in his thick hair, but he didn't mind or notice. He was relentless, licking and sucking at her with his tongue while his finger teased her tight passage. The pressure building inside her was too much, and she exploded in an orgasm, her body shaking as tremors of pleasure passed through her.

As she recovered, he got on his knees and reached for the belt of his robe. Pulling at the knot, he shrugged the garment off his shoulders. This time, she was the one feasting on him. Her eyes devoured his broad, muscled shoulders, the well-formed chest and the soft mat of hair sprinkling it leading to a delicious trail down his abs and lower still to his fully-erect cock. Though the low light of the room kept most of him in shadows, her own desire and want made her boldly reach out for him. He didn't move but allowed her to wrap her fingers around his shaft. She held her breath, feeling his warm, male hardness. Like steel covered in velvet.

"Elise," he whispered as he gently took her hand away. He moved between her legs, spreading them apart until his hips were at level with hers. "I'm sorry." He kissed her forehead, then her cheeks, then claimed her mouth again. "I have to hurt you."

His words were like a knife, gutting her. "You can't hurt me. Please, Reed. I need you."

She braced herself as he nudged the tip of his cock against her entrance. His face was twisted in concentration as he filled her, inch by inch. When he stopped, she knew it was going to happen. Arms went around her, and she clung to him, desperate and wanting him. He pushed his hips forward one more time until she felt pain. It was brief, but as her mouth cried out, he smothered it with his, desperately kissing her pain away. Her body relaxed as the throbbing subsided.

He pulled away from her and stared down into her eyes. "You're beautiful." He kissed her gently now, reverently caressing her mouth with his. Her power hummed inside her, but instead of unleashing a torrent of uncontrolled electricity, it stayed contained. There was no more fear inside her. She didn't even question it, why her power remained stable around him. She only knew it to be the truth.

"Reed, please." She arched her hips up at him, wanting him so bad.

He grunted, then braced himself on an elbow. A hand moved down, cupping the back of her knee as he pulled her up. The motion buried him deeper in her, and she gasped at the sensation, her leg wrapping around him automatically.

Lips crushed against hers as he began to move. Short, shallow strokes, allowing her body to adjust to him. He slipped his arm around her and pulled her so tightly to him she couldn't breathe. He drove into her, his movements now hard and fast, driving himself to the hilt each time. Her body seemed to have a mind of its own, arching into him, seeking his body as she enjoyed the feel of him inside her, on top of her. His chest pressing against her so she could hear his hammering heart and his powerful thighs driving his hips into her. Pleasure built inside her in a frenzy sending streaks of ecstasy through her like lightning.

Reed's body moved erratically, his back spasming and shuddering as she clasped around him. With one last thrust, he drove into her, jerking violently as he cried out in pleasure. She felt him pulse inside her, filling her with his warm, hot seed as her body clamored for more.

When he finally slowed, she let out a satisfied sigh. He rolled to his side, taking her with him so she lay tucked against his side. An arm came over her possessively, and she felt his lips press a kiss to her temple. She relaxed against him, forgetting everything that was beyond this bed and room. This was what she wanted. This was the only thing she could have, really, and so she would keep this moment and treasure it forever.

CHAPTER FIFTEEN

THE KNOCK AT THE DOOR CAME AT AROUND DAWN. REED was so in tune with his body's inner clock that he knew the sun was just rising as he opened his eyes. The scent of citrus and strawberries hit his nose and he came instantly awake.

A warm, soft body pressed against his, and he knew last night hadn't been a dream or hallucination. Elise did come to his room, and they spent the night together. After the first time, he woke her up twice more to make love to her, giving her endless pleasure until she begged him to stop. A smile made his lips curl up. She was magnificent, even in her innocence. So eager to please him, and he had never wanted anything more in his life than to watch her body burn with desire and explode into orgasm.

As the knocking became more insistent, his smile turned into a frown. What the devil could that be about?

He moved swiftly so as not to disturb Elise—she looked so beautiful as she slept that he could watch her for hours. Grabbing his dressing robe, he yanked it on and headed for the door. "What the bloody hell is it?"

Neville stood on the other side, already impeccably dressed. "Your Grace, I'm sorry to disturb your sleep, but the Alpha of Caelkirk is here."

Hell's bells.

He raked his hand through his hair. "I'll be down in five minutes. Please show Lord MacDonald to my office."

"Yes, Your Grace."

Closing the door gently, he let out another curse. His gaze strayed to Elise's sleeping form. He was loath to leave her now, but he didn't want to wake her up either. *I'll just go down and greet Uncle Alec*, he told himself. He'll probably be exhausted himself, as he and his men traveled for five days straight to get here. Then he could come back here and maybe wake up Elise with another round of lovemaking.

Not wanting to call his valet, he dressed himself in a shirt, breeches, and boots. Uncle Alec was family, after all, and Scots didn't care much for formalities. He made his way to his office, whistling some long-forgotten tune.

"Reed, my boy," Alec MacDonald, Earl of Caelkirk and Alpha of his clan greeted as he entered the office. He was just as big and tall as Reed remembered, though the shock of red hair and most of his beard had turned silver. Strong arms wrapped around him and brought him in for a hug.

"Uncle Alec," he greeted back. "Thank you for coming on such short notice."

"Ach, no need for thanks, boy," he said, slapping him on the back. "We're family, and when family needs ye, ye come." He motioned to the others around him. "I have my best men with me. Plus I've also picked up some help along the way." He nodded to the tallest and burliest of them all—a great mountain of a man with long, dark reddish hair, a thick beard and bright green eyes. "This here's Connor MacDougal. Second son to the Alpha of Glenmore."

"'Tis an honor to meet you, Alpha." Connor MacDougal bowed his head reverently. "Thank you for allowing me into your territory."

"I've been meaning tae meet with his father for the last few years now," Alec began. "But he's just so far away from us. So, I thought I would pay my respects as we had tae pass through his territory anyway bein' that it was the fastest way. When I explained tae Laird MacDougal why I was comin' through, he insisted sending a few more of his Lycans to help."

"Thank you for coming to our aid," Reed said to Connor. "I'm sorry to trouble you."

The other man grinned. "No trouble at all." His brogue was even thicker than Alec's. "We've been looking for an excuse tae kick some Sassenach arse—er, warlock arse."

"Well, there's only one we know of," Reed said. "And he's not a warlock. He's a mage." He quickly explained the difference to his new guests. Seeing as Elise was quite passionate that the two be differentiated, he wanted to make sure they knew. Speaking of Elise ... "Uncle, you look exhausted. You should get some food and then rest."

"I've got the strength of a man twenty years younger than me, boy," he protested.

"Still, you've been riding hard for five days," Reed said. "And we'll need you at full strength tonight."

"I suppose yer right, boy," he conceded. "A warm bed would do me good. It would do all of us good." There was a murmur of agreement among all the other men. "All right boy, we'll get rested up for tonight."

Reed called in Neville and instructed him to get their guests settled in. He spoke for another few minutes with Uncle Alec before he finally bid them goodbye. Eager to get back to his room, he practically sprinted back upstairs.

"Elise?" He called as he approached his bed. But it was empty. Had it not been for her lingering scent mixed in with the smell of sex, he would have thought he'd dreamt it all. A foreboding thought entered his head, but he brushed it aside. It was already eight o'clock and the servants were up and about and soon so would his grandmother and sister. *She probably woke up and realized that she had to get back to her own room before anyone found her.*

It was unnerving to say the least that she would creep out of his bed. But it didn't matter. As soon as this whole mage affair was done, he would offer for her hand in marriage. He would need a special license which he could easily procure as he would not wait a second longer than he had to. Cross might object, but he was not waiting another three months or so to obtain her father's permission. Not if she could be carrying his heir.

Not if, he realized. She was already carrying his pup. Elise was his True Mate.

The thought elated his wolf, and, *hell's bells*, he was damned happy too.

"Er, Your Grace?"

He turned his head toward the door where Morgan was standing, his mouth open. "Good morning, Morgan," he greeted.

"Uh, good morning, Your Grace. Are you, er, quite all right?"

"Hmm?" he said absentmindedly. "I'm fine, what is it?"

"Er, I thought maybe there was someone else in here ... the maid or something, as I heard whistling."

"Whistling?" He chuckled. "Yes, that was me. I just had an ... urge to whistle."

The valet stared at him as if he said he wanted to go on a murder spree across London. "Er, so would you like the navy or the tan jacket today, sir?"

He shrugged. "Whatever you pick is fine." His mind drifted off to Elise as his valet went about his business. Once he was dressed and ready, he thanked Morgan and headed downstairs to breakfast. He wondered how Elise would react to him this morning. He had an urge to sneak into her room, but seeing as her guardian and her cousin was in the same wing, he couldn't risk it. Not that it would matter, seeing as they would be married soon enough. Still, he didn't want to risk any scandal to the future duchess of Huntington.

When he came to the dining room, he was disappointed that only Jeremy, William, Cross, and Signori Rossi were there. "Where is El—I mean, the ladies?"

"Grandmama whisked them away to Madame Marie's," Jeremy explained. "She said that they had to have new gowns fitted for tonight, and"—he lowered his voice—"she mentioned something about not being too fond of our new guests."

He let out a laugh. Grandmama and Uncle Alec got along like oil and water. No wonder his grandmother chose to leave for the morning.

"Er, are you all right, Hunter?" Jeremy asked.

"Me?" As he came up to the head of the table, he ruffled William's hair affectionately. "I'm fine. Why?"

"I've never seen you this cheerful early in the morning," Jeremy remarked. "Or, uh, anytime."

"I'm just ... having a good start," he said as he sat down. He even managed a smile at Cross and Signori Rossi. "How is your painting going, Signori?"

"*Eccelente*, Your Grace, it is almost finished," the Italian declared. "I do hope Her Grace likes it enough that she will allow me to do your portrait."

"I'm sure it will be amazing."

Jeremy looked at him strangely again, but he ignored it. They resumed their normal conversation, and as soon as breakfast finished, he, Jeremy, and Cross went to his office to continue their planning for the evening. Sometime before noon, their Scottish guests joined them so they could be updated on their strategy.

"We want the mage to think that he has a chance to hurt Reed," Jeremy said. "Otherwise, if he thinks we are too protected, he might not take the risk."

"That's why, except for Uncle Alec and one or two of his men, we'll be asking most of you to stay hidden around the house," Reed continued. "Once the mage reveals himself, then we can contain him. The males will attack, while the females have been instructed to get the humans and other vulnerable people out of the room and keep them safe."

"What powers does he have?" Alec asked.

"As far as we know, he can create fire with his hands," Cross said. "There are mages who have the ability to take the power of other blessed witches and warlocks, so we must be prepared for any eventuality."

They continued their discussion, with Connor adding a few smart suggestions that they incorporated into their strategy. It was two o'clock when they finished, and they left for the dining room where Neville had set up a late lunch. As they went past the main foyer, he saw Julianna and Elise walking up the stairs. His heart stopped when he saw her in profile looking magnificent in a violet morning gown. He urged the others to go ahead without him as he headed toward the stairs. Much to his surprise, both women were gone. *Strange*. It didn't take him more than a few seconds.

"Reed!" He turned around and saw Bridget walking toward him as she came into the house.

"Hello, Bridget, how was Madame Marie's?"

"'Twas all right, though it took a little longer than usual." She frowned.

"Really? How so?"

"Elise was just being fussy and—" She stopped suddenly and her nostrils flared. "What is *that*?"

"What is what? And what did you mean Elise was being fussy?"

"That smell!" A smile lit up her face. "Oh, it smells so good." She sniffed the air, her head turning left and right. "It's like ..."

"Bridget," the dowager called as she entered the front door. "We must head upstairs if you are to be ready in time."

"Yes, Your Grace," she replied. "Sorry, Reed, I should get going." She curtseyed and then bounded up the stairs.

The dowager shook her head. "Everything is all right, I presume?" she asked Reed.

"Yes, Grandmama." He gave her a kiss on the cheek. "Are you sure you won't reconsider staying at your home tonight? It will be much safer. I can spare one or two of our clan members to guard you."

"Nonsense," she insisted. "I will watch you ascend tonight, nothing will stop me, not even some odious mage." She turned on her heel and marched up the steps.

As he turned to go to the dining room, he had a strange feeling in the pit of his stomach. His wolf, too, was uneasy having been away from their mate for a few hours. It prowled inside him, urging him to go see her and make sure she and their pup were all right.

He shook his head. *Don't worry*, he assured it. *We'll see her soon enough.* Another emotion shot through him, something he'd never felt before. *Fear.* He was afraid for her. What if the mage got to her?

No, he would never allow it. She would be safe. Besides, now that she was with child, she was safe from anything. And she'd handled the mage previously. That bastard should be afraid of her, and not the other way around.

Turning on his heel, he walked toward the dining room, wondering if Elise preferred a diamond or sapphire engagement ring, to match her eyes. *Maybe I shall get her both.*

"Are you all right, Reed?" Jeremy asked.

"Why does everyone keep asking me that today?" Reed answered in an irritated tone.

"Maybe because you're worse than a woman," his Beta quipped. "One moment you're whistling a happy tune, and now it's like you want to murder someone."

"Ye best be savin' that for the mage, boy," Alec said. "But for now, try not to scare anyone away, ya ken?"

"I'll try." But he was thoroughly annoyed. No, he was spitting mad.

At first, he thought he was imagining things. After lunch, he tried to see Elise but her maid told him that she was sleeping. When he waited at the foot of the steps for her to come down for dinner, she didn't show up, and Julianna told him that she ate something that made her sick and was still recovering, but she would definitely be at the ball later that evening.

Since the ascension ball was for Lycans and alliance families only, the social rules were much looser, but he still had to open the ball by dancing with his grandmother. Elise had definitely been announced, and he thought he saw her from the corner of his eyes, but whenever he tried to find her, she was gone.

Individually, he would have brushed off all these events, but together, he knew it was not coincidence. Elise was avoiding him.

He would understand if she was some shy miss, but she was the one who'd seduced *him*. And for God's sake, they were True Mates, so there was no need to act ashamed. Fate had meant for them to be together, and soon, she would take her rightful place at his side.

"Congratulations, Your Grace," Lord Finnerly greeted as he came up to them, Lady Finnerly on his arm. "I must say, if he were here, your father would be proud of you."

"Thank you," he said. "I—" He stopped short when he spied Elise across the ballroom, looking resplendent in her emerald green gown. She was laughing with a few of the London clan Lycans, looking so carefree and happy. "Excuse me." He didn't bother waiting for a response from his companions, and using his Lycan speed, crossed the room in no time. "Miss Henney, may I have this dance?"

Blue eyes widened in surprise, and she looked around as if searching for an escape. Well, there would be no escape because he didn't bother waiting for her to agree. Instead, he took her by the hand and dragged her to the dance floor.

She stood in his arms like a limp doll.

"Put your hand on my shoulder," he hissed.

She startled at his tone but followed his command. He led her into the waltz twirling her around the ballroom. Much like the last time they danced, she was once again looking around, anywhere but him. This time though, he was not going to be subtle. He maneuvered her toward the edge of the ballroom, and before anyone noticed, spirited her away to the nearest terrace.

"I—Your Grace!" she exclaimed when she realized they were outdoors, alone. "What are you doing?"

"Reed," he corrected.

She pulled away from him. "Your Grace, please, it's not proper."

"You called me Reed last night. Over and over again as you came apart in my arms."

Even in the dark he could see her turn bright red. "I ... please, we shouldn't be out here alone, Your Grace."

He seized her arms and then pulled her to him. "Reed. My name is Reed. Say it," he commanded.

"I ..." Her lower lip trembled. "Reed," she whispered.

"Good girl." He lowered his mouth, pressing it against hers in an urgent kiss. Instead of responding, she squirmed in his arms, a move that infuriated him. "You're mine," he growled, unable to control his own words. His wolf urged him to prove it to her, to the world that she and the pup she carried belonged to him. "Say my name again."

"I ... Reed!"

He pressed his lower body to her so she could feel the evidence of his desire. "That's right. My name is Reed. And I'm your True Mate."

Her entire body went stiff. "You can't ... but you didn't ... you didn't recognize me!"

So, she knew about that? Damn it all to hell. Someone—Eleanor or Bridget—must have told her. He wished they didn't because how was he supposed to explain it to her? That he didn't want her at first, but now he did? "You're my True Mate. I know it. And now"—he slid his hand down to her belly—"you're already with child. Our pup and my heir. We shall be married in a week—"

"No!" She wrenched herself away from him. "Reed ... no ..." She shook her head. "It can't be ..."

"Of course it is. Is that why you were avoiding me? Because you thought we weren't mates?" He reached out to her. "I'm sorry, love. It's hard to explain."

"I ... Reed, we can't!" Her voice was shaking, and so were her hands.

"Then why did you come to me last night? Why did you give yourself to me? Don't you feel anything for me?"

"It's not ... I can't explain it."

"Then try!" What was wrong with her? He was giving her the world—a coronet, his wealth and protection, the lofty station of being his duchess and Lupa. What more could she want? "Is there someone else?" He'd always suspected there was something strange about her relationship with her "cousin." Or maybe it was Simon Richardson.

"No," she denied. "I just ... Reed ..." She hesitated. "Reed, I've been lying to you. We've all been lying to you."

Her words stunned him. "You're not from America?"

"No. I mean, yes, we're from America. But not from now."

"Elise, love, you're not making any sense." He wrapped his hands around her upper arms. "Please, explain it to me."

"Reed ... Julianna, Cross, and I, we're not from this time. Not 1820. We're from the future. Over two hundred years into the future. My father is the Alpha of San Francisco and I was attending Lucas Anderson's—that's the Alpha of New York's ascension—when I was kidnapped by the mage. Somehow, the dagger they were using for his ceremony turned out to be this magical artifact and ... I can't explain how but we were transported here. We weren't supposed to show ourselves to you but then William was almost run over and ..."

"Elise, this is madness." What was she saying? "You're not making any sense."

"Please, believe me. Reed, that mage that attacked us, he's the same one who kidnapped me. We unknowingly transported him back here, and now he wants the dagger. Your dagger. So he can go back home. And he's going to—" She covered her mouth with her hands.

"He's going to what?"

"Reed ... I'm sorry." She pushed at him. "I can't ... we can't be together. It's not meant to be. I d-d-don't care for you at all."

Her words sliced through him like a dull knife. She was making up this insane story all because she didn't want to be with him. Once again, he had fallen in love with a woman who didn't want him.

Things were different now, though. He was much older and wiser. Ice filled his veins, as numbness began to come over him. He dropped his hands to his sides. "If you didn't care for me at all, then all you had to do was say it. There's no need to concoct a silly story."

"Reed, I'm not—"

"We shall talk about this later," he said. "Don't even think of running away from me now. Because if you are carrying my heir, then I will take that child, one way or another. But," his voice turned edgy, "once I do, you shall be banished from my territory."

She went white as a sheet but said nothing. He turned on his heel letting the numbness take over as he went back into the ballroom.

CHAPTER SIXTEEN

Elise couldn't move. She couldn't breathe, she couldn't say a word, she couldn't even think clearly. Not when her heart felt like it was shattering into a million pieces.

Yes, she did everything she could to avoid him today, even delaying at Madame Marie's. What could she do? Going to him last night was a mistake. But she just wanted one sweet memory of him to last her for the rest of her life before she went back to her own time where she belonged. She thought that maybe, since he was such a rake, that he would be glad she wasn't demanding him to marry her after last night.

But Reed seemed to think otherwise. And True Mates? Was he crazy? If that were true, why didn't he recognize her when they first met the way Bridget said he was supposed to?

No, they couldn't be together. She just couldn't hold on to that piece of hope, not when he was going to die tonight.

The terrace doors flew open, and for a second, fear gripped her as she thought it was Reed coming back.

"Where the hell have you been?" Julianna exclaimed as she burst out into the terrace. "We're supposed to stick together inside where Cross can see us at all times." That was part of their plan so they were ready when the mage attacked. "What the hell—Elise, are you okay?"

"I—" She couldn't find the strength anymore to hold back, and she burst into tears. "Julianna," she cried.

"Oh my—Elise!" Her arms wrapped around her. "What's the matter? Tell me."

She took a deep breath and told her friend about what happened last night with Reed until the moment he walked away from her. She did, however, leave out the part about True Mates. She just couldn't say it out loud, as if saying so would make it true.

Julianna grew quiet, listening to every word she said. Elise expected a lecture or scolding, but to her surprise, the other woman hugged her tighter. "Elise, I'm sorry." She looked her in the eyes and wiped a tear from her cheek. "You love him, don't you?"

She nodded. "I do. But ... it doesn't matter. It's not meant to be. I was stupid for falling in love with him in the first place."

"There must be something we can do. Did you ask Cross if there was any way we can save him?"

"I did, and he said no." She took a deep breath. "Reed doesn't believe me anyway. He thinks I made it all up because I don't want to be with him." That was the irony of it all. She would have done anything to be with him.

"Elise, I'm sorry," Julianna said. "I really am."

"I know." *And so am I.* There was nothing she could do about it now. "We should head back inside." She gave Julianna a squeeze on the shoulder. "Thank you for listening."

"Hey, cheer up, we'll be home soon." She put on a big smile. "I can almost taste the big juicy cheeseburger I'm going to have the moment we get back."

She returned Julianna's smile. "I'll join you for that cheeseburger."

Hand in hand, they re-entered the ballroom. Everything seemed to be normal so far, as the orchestra continued to play, and the guests danced, drank, and continued with their celebration.

"Julianna! Elise!"

They both turned around and saw Bridget running toward them. Her face was red and her pretty blue eyes were sparkling, like she was keeping some secret.

"I was looking all over for you two," she said, her cheeks puffing up with excitement. "I've the most wonderful news!"

"What is it?" Julianna asked.

"I've met him!" She clapped her hands together. "My True Mate! I've met him!"

"You have?" Julianna looked around. "Where? Is he from the London clan? Where is he?"

"He's hiding in the bushes," Bridget exclaimed.

"Bushes?" Elise and Julianna said at the same time.

Bridget laughed. "It's a long story. I was outside, trying to get some fresh air when he popped out of the bushes and declared me to be the 'bonniest Sassenach he'd ever met.' Before I could tell him I was no Sassenach, it happened! I felt it and I knew it was him!"

"What's his name?"

"Er, I don't know yet," Bridget said. "One of his friends called him away before I could say anything. But," her smile became dreamy, "isn't it wonderful? And he's a Scot too!"

Julianna glanced at Elise as if waiting for her to say something. So, she reached out and squeezed the other girl's hand. "I'm so happy for you."

"You are?" She pulled them both in for a fierce hug. "I'm so glad. You two ... I don't have any women in my family, you know? My ma died after giving birth to me, and I haven't any sisters. I feel like ... you're my sisters."

Her throat closed up with emotion, and when she looked over at Julianna, she saw her tearing up too. "Thank you, Bridget. You're like a sister to me too."

"Me too," Julianna sniffed. "I feel closer to you than my own little sister."

"What are you three doing here?"

Julianna's expression turned sour. "Well, hello, Your Grace," she said as she turned to face the dowager.

"Why aren't you out there, dancing with every available gentleman?" she scolded. Dressed in a rich purple velvet ball gown with ostrich feathers in her hair, the dowager duchess looked even more imposing than usual. "You're wasting valuable time and all the lessons I've taught you."

"Listen here, lady." Julianna rolled up her non-existent sleeves. "I've just about had it with you."

"Julianna, please," Elise warned.

But she didn't pay her any mind. "Look, after tonight, you won't have to worry about us. Bridget has found her True Mate, which means she's off the market. And Elise and I will be leaving soon, so I won't be disappointing you any longer."

At that moment, Elise saw something that she'd never seen before. The dowager duchess's face lost its severe expression. "My dear, whatever gave you the idea that I was disappointed in you?"

"What gave me the idea?" Julianna huffed. "Just about everything you do and say is to criticize me for every little mistake I make!"

The duchess laughed. "And if I praised you at every turn and lauded every little accomplishment, would you have worked so hard? Would you have done everything you could just to prove me wrong?"

Julianna opened her mouth and then shut it again.

"I'm proud of all of you," the duchess declared. "Bridget, I'm very happy that you've found your True Mate."

"T-thank you, Your Grace."

The dowager *tsked*. "What's with this 'Your Grace' nonsense? You are cousin to my grandchildren and the future countess of Caelkirk, therefore you must start calling me grandmama."

The young woman's eyes widened. "Yes, your—er, Grandmama."

"And as for you," she turned to Julianna, "I'm most pleased with you. You've exceeded all my expectations. If you are leaving after tonight, then I wish you all the best and that you find a husband worthy of your spirit. It's obvious that you're not meant for an Englishman. You'd run circles around one."

"What?"

The dowager ignored Julianna's slack-jawed expression and turned to Elise next. "But what about you, my dear? Is my grandson still being a stubborn mule?"

Elise blinked. "E-e-excuse me?"

"Don't play dumb, my dear. It doesn't suit you." The duchess's haughty expression came back. "And don't treat me like a senile old fool. I know what's going on between you two."

"It's not—"

"Poppycock! I've seen that look on his face before." Her eyes softened. "It was the same one my son had when he looked at his True Mate. I've always ... felt regret about the way things were between Annabelle and I. And I never got the chance before she ..." She cleared her throat. "I only hope that I can be better with you."

Bridget gasped and Julianna's mismatched eyes widened.

"He doesn't ... it can't work out," Elise stated. What else was she supposed to say? Her emotions felt like they were spinning around in a tornado.

"Nonsense." The old woman tucked Elise's arm into hers. "Come. The ceremony is about to start. You'll be right up front with us, his family—where you belong."

Confusion fogged her brain and her heart, which was why she allowed the duchess to drag her along, all the way to the front of the ballroom. There was a small dais set up where five men were standing with Reed. He had his back to her, so he didn't see that she was there. When the dowager pulled her to stand with the rest of the family, Eleanor beamed at her, but said nothing. It dawned on Elise that both the dowager duchess and Eleanor suspected that something had been going on between her and Reed.

In her time, during the ascension ceremony, the would-be Alpha made their vow to protect their clan and their secret by gripping the blade of the ceremonial dagger and sealing their vow in blood. It seemed the ceremony was pretty much the same now.

"... to show your commitment to the position," the man in

front of Reed said. He was likely the head of the Lycan High Council. "You must make your vow with blood." He raised something metallic in the air. She couldn't see the dagger clearly, but she saw Cross and Julianna take their place on the other side and the younger woman nodded, signaling that it was the same dagger Lucas had used.

Reed reached out, then turned to the rest of the people in the ballroom as he held the blade with his hand. He didn't even flinch as he gripped harder, staining the dagger with his thick, bright red blood.

"The vow has been spoken and sealed with your blood. And now—"

A loud, crash of thunder interrupted the head of the Lycan High Council. Another one came, so loud that it shook the glass panes of the windows in the ballroom.

Eleanor glanced around. "What in the world?"

A deafening boom filled the room as the wall behind Reed and the High Council exploded, sending chunks of the brick wall and debris flying everywhere. Elise instinctively covered the dowager's body with her own, wrapping her arms around the old woman. Smoke and singed wood assaulted her senses, but she forced herself to look up.

"Well, well, it seems my invitation got lost in the mail."

Three figures in red hooded robes stood amidst the pile of rubble created by the flaming, gaping hole in the wall.

"Get everyone to safety," Jeremy said to Eleanor.

His mate nodded. "I will. I love you."

"I love you, too." Jeremy pulled her in for a quick kiss. "Go now, my love."

Elise unwound her arms from the dowager. "Go with your granddaughter, Your Grace."

The older woman nodded. "You take care of him."

"There's no time to waste!" Eleanor already had William in her arms. "Let's go, Grandmama, Elise."

"I'll be staying," she said. Before Eleanor could protest, she put a hand on her belly. "I'll be safe. You *know* it." She wasn't 100 percent sure right now if she was pregnant with Reed's baby and that she was invulnerable, but at least that would make them leave without her.

Eleanor gasped. "You're already ... all right. You take care of yourself too." And with that, she led the dowager away toward the exit doors just as they had planned. The rest of the guests were already on their way out as several Lycans began to surround the dais forming a protective wall between the mages and the escaping guests.

Julianna and Cross were already at her side. "Three mages?" Julianna exclaimed. "How can there be three of them?"

"How dare you?" Reed shouted, his voice full of power and authority. "You dare come into my home and territory, mage?"

The hooded figure in the center of the trio stepped forward. "It seems your visitors have told you about the existence of my kind. Did they also tell you where—or rather, when—they are from?"

"Who are you?" Jeremy said. "Stop being a coward and show us who you are."

The man laughed. "I wasn't planning on keeping that a secret. After all, you should know who your future ruler will be." He pulled the hood down.

"Lord Daly?" Reed said. "I don't understand."

Elise felt like she'd been struck by lightning. Glancing at Cross and Julianna, they seemed confused too.

"That's not the mage who attacked us," Julianna whispered. "He's way older."

Elise thought back to the man who asked her for a light on the street. No, it couldn't be! That man was about their age. Who was this, then and who were the other two mages with him?

"Yes, I'd expect you'd be confused." But he wasn't looking at Reed. He was looking right at Julianna, Cross, and Elise. "I was a much younger man when you met me. About thirty years ago, at least for me." He laughed.

Her skin crawled as she recognized his voice. 'Lord Daly' dropped his British accent and now it was clear who he really was. *Malachi*. The same mage who kidnapped her and attacked them at Lucas's ascension ceremony.

"Funny thing with unintentional time travel. I arrived in England in 1790, right in the middle of the docks. A press gang kidnapped me and put me to work on a boat on the way to West Indies. Of course, as soon as we got to the Caribbean, I escaped. For years I survived, building up my power as best I could. Then fate brought along these two." He motioned to the two beside him.

The two figures shrugged off their hoods, revealing Simon and Beatrice. "Hello, Your Grace," Beatrice purred.

Reed's face went white. "You ..."

"I found them being held on a sugar plantation by the native workers there. Their mother was some doxy in America and gave them to their father, a sea captain, who took them to live aboard his ship. When the father died in the islands, the children were left abandoned."

"We were begging for scraps when Beatrice accidentally unleashed her power," Simon continued. "The natives were so scared that they captured us and kept us tied and locked up."

"They thought them witches," Daly guffawed. "They were right. A blessed witch and warlock."

"Father found us." Beatrice looked adoringly at Lord Daly. "And freed us so we could get our revenge."

"As they got rid of the workers, I disposed of the plantation's owner and took over his identity. Now," Daly nodded his head at the dagger in Reed's hand. "Hand that over to me, Your Grace."

"This?" Reed held up the dagger. "What do you want with this?"

"He needs it to go home," Cross said.

"Home?" Daly laughed. "Are you kidding me? I have three estates, a fleet of ships, a sugar plantation in the West Indies, and a palace in India. Why the hell would I want to go back home to the shit hole that is New York?" He shook his head menacingly. "I have much bigger plans. I already have one artifact of Magus Aurelius which will allow me to create portals to travel through space." He grinned. "And I know the location of the other two as well, not to mention," he turned toward Reed, "a supply of double Alpha blood to magnify their powers. Beatrice!"

The witch raised a hand, sending a small bolt of lightning from the sky straight at Reed. His body convulsed, and he fell to the ground, sending the dagger skittering across the floor toward Daly.

Elise cried out, but when she tried to run to Reed, Julianna held her back.

Daly picked up the blood-soaked dagger. "When I have all three and I have drained His Grace's body of every drop of blood, the world will see a darkness like it never has."

"I won't let that happen," Reed growled as he struggled to get up. "I'll die first!"

"No need to be dramatic, Your Grace," Daly mocked. "Besides, if you don't come with me, I will hunt you down and kill every last one of your clan and your family. You can't run anywhere I won't find you. My children will burn London down to rubble to get you."

Simon raised his arms, a fireball forming in each palm. Beatrice waved her hand and a bolt of lightning sent a piece of the ceiling crashing down a few feet away from them.

"I'm not going to run," Reed said. "We will fight you and defeat you."

"If you come with me now, Your Grace," Daly said. "I won't kill your family."

"You'll kill them anyway," Reed shot back as he got to his feet. He signaled to the other Lycans. "Change. Now!"

"You can't—" She struggled as Julianna held on to her tighter. "Please, let me go! I can't let them kill him. Or anyone else."

"We can't change the past," Julianna said. "We stick together and grab Daly— or Malachi or whatever the fuck his name is—while you fire up the dagger."

"What about Beatrice and Simon?" she asked. "Will we let them kill the others?"

"When we take Daly with us, they won't be able to do anything," Cross said. "They haven't begun their transition into mages yet. Plus, with over thirty Lycans here, they'll be defeated in no time. We already know what will happen, Elise. I'm sorry, but we can't change it."

Helplessness and despair made her heart ache. "I—"

A streak of lightning sent more of the ceiling crashing around them. Many of the Lycans in the room had already changed into their wolf forms, but Simon's fireballs were keeping them away while Beatrice's lighting strikes scattered them before they could come any closer.

"Get the hybrid!" Daly screamed, pointing to Cross.

Simon turned his attention to them as a giant fireball formed between his hands. In a split second, Cross disappeared with a soft pop before reappearing behind Simon. His hands wrapped around the man's head and snapped his neck. His eyes rolled up and his body crashed to the ground.

"You bastard!" came Beatrice's anguished cry. "I'm going to tear you apart!" She raised her hand to bring another streak of lightning down, but Julianna jumped at her, sending both women to the floor.

"Give up, Daly." Reed approached the mage. "Powers or no, we've got you outnumbered."

"Never," Daly snarled. "I still have you and I have this!" He raised his arm and sunk the end of the dagger into Reed's chest. Daly's face twisted into hate as he held onto the dagger and began to chant some spell and the air around them began to shimmer and distort. Reed grew pale as he sank to his knees.

"No!" Elise tore her gloves off as she dashed toward the mage. "You monster!"

The power building up inside her burst from her fingers, firing streaks of electricity at the mage. His body contorted but he held on, and Elise could feel the power from the dagger emanating like waves.

"Julianna!" she heard Cross scream. "Let's go."

As Reed's body collapsed to the floor, Elise let all her rage flow through her, sending thousands of volts of electricity into Daly. The stench of burned flesh permeated the air as he let out a long, blood-curdling scream.

Hands wrapped around her arms, and a familiar feeling washed over her as the floor seemed to disappear beneath her feet. She directed the electricity coursing through her, keeping it steady as she felt the force pulling her body back before releasing her into the dark, cold, endlessly spinning vortex. Her last thoughts were of Reed and his limp, lifeless body.

CHAPTER SEVENTEEN

THE BRIGHT LIGHT AND THE SHARP RINGING FADED AWAY as the feeling came back to her body. Surprisingly, she landed on solid ground, unlike their previous trip through the tunnel that had sent them sprawling across that field.

"Elise!"

She heard someone call her name. Someone familiar, but whose voice she didn't expect. A sob escaped her mouth.

Lara's arms wrapped around her. "Elise. Oh, Elise, I thought you'd ..." She trailed off as she choked on her tears.

"Cross!" Aunt Meredith also came running at them and embraced Cross as she began to bawl. "What are you wearing?" Her tears halted as she cocked her head at her son's formal evening wear. Then she glanced at Elise and Julianna, who were both wearing satin ballgowns. "Wait, what are you all wearing? And Julianna—your hair!"

"What happened?" Lucas Anderson's voice was calm, though it had the unmistakable power of an Alpha. Elise's heart sank, as her thoughts once again went to Reed.

"It's a long story." Julianna sighed and scratched at her

scalp. "A very long story." When she met Elise's gaze, her expression turned sympathetic.

Grant Anderson pulled his daughter into a fierce hug. "But you were only gone a minute or two."

"Like she said," Cross said. "It's a very long story."

Daric came forward and untangled his wife's arms from his son, then pulled him into a hug. "Then perhaps you should begin."

Cross began to tell them all that had transpired in the last two weeks—at least it had been two weeks for them, because apparently, no time had passed for the people in the present. Elise sank deeper into her mother's arms, trying to stop herself from crying out in agony as she thought of Reed. *I'm sorry, my love,* she said silently. *I couldn't change the past, and I couldn't stop time.*

"That's incredible!" Meredith exclaimed. "So, he's dead? You're sure?"

"Elise burned him up."

Lara suddenly stiffened, and she pulled back from her daughter. Her expression changed as she looked down at her and Elise's linked hands. "Darling! You're not wearing gloves!" Lara's hands tightened around her bare hands. "Oh my ... you've done it. You've learned how to control your powers."

Elise didn't even realize it. "Mom," she whispered as she touched her cheek to Lara's. It felt so good, feeling her mother's bare skin. "Oh, Mom. I have something I need to tell you."

"Whatever you want, darling." Lara was crying, tears streaked down her smooth cheeks. "Tell me. What is it?"

"There was someone—"

A loud growl interrupted her, and every single Lycan in the room went on full alert. They all turned to the source of the sound—a large, gray wolf slowly padding toward them.

"Who the hell is that?" Lucas asked.

Beside him, his mate, Sofia frowned. "He's not one of yours?"

He shook his head. "I don't recognize him."

"I thought ..." Sofia's expression turned serious. "He was outside, begging to be let in, so I let him inside!"

"You what?" Lucas's eyes began to glow as he turned toward the unknown wolf. "Get him!"

Several of the Lycans approached the wolf, but stopped as it began to shift. Slowly, limbs began to shorten and fur receded into skin.

When the man stood up, Elise felt her heart slam into her chest.

She was dreaming.

This wasn't real.

It can't be.

He *died*.

"Reed?" The name came out like a rasp.

Brilliant onyx eyes turned to her. "Elise."

She broke away from her mother's arms and began to walk toward him. Everyone was talking around them, but she didn't hear anything. The only thing she could focus on was Reed standing right there in the room. As she drew closer, her eyes devoured the sight of him. She recognized his handsome face, though half of it was covered with a thick beard. When she was inches away, she focused on his chest and let out a gasp. There was a large scar on his chest that wasn't there before. She reached out to touch it, feeling the long, raised bump under her fingers. "Is it really you?"

He smiled. "Yes, love, it's me." He sucked in a breath and wrapped a hand around her wrist. "I've been waiting so long for you."

The ache in his tone was so real, she had to believe it. "Reed."

Strong arms came around her and pulled her to him. His firm lips came on top of hers in a desperate kiss, like he was a man drowning and she was his only source of air. His scent, oh his delicious scent, tickled her nose, and her wolf came alive knowing their mate was here. "I love you," she whispered when he pulled away for a second. "I only said I didn't because I knew you were going to die."

"*Ahem.*"

They turned and saw Lara with her arms crossed and a delicate brow raised. "Will one of you please explain?"

"Hello, Your Grace," Cross said as he approached them. "Welcome to the future."

"I believe 'welcome back' is more appropriate at this moment," Reed replied. "And please, you don't have to call me that. It's just Reed now. Reed Wakefield."

"I don't understand," Elise said. "I saw you. You died. And now you're here!"

"I'm not sure what happened myself," Reed began. "I felt the dagger in my chest and then the lightning—er, electricity—flowing through me. Then I was going through this tunnel and then I landed on the street. Little did I know I was in the East Village."

"You arrived in New York with us?" Elise said. "How did you come here so quickly?"

"Elise, love." He took her hands in his. "I landed in New York all right. About three months ago."

"Three months?" She felt her jaw drop to the ground. "Why did you just come now? What have you been doing? Why didn't you get help from the clan?"

He chuckled. "Can you imagine how that would sound? That I was a Lycan from two hundred years in the past? No one would believe me." His voice turned somber. "I didn't believe you."

He was right, though. If Reed came to her months ago, she would have thought he was a crazy person. "But, all this time ..."

"It was worth it," he said, beaming at her. "It was the middle of winter when I found myself on the street, bleeding to death. These kind gentlemen saw me and brought me to the emergency room. After I got patched up, the same people helped me get to a homeless shelter. I've been living there ever since."

"A homeless shelter?"

He chuckled. "I know, it's a far cry from Huntington Park. But I realized that you were telling the truth. About traveling through time and such ... and so my new friends at the shelter showed me this wonderful tool. It's called Google." Elise laughed, and he continued. "I tried to remember all the details you told me. I found the website of the animal shelter where you worked in San Francisco, and I had a detective get more information on you, which led me to the New York clan." He looked over at Lucas. "Please forgive me for hiding out in your territory."

"Under the circumstances, you're forgiven." Lucas

massaged the bridge of his nose. "I'm still trying to wrap my head around this, but please continue."

"I was here for your first ascension ceremony, Alpha. I thought that would be the time Elise, Cross, and Julianna would travel back to 1820, but I was wrong." He looked down at her tenderly. "The first time I saw you again, I thought my heart would burst. I wanted to come to you and tell you who I was, but I couldn't. I knew I would have to wait until you traveled back. I befriended a few Lycans at Blood Moon, and finally, I got news about the new ascension ceremony. And I realized tonight was the night." He gritted his teeth. "I followed you today. From Bloomingdale's all the way to Tribeca."

"That was you!" She cried. "Someone was watching us from across the street when we came out. I thought it was the mage."

"It nearly killed me letting Daly kidnap you." His chest rumbled as his wolf reached for the surface. "But I knew I had to let it happen. So that you would come back to me."

"Oh, Reed, I—" She frowned, then looked at Cross. "You said he was going to die. That William would be Alpha. What happened?"

Cross thought for a moment. "He did die, in a way. Reed came to the future, and he never became Alpha. His family must have seen him disappear and declared him dead."

Elise felt a pang in her heart. Oh no. Eleanor, Jeremy, William, the dowager. They were all gone. "Reed. I'm so sorry."

There was a sadness that passed over his face as he squeezed her to his side. "We'll talk later."

"Oh God, this whole time-travel paradox is giving me a headache again!" Julianna exclaimed.

"Yes, it's giving us all headaches," Lucas declared. "Why don't we all get cleaned up and, uh," he glanced at Reed's naked form, "dressed, and we can all debrief? The mages are still out there."

"The mages!" Julianna exclaimed. "Where's the dagger?"

"Here," Cross said as he held up the dagger. "I secured it first chance I got." He turned to Reed and waved his hand, and suddenly he was dressed in a white shirt and tan colored breeches.

"Thanks," Reed said. "I prefer jeans though."

Elise laughed as happiness bubbled inside her. She couldn't believe it, but the proof was standing right next to her. Reed was here, in her present. And he was here to stay.

"Elise, darling," Lara began as a knowing smile formed on her face. "Anything else you want to tell us?"

"Yes," she looked up at Reed. He looked different with his beard, but also, there was something different about him she couldn't quite put her finger on. "But maybe I'll tell you later."

CHAPTER EIGHTEEN

The debriefing didn't take too long, as almost everyone already knew the story of their time traveling escapades, and Reed had mostly filled them in on what had happened to him when he landed in New York. Lucas declared that they were going to put the dagger in a safe place, while also begin searching for the only missing artifact —the ring of Magus Aurelius—as part of their overall strategy to defeat the mages once and for all.

However, dinner took much longer as Julianna ate five cheeseburgers, French fries, two pizzas, and four milkshakes in one sitting. Reed surprised everyone when he volunteered to order all the food using his smartphone. "I swear, these things are like magic," he had declared. "All I have to do is think of something, and someone will come by and bring it to me!"

Yes, he'd had three months to explore this strange new world, but all of that paled to the wonder of the woman standing beside him. The Alpha had generously offered them a suite in The Enclave to use for the time being. Reed heartily agreed, seeing as he really couldn't see bringing Elise to his bachelor room at the homeless shelter he had lived in for the past three months.

And now, here they were alone, and he was speechless. One would think he would have spent all this time practicing what he was going to say to his True Mate, the love of his life, but right now, all words escaped him.

So, he decided not to use any words. He took her hands, pulled her close, then lifted her up into his arms to carry her to the bed. She didn't protest at all, in fact, she was an eager participant as he helped her take off her gown.

He made love to her like he'd dreamed of doing all these lonely months. Slowly, eagerly, aching, and full of love. She was amazing, and though his memory of their last encounter was burned into his brain, it was just as beautiful as he remembered, and more so. When she came apart in his arms, he thought for sure that he had really died and gone to heaven.

They lay in the dark afterwards, arms around each other, enjoying the silence.

"I think I'm about as speechless as you are," she began, a blush creeping into her cheeks.

"I don't know what to say either," he began. "So, let me start by saying the words I've been wanting say. I love you, Elise." Sliding his hands down her back, her pulled her closer to him, inhaling that wonderful scent of hers. "I've been going crazy all these months waiting for you."

"I can't believe it ..." She looked up at him with those luminous eyes of hers. "Three months. What have you been doing?"

"A lot," he said. "I told you about that shelter, right?

Well, they had tons of books and a computer. Within a month I'd read every single book there and I became proficient at 'Google-fu.'" She laughed. "The shelter was so run down, and they needed so many things. I guess you could say I put my business experience to use. I helped them get more donors, and then I invested that money for them so they could buy more beds, clothing, and food for the residents."

"Wow," she said. "You *have* been busy."

He smiled. "I had to do something while I was waiting for you." But truth be told, he enjoyed his time at the shelter. Helping other people instead of making himself rich brought out a different feeling in him. The director was so happy that he gave Reed a job managing their finances and his own apartment at the shelter since he refused a salary because the residents needed every bit of money they could scrounge up. "Are you disappointed that I'm just a 'mister' and not a duke anymore?"

She chuckled. "Like I care about that. I can't believe you're here!" Reaching up, she ran her fingers through his thick beard. "All this time ..." Her expression changed.

"What is it, love?"

"It's been three months," she said. "And you've probably experienced so many things. Maybe you might even want to explore more about what this world has to offer—"

"I have." He covered her hands with his. "This is a wonderful, crazy world, and I know I've only seen a small portion of it. But, don't you know I've been waiting for you to come back to me? Do you know how hard it was not to approach you all this time?" He planted a kiss on each palm.

"You *have* changed," she declared. "I thought I saw it

earlier tonight. I couldn't put my finger on it but ... Reed, you seem happy. Really, genuinely happy."

Her words struck him. "I am," he realized. "I truly am happy. Happy you're here, but also, happy with myself." Being independent and having to start from scratch here had given him a purpose. "And I have you to thank for that. I think ... I think I wanted to be better for you. To be worthy of you." He planted a kiss on her mouth to stop her from protesting. "All this time, I've been so bitter and cold because of what happened with Joanna."

"I overheard your grandmother talk about her," she confessed. "I hope you don't mind."

His chest ached, thinking of Grandmama. Some nights, he allowed himself to grieve for the loss of his family, but he knew he couldn't focus on that. They would have wanted him to be whole and happy for the time when Elise came back. "You were meant to be mine, Elise."

"Reed," she began. "I thought I wasn't meant to be with anyone." She told him about her former best friend, and his heart ached for her. How lonely and sad she must have been, not being able to touch anyone. "And then I met you and I fell in love ... I came to you last night because I thought it was the last time I would see you."

It was strange that for her, it was only last night, while it had been months for him. He held her tighter. "I'm here now, love. And I will love you and our pup." he slid a hand down to her belly, where he was certain that life grew, one that was half her and half him. "I loved you two hundred years ago, I love you now, and I will love you two hundred years from now."

She moved her head up to kiss him, her lips moving over

his in a sensuous caress. "I love you, Reed. In any lifetime, I will love you."

Despite the loss he had experienced, Reed's heart had never felt fuller than at this moment. And he had this brave, beautiful woman who'd traveled through time to banish the darkness and numbness from his life to thank for that. Inside him, his wolf snorted haughtily, and for once, he conceded to the animal. *You're right*, he told his inner wolf. *All this time, you were right.*

EPILOGUE

A few months later ...

"Are you all right, love?" Elise asked as she slipped her fingers through Reed's, her shiny white gold wedding ring a stark contrast to his tanned skin.

"I'm fine," he said through gritted teeth. "This gets easier, doesn't it?"

She chuckled. "Not until you've done it a few times. Have you changed your mind—"

"No, I—" He stopped when the lights dimmed. "Besides, it's too late to call your father now to ask to borrow the jet."

She patted his hand. "You'll be fine. We'll be fine."

"Right." He looked straight ahead at the back of the seat in front of him. "We're only inside a metal tube that's about to hurtle across the sky, ten thousand feet in the air. What could go wrong?"

Rolling her eyes, she reminded him, "*You* were the one who wanted to fly commercial."

"I was told it was an experience."

"You'll do great." She felt his fingers grip hers tighter as the airplane picked up speed for takeoff. "Just breathe."

Most people would have laughed at Reed being so anxious at flying in an airplane, but this was only his second flight ever. The first was in her father's company jet when he finally moved to San Francisco about a month after their reunion. Reed had been reluctant to leave New York because of his job at the shelter, but Elise lived in California. One of them had to move and he was the more flexible of them both. So, after helping the homeless shelter's director find a replacement—and promising to be available anytime if they needed help—he packed up his small apartment and moved to California to be with Elise and pledge to the San Francisco clan. Soon after, he proposed to her and they were married in a simple ceremony in Napa Valley.

Reed didn't have a real plan on what he was going to do in California, so he started volunteering at the animal shelter where Elise worked. Turns out, he was so good at fundraising and charming donors from their money, so the shelter hired him part-time. On his days off, he took business classes at the local college as he tried to figure out what else he wanted to do now that he lived in this century.

Elise had accepted the position of director at the shelter. However, Shelley said she would wait to leave until early next year to give Elise time to bond with the baby after she gave birth. So, she and Reed decided it was time to take a vacation now, while it was still comfortable for her to travel, as well as do the one thing they had been putting off for months.

They both knew they would eventually have to go to London and visit Hunter House and Huntington Park.

Though Cross had given them his research into what happened after Reed "died", they decided that going there was something they had to do, to give closure on the events of what happened back in 1820 and finally move on with their lives.

Elise was concerned at first, but Reed was insistent. "If I don't do this now, I may never find the courage to do it at all," he had said. "And I don't know what kind of father I would be if I can't face this."

And so, they both put in for vacation time and planned their trip. To help ease them into it, they decided to go to Scotland first, to visit his parents' graves, before proceeding to England to pay their final respects to his grandmother, Eleanor, Jeremy, and yes, even little William.

The first leg of their trip was a commercial flight to New York. Reed insisted on paying for the trip, at least part way, which is why they were now stuck in row sixteen, seats B and C in front of a toddler who wouldn't stop kicking Reed's seat and behind a woman who played her videos loudly without earphones. Elise couldn't stop herself from smirking as her husband let out the one hundred and thirty-seventh long-suffering sigh. Thank goodness they were only doing this for the first leg, as they were stopping in New York to switch to Grant Anderson's private jet that would take them directly to Scotland. It was a long-delayed wedding gift from the former Alpha and his family, plus they were also picking up another passenger.

The plane landed five hours later at JFK, and a limo was already waiting for them outside the terminal to whisk them off to the private airstrip outside Jersey City. After slogging through Manhattan traffic and the Lincoln Tunnel, they made it to their destination. The limo stopped on the tarmac, right beside the sleek private jet waiting for them.

"Elise! Reed!" called a familiar voice as soon as Elise stepped out of the car. It was Julianna, running out of the black SUV parked not too far from them. "It's so nice to see you!" she exclaimed, pulling Elise into a tight hug. "Oops! Sorry!" She stepped back looking down at Elise's stomach. "Hey, momma, you popped!"

Elise laughed and Reed came up behind her, a hand slipping over her round belly protectively. "She has and she's beautiful. How are you, Julianna?"

"I'm great."

But something about the way she said it told Elise that Julianna was the opposite of *great*. Maybe it was the flatness in her voice or the way her smile didn't quite reach her mismatched eyes.

Once again, that nurturing, witch part of her could sense something was off about the younger woman. She sensed it days ago too, when Julianna called out of the blue asking if she could join them on their trip, explaining that Lucas had asked her to be his envoy and meet with the Alphas of Caelkirk and London. Apparently, he thought it was a good idea to start meeting with other Alphas from around the world to forge alliances and inform them about mages. When she spoke to Reed about it, he of course agreed to let her come.

"I see you haven't cut your hair as you threatened a million times," Reed teased.

Julianna smirked and flipped her long braid of hair over her shoulder. "It's growing on me. Thanks again for letting me horn in on your babymoon."

"Babymoon?" Reed asked.

"You know." She pointed her chin at Elise's bump. "Last chance to get some alone time before the baby comes."

"Ha! My parents and siblings are so excited and preparing to come visit us all the time that I doubt we'd even have time with the baby when he or she comes." Elise glanced up at the waiting plane. "Should we get going? We want to get there by morning, right?"

They headed into the plane and were welcomed by the steward with flutes of champagne and orange juice. She gave Reed a teasing smile as he eased into the plush leather seats. "You told me so," he said but grinned at her.

She gave him an innocent smile. "I wasn't going to say it."

The seven-hour flight to Glasgow was uneventful, and Elise was glad to have a real bed to sleep on for this last leg. She had retired to the private bedroom right after dinner, though Reed stayed behind to chat with Julianna. By the time she woke up, it was time to land, and Reed was just emerging from the bathroom, already dressed.

From Glasgow airport, they rented a SUV for the four-hour drive to Caelkirk, with Julianna in the driver's seat. As the vehicle drove through the Scottish countryside, Elise couldn't help but marvel at the wild beauty of Scotland, with its green rolling hills dotted with purple-pink heather, cozy little villages, and rugged mountainscapes.

"I can see why your mother loved it here," Elise said as she popped her head between the front row seats and reached over to place her hand on Reed's shoulder. "It's beautiful."

"Did you come here a lot?" Julianna asked.

"I've only been three times," Reed said. "Twice when I was younger and then ..."

When he drifted off, she squeezed his shoulder. "I'm sure you had a lovely time."

He guffawed. "Yes, I did, if you define 'lovely time' as being plagued by pranks from my mother's cousins for being a 'Sassenach.'" But there was a fond smile that touched his lips.

Julianna slowed the vehicle as she flipped on the turn signal to take the next exit. "So, are we going to stay with the clan?"

Elise nodded. "Dad took care of everything and contacted the clan on our behalf."

"He told their Alpha the story of me being adopted and never knowing my true nature until I met Elise," Reed continued. "And that I was probably from the Caelkirk or London clan and wanted to research my roots."

Aside from getting him a new birth certificate and other papers, the New York and San Francisco clans used their resources and favors to make Reed Wakefield a real, legal person in the eyes of both human and Lycan law. "The Alpha agreed to host us at Castle Kilcraigh and allow us to tour the grounds," he continued. "According to Cross's research, he's Bridget's direct descendant."

"I'm really glad Bridget met her mate," Julianna said. "And you said that Connor guy was okay?"

"I only met him for a moment," Reed confessed. "But he seemed a decent sort to me."

Elise could sense that Julianna seemed less tense today, and the fact that Reed was talking about someone from the past was a good sign. Truth be told, she had been anxious the whole time, and she wondered what Reed and Julianna talked about on the flight there. She wasn't jealous or anything, but she knew that there were probably some things Reed couldn't open up to her about as he was always afraid of stressing her and their pup out. She had to remember that right now, aside from herself, there were only two other people in the entire world who'd had the same experiences as Reed. And it wasn't like Cross was around to have a heart to heart talk with. In fact, according to Lara, Cross had not been around a lot at all, as the Alpha and Grant Anderson were sending him out on more missions to try and find the last artifact before the mages did.

"We're here," Reed said as they drove past an imposing moss-covered wall. "Look."

Julianna whistled. "Wow."

As the estate came into view, she held her breath. While Huntington Park was breathtaking in that perfectly manicured way, Castle Kilcraigh was rough and wild, but still beautiful, just like Scotland itself. It wasn't as big as Huntington Park, but the stone walls, spires, and turrets evoked a fairy-tale like quality.

Though Castle Kilcraigh itself was old, it was obviously well-cared for and modernized. The road sitting across the manicured lawn was paved, and the car stopped just outside the castle. By the time they exited the SUV with their things, there was already someone waiting for them at the doorway.

"Ye must be our guests from America," the man greeted. He was in his 40s, tall and slim, and wore a tweed suit. "I'm Gerald MacDougal, Beta of the Caelkirk Clan."

"Thank you for welcoming us and allowing us into the territory," Reed greeted back. "I'm Reed Wakefield, this is my wife Elise, daughter to Liam Henney, Alpha of San Francisco, and Julianna Anderson, envoy and sister to Lucas Anderson, Alpha of New York."

"Thank you for welcoming us," Elise greeted back.

"Nice tae meet ye all," he said as he shook hands with Reed.

Elise offered her hand which he shook, but when he did the same with Julianna, he paused. "Do I know ye?" His eyes narrowed at her.

Julianna shrugged. "I don't think so? Have you ever been to New York?"

"No, but it's like ... I could have sworn ..." He scratched at his chin. "It's like I've seen ye before." Shaking his head, he let go of her hand. "I'm sorry my Alpha's not here tae greet ye. He and his son had a sudden meeting in town, and he's not sure when they'll be back. But, don't ye worry, we're all ready for ye." He nodded to the older woman walking toward them. "Mrs. Carter, she's the housekeeper around here, will have yer things sent up tae yer rooms. Unfortunately, I'm about to pop into a conference call myself, but please feel free to look around the grounds. I'll be out around two and we can take a tour of the castle after we have tea."

"Excellent idea," Reed said. "I would like to go for a walk."

Elise slipped her arm into his. "I'll join you. It'll give me a chance to stretch my legs."

"I'm pooped." Julianna yawned and then stretched her arms over her head. "If you wouldn't mind, I need a shower and a nap, but that tea and tour sounds great."

"It's all settled then," Gerald clapped his hands together.

"Julianna, ye can follow Mrs. Carter, and we can all meet here at two."

As Gerald and Julianna and Mrs. Carter went their way, Reed tugged her toward the door.

"Is it just like you remember?" she asked in a quiet voice.

"Mostly," he said. "It's definitely more modern, but there's something about it ... it feels the same."

She stopped before they reached the outside. "Reed, where are we going?"

"To the family cemetery."

"Oh." She placed a hand on his arm. "We don't have to do this right this moment. How about we wait until tomorrow?"

"No, I want to do this now," he said. "It's the perfect timing. I don't know what our host has planned, and I'm not sure how I'll be able to explain why I want to schedule time to visit his dead ancestors."

She gave him a tight smile. "All right, love, whatever you want."

―――――

The Caelkirk clan's family cemetery was about a thirty-minute walk, down a path that led them halfway across the castle grounds. Though Reed only relied on his memory, he didn't have trouble finding the old chapel and a small house surrounded by a short stone wall. He explained to Elise that in his time it was a parsonage, as the clan usually had its own clergyman living on the estate. Though they seemed well-kept, both the clergy house and chapel were abandoned. He led her to the back of the chapel where he knew the family cemetery was located.

His parents' burial was the first and only time he'd been here. In his mind, it had only been a year since their deaths. But looking at the gravestones and markers around him, it really hit him that over two hundred years had passed.

Slowly, he made his way to the back of the graveyard, to what had been, at the time, the newest headstones. While they had just been installed when he was last here, time had obviously made its mark, the stone covered in moss and the words nearly faded. His parents' name was still clear, but the words "Beloved Mother and Father" had nearly worn off.

"I thought this would be the easy part." He had said the words after what seemed like an eternity of them standing there. "I was here a year ago, throwing dirt on top of their coffins. But it still hits me. It hits me now, and I'm reminded that they're gone. They're ... all gone."

Elise's fingers threaded into his. "I'm sorry, Reed. I'm so sorry."

"You know," he began. "It was my mother's last wish to be buried in her homeland. My father wouldn't have cared where he was buried, as long as it was with his True Mate." The tears burned in the back of his throat, but he swallowed them down. "Grandmama fought me tooth and nail, declaring that they were the duke and duchess of Huntington, and every single duke and duchess before them was buried in the family plot at Huntington Park, and she'd be damned if my parents weren't. It was the only time I had defied her."

"Reed." She leaned her head on his arm. "There's something I just remembered. Right before we ... we left, your grandmother came to talk to me."

"She did?"

"Uh-huh. She told me ... she knew about us being True Mates."

Now *that* was a surprise. "What did she say?"

"She said ... well, she said she regretted how things were between your mother and her. And that she wanted to be better with you and me and—"

A sob was threatening to escape his mouth, so he gathered her into his arms and pressed his lips to her. With their pup growing inside her and cradled between them, he poured every ounce of love and sadness and regret into their kiss. When he felt the wetness on his cheeks, he couldn't tell if they were hers or his.

"I love you," he murmured when he pulled away. He placed a hand on her belly and he felt a movement there.

Her lashes wet with tears, she looked at him. "I love you too."

He cleared his throat and brushed his fingers across her cheeks. "You and our pup must be getting hungry. We should go back."

They went on a more leisurely pace, enjoying the beautiful grounds of the castle, and simply content to walk in silence in each other's company. When they reached the castle, it seemed they were just in time. Gerald and Julianna, who had changed clothes and looked refreshed, were waiting in the foyer.

"Did ye have a nice walk?" the Beta greeted.

"We did." Elise gave Reed a knowing smile.

"Good," Gerald declared. "We can start in the library

where I have tea set up." They followed him down a long hallway on the right, then into the last room. "Here we go." He led them inside and gestured to a sitting area next to the fireplace where a multi-tiered cake plate was piled with pastries and sandwiches, and pots of tea sat on top of candle-lit warmers. "Let's—oh." Gerald stopped in his tracks, looked at the fireplace and then at Julianna. "I thought I had ... but how ..."

Reed followed the Beta's gaze, retracing them as he set his eyes on the mantle above the fireplace. Or rather, the painting above the mantle.

"Oh." Elise's jaw dropped. "Oh my."

Looking back at them with her mismatched green and blue eyes was a portrait of Julianna, sitting on top of the mantle as if she belonged there, her dark hair flowing down her shoulders. It was unfinished, as the edges of the painting had exposed canvas, but it was obvious which painting this was. It was a beautiful portrait, really, and Rossi really captured Julianna's personality—with her mischievous sparkling eyes and that impertinent mouth that more often than not got her in trouble with the dowager duchess.

Julianna stood there, frozen, looking up at her doppelgänger.

"Are you all right?" Elise asked.

"I'm great," she said, seemingly snapping out of her trance. "Dandy. I should—I need—I'm—" She spun around and dashed toward the door like Satan himself was on her heels. Unfortunately, she didn't quite make it outside as someone else was coming through the doorway at the exact moment.

"Whoa!" Julianna staggered back, but the other person

managed to catch her before she tumbled over. "I—" She sucked in a breath and stood very still, her neck craning up to look at the man who was holding her.

The man stared down at her, bright green eyes growing large. "It's you," he said, his voice in awe. "It's really you."

———

I have some extra HOT bonus scenes for you that weren't featured in this book - just join my newsletter here to get access:

http://aliciamontgomeryauthor.com/mailing-list/

You'll get access to ALL the bonus materials from all my books and my **FREE** novella **The Last Blackstone Dragon.**

ABOUT THE AUTHOR

Alicia Montgomery has always dreamed of becoming a romance novel writer. She started writing down her stories in now long-forgotten diaries and notebooks, never thinking that her dream would come true. After taking the well-worn path to a stable career, she is now plunging into the world of self-publishing.

- facebook.com/aliciamontgomeryauthor
- twitter.com/amontromance
- bookbub.com/authors/alicia-montgomery

Printed in the USA
CPSIA information can be obtained
at www.ICGtesting.com
LVHW091804241023
761966LV00002B/227

9 781952 333057